# The Cry of the Dunes

*LL Goulet*

ISBN 978-0-615-43832-0

Cover design by JTG

*To Jerry*

*For his enthusiastic support*

# CHAPTER 1

The smiling eyes did not conceal the warning. *Everything you hear about us will remain within these walls.* Sheri's stern instruction echoed in Janet's mind as though she had heard the words the day before.

*People who have it all.* The image on the magazine cover floated before Janet. Did they really have it all? The troubling words kept swirling in her mind. To be sure, Lars Van Reef was a wealthy and successful businessman. His wife Sheri, a beloved television personality, was probably the most written about woman in society pages.

Why then did Janet feel that everything was not as it seemed? Was it her imagination or had she sensed sadness behind Sheri's radiant smiles?

Were cracks developing in the perfect façade?

The frown on Janet's face deepened at the memory of her first encounter with Lars. Even though she stood inches away, he had looked past her as if she had not been there.

*The air of aristocracy;* the media gushed annoyingly. She found him cold and aloof. Still, one could not deny he was a handsome man. Together, Mr. and Mrs. Van Reef made a striking couple, reported to be the envy of many, even in high society.

*People who have it all.* The crashing waves seemed to shout with every surge. The Van Reef world was nothing like her own. And yet, in an unlikely way, Janet's life had become entwined with that of Sheri van Reef.

She recalled the cold winter day more than two years before, when their paths first crossed.

»«

Getting a foothold in the world of newspapers had been anything but easy. Janet winced, remembering the lean stretches; there had been many. She regularly scanned local papers for a second job to help cushion the dry spells.

One such advertisement was placed by Sheri Van Reef, in search of a dog walker. Janet had no particular qualifications but had been honest about her situation. She felt a connection with Sheri. Much to her relief, she had been hired.

At that time, Janet told herself it was a temporary job. A month, two at the most, until a substantial newspaper assignment came along.

*And here I am, still*; Janet's eyes travelled over the gentle sand dunes back to the crashing North Sea surf. Days had turned to weeks and two and a half years later, she was still walking the famous collies.

Freelancing for the European Daily, she earned enough of a living but knew that a steady income was never a guarantee. Even if it was, the salary probably would not come close to what she was paid by the Van Reefs.

"Come on, it's time to go. Rocky. Coco." Janet clapped her hands and urged the collies toward the van.

As the vehicle turned the corner and the red tile roof came into view, Janet thought of the very first time she had driven down the road to no. 32.

»«

Pausing before the high gates of the imposing white building, Janet had been overcome with self doubt. Despite wanting to run, she had decided to proceed with the interview. Embarrassed by her rusty van, she had parked it several doors down and walked to the famous no. 32.

The singular impression Janet received at the interview was only the beginning. Once acquainted with the Van Reef name, she began to see it in many a magazine article and hear it on most television programmes. Sheri Van Reef was more of a household name than she ever knew.

Janet frowned, remembering the magazine's overly generous compliment, declaring Sheri to be 'Holland's First Lady'.

Lars van Reef was less well known but the surname was familiar among old families. He was an unmistakable member of the old money club.

After the first several months of working for the Van Reefs, Janet had drawn her own picture. Lars was wealthy but Sheri was the more accomplished partner. Her beginnings had been modest but she had received recognition as a violinist. Her good looks had proved to be an asset and her career in television had progressed quickly.

Their wealth, fame and visibility made the Van Reefs a target of unwelcome onlookers. This resulted in life behind the high walls of their guarded residence. Janet wondered about the need for all the security. The noisy collies would have been enough of a deterrent.

She could not help thinking that this was all part of an image.

The mansion, situated on the shores of the Kaag lakes, was also the subject of articles. The building style was described as Mediterranean, drawn from the family's holidays in southern France and Italy.

Interactions with Sheri were frequent but brief. Janet thought her nice but wondered if Sheri would be as agreeable if someone crossed her, either socially or in her profession.

*It isn't something I need worry about;* Janet concluded. *Our paths will never cross on either of those planes.*

»«

"Good morning Miss." The guard's scratchy voice interrupted Janet's daydreaming. He stood holding the gate open. The rattle of her approaching van was the signal each morning.

"Thank you. Looks like it's going to be a nice day."

Weather was always a safe topic. Janet could not think of anything else to say to the stocky man with the shaved head and tattoos. Even the brief eye-contact was uncomfortable.

As Janet stepped off the van, she heard a shout over the excited barking of the collies. The words were barely discernible but she guessed what was being said; *come in for a cup of coffee Janet;* Van Reefs' housekeeper stood at the back door, waving her in.

"I'll be right in." Janet shouted back, ushering the dogs into the pen.

As she walked into the house, the aroma of baking bread wafted in from the kitchen.

"Thanks for the invitation Mrs. Steen."

The exchange began the same way each day. Despite the predictable conversation, the morning coffee session was often the highlight of Janet's day.

Her eyes wandered to the silver tray on the dumb waiter,

4

ready to be loaded. Although a modern version, she felt the accoutrement was something which belonged in a castle. It was too gaudy, even for the elaborate Van Reef residence.

"Madam's inspiration. You know, she toured many castles to come up with the perfect one." The housekeeper purred the *R* in *perfect*.

"A few turrets and a moat, this house could be a proper castle!" Janet threw her head back and laughed.

"You're funny schatje." s*chatje* – darling. Only her grandmother called her that.

Janet moved close to the oven and stood with her back to it. *On rainy days the house does feel damp like a castle;* she thought; *damp, cold and gloomy.*

Was that feeling because of the long rainy days? Did the high ceilings give the house a remote feel? Or did her mood in some way reflect on the residents of the mansion?

Janet carried her cup to the breakfast nook and pulled out a chair. "Does the family ever eat at this table?" she asked, surveying the bay window reaching all the way to the top.

"Not much. Madam likes spending time in the sun room." Mrs. Steen pointed to the second level.

When Janet toured the house and stood in the glass enclosed terrace for the first time, she was struck by the views of the lake all around. She recalled the room's other dominant feature; a mosaic top table, reportedly custom made for Sheri in Morocco.

"Tut-tut."

Janet turned to see the Mrs. Steen shaking her head.

"What is it?" She walked over and peered at the notebook in

the housekeeper's hand.

"Mrs. Van Reef wants me to plan a party in June. There is much to do and not enough time." She picked up the pen and scribbled on the notebook.

"Now I understand why you're so quiet this morning." Janet sympathised.

The news of a Van Reef social event had pushed aside the usual familial anecdotes.

"It's going to be a big one Janet. I hear some Royals might attend." Mrs. Steen beamed.

Working for the Van Reefs for nearly two decades, the housekeeper had seen many celebrities come and go. Dutch Royalty however, was beloved and much revered.

Janet sipped the last of her coffee. "Do you want me to help with the party?"

She remembered her first Van Reef social event and the generous compensation which had followed the evening's work.

"You are on the list already, see?" Mrs. Steen waved the pad.

It was no surprise to Janet that planning had begun with more than two months to spare. The Van Reef parties were grand and a showcase for all present.

"I'll mark you down as a yes, Mr. Flanders will want to know."

*Oh yes, Maurice Flanders will definitely want to know.* Janet's brow creased. *Mr. Flanders has to know everything that goes on here.*

Flanders had been introduced to her as the 'butler' but Janet realized quickly that he was much more. His exact duties were unclear but she knew he was important. He went regularly to the upstairs office, for meetings with Mr. Van Reef. Janet could not think of anyone else working in the mansion with such access to Lars.

Flanders was polite and courteous but something about him made Janet flinch. Was it the person himself? She wondered; or was it his close association with Lars Van Reef?

As the gates closed behind the van, her mind moved away from the Van Reef world to the articles she had yet to invent.

# CHAPTER 2

*This has to sound more exciting.* Janet stared at the scribbles on her notepad. The elections were the most talked about topic and yet not the most exciting reading. Long campaigns and repetitive rhetoric resulted in readers straying away from the European Daily. She had to convince the newspaper that her articles would grab the readers' attention and maintain it week after week.

A long line of men and women vied for the post of Prime Minister. The public was well acquainted with the leading contenders but did not know much about the others. Janet underlined the names of the outsiders, especially the more colourful and controversial figures.

Deep down she knew these stories would be heavy on personalities and light on policies. Janet began typing.

Morning turned into afternoon and soon night fell.

*What is that harsh ringing?* Janet sat up and looked around the dark room. Her watch glowed five past eleven. *Where am I?* Then she remembered; she had stretched out on the sofa earlier, for a break from the typing.

The noise came from across the room. It was the telephone. Who was calling at this late hour? Scrambling, she reached it on the sixth ring.

"Hello."

"Janet, it's me."

"Rosie? What's wrong?"

No jokes. No small talk. Something was amiss. Rosie did not sound like herself.

"Janet, are you awake?" The voice had an edge.

"Yes. What is it Rose?" Janet came to the point. She sensed urgency and this was not the time for chit chat.

"Grab some paper and a pen."

Janet was ready with the pad. "I'm listening."

"Someone's been killed." The speech was abrupt, not wrapped in witticisms as was usually the case.

"Can you speak up?" Traffic noise in the background drowned out much of what was said. Janet knew Rosie was calling from a phone booth.

"Someone's been killed."

"Murdered?"

"Yes. And I don't think it's your average street knifing."

Janet suddenly realized this was a tip. "Do you know who it is?"

"Not at this point. Looks like someone important."

"Where?"

"On Java island. Let's see, not far from the Caribbean restaurant. Remember we met there at the bar once?"

Janet pictured the neon palm tree on either side of the restaurant's name. She scribbled *Bahamas on Java Island.*

"Damn." She mumbled under her breath as the pencil lead broke. She opened the drawer and grasped the first pen she felt. Rosie had been reeling off street names and Janet scrambled to write them down.

"Thanks Rosie. I'll head out there now." Many questions were popping up in her head but she knew not to push. Besides, she felt that Rosie did not have further details.

*If she does, she isn't saying.*

It was as if her thoughts were heard. "Can't tell you too much more."

Who was that person? And when? What else was there to it? The questions would not stop. "Do you..."

Click, the line went dead.

Janet thanked her friend silently. This was not the first tip Rosie had supplied but was nothing like the other two which had been about a hold up and a raid.

This was huge.

There was no time to waste. She hoped she had not been half-awake and missed anything of what Rosie had said. She surveyed her notes. The words *Java Island* stood out. At least she had a destination.

Janet began to think of the fastest route to the islands. *Back roads or the highway?* A4 was faster; she decided.

Java was a mile Northeast of the train station. 'Islands' was the word Rosie had first used to describe the small strips of land separated by channels and connected by bridges.

The landscape had struck Janet as odd, a combination of swanky, high-rise residences and run down warehouse buildings immediately next to them.

In the midst of all that was *The Bahamas,* where Rosie and she had met for a drink.

Now it was a crime scene.

Janet pulled on a sweater over her pyjama top. The coke bottle glasses were hideous but contact lenses would cause further delay. Shoe laces would have to wait till some traffic light. She grabbed her backpack, crammed ready with her minimal necessities; pen, pad and camera.

The traffic in the middle of the night would be considered nearly nothing at any other time. But tonight, she needed to drive the twenty miles in a hurry. To report an incident before it was yesterday's news. She counted six traffic lights over five miles. Why the hell were so many signals necessary at this time of night? She rapped her knuckles on the steering wheel. The clock on the dashboard glowed eleven fifty.

After twenty five minutes of driving, Janet was on the island. She did not have to look at street signs. In the moonless night, police lights were visible from far away.

*No time to look for a proper space;* she decided to chance a parking ticket and drove the van onto the curb. As she stepped off, Janet felt a shiver. The darkness combined with the mist on the water and the flashing lights gave the area an eerie feel.

She began running toward the crime scene. Three blocks later, she paused at the intersection. On the other side of the street was the brick building which occupied the entire block.

*This must be where it happened.* She walked briskly as she pulled the camera out of the backpack. The press badge hung around her neck but she kept touching it, to be certain it was still there. Weaving her way between the police cars, she arrived at a barricade.

A policeman hovered at the roadblock. Hearing her footsteps, he turned around.

"Good evening officer." She lifted the badge up to him.

The man grimaced but let her through. As she walked to the edge of the scene, Janet scanned the crowd. A television camera with the blue 'Nederland' sign was perched at the corner, furthest from where she stood.

*It isn't crawling with reporters.* The scant presence of the press was surprising. Word had not yet spread.

Rosie had not wasted time.

Two ambulances blocked her path. Holding up her badge, she made her way past the emergency personnel to the area cordoned off with police tape. *One, two...;* she counted five businesses housed in the building. The police cordon surrounded the part of the parking lot in front of the restaurant. Bahamas was the only business operating at the time of night.

Janet's eyes travelled to a cluster of people in the middle of the parking lot. A body was on the ground. It was a man. From what she could see, his face and torso were covered with blood. He wore what looked like a tuxedo.

*Probably dressed for an important event at the restaurant.* Janet thought sadly. *What a way to end an evening. What a way to end your life.*

*Stop*; she reminded herself; this was no time to get emotional. There was work to do.

"Excuse me." She waved her hand at a few workers, each preoccupied with some task.

The forensic team with white overalls shuffled about, collecting bits and pieces strewn about the body. They were

13

not too far away to hear Janet or see her but did not glance her way.

She walked up and down the yellow and black ribbon trying to get someone to talk to her.

"Hello, Sir."

A man in uniform turned around. He did not seem much over twenty years of age.

"*Meneer*, could you tell me who it is?"

"Sorry." He shook his head.

*He's following rules.* She had to persevere but knew he could very easily walk away or tell her to leave. But he had not. He was young, polite, not yet hardened.

*He* was her chance.

"Sorry Sir, but do you know the identity of the person?" She tried again in a low voice, almost a whisper. Pushing too hard might just drive him away. The young man turned his back to her, as if no longer talking to her.

*I've lost him.* She looked around for another person to talk to but stopped at the slight jerk of the young policeman's head.

His face was still turned away from her but Janet thought she heard him mutter something. It sounded like *Santiago*.

*Santiago? The director of internal security? No, that could not be, it was some other person with the same name.*

"Jose Santiago?" Once again she saw a slight movement of his head. From his body language it was clear he did not want to be seen talking to her.

*There must be some mistake.*

"Director Jose Santiago?" The words felt as though they

were stuck in her throat but she had to ask again.

Her voice was so low, she wondered if the young policeman heard her. She tried looking at his face but he was walking away from her. *Damn, I nearly had the answer.* She moved along the barrier and kept pace with him to see if she could look at his face.

He swirled around and scanned the small crowd that was gathering. Pausing and looking directly at Janet, he nodded. He then turned away and his silhouette disappeared into a blur of white overalls.

Janet stared at the corpse. The dead man was indeed Jose Santiago. How could that be? She had just been profiling him as one of the candidates running for office. The introductory line was fresh in her mind; *Jose Miguel Eduardo Santiago, second generation Dutch of Venezuelan parents, forty seven years of age.*

She stood staring at the jumble of feet around the corpse. The keys were in her hand but she could not tear herself away from the scene. Lying before her was the man on whom millions had pinned their hopes. She took another look to pay her respects before departing. The body could have been Santiago's but it was impossible to say. Whatever was left of the face was unrecognizable.

Janet felt a chill. The man gunned down was none other than the chief of Internal Security. The very person who was in charge of preventing such crimes.

Santiago was thought as the most likely candidate to be elected leader of the country.

Not now. Not ever.

She felt sick to her stomach. But she had to keep going. She had a job to do.

On the way back to the van, Janet shouted out to two policemen looking in her direction. She hoped for a few more facts but neither responded. The usually grinning, relaxed faces of the Dutch police were rigid this night.

Rigid with horror. With sadness. With disbelief.

The crowd had grown and the chattering voices became louder and louder.

"This was no ordinary killing."

"Who is he?"

"He must've crossed somebody powerful."

"What is the country coming to?"

The words were becoming jumbled into an incomprehensible hum. Janet's head whirled. Her feet felt like lead as she made her way back to the van. She knew she could not expect any statements by the police tonight.

An official comment would be made after the person was formally identified and the next of kin informed. They would say something about launching an investigation. There would be claims that no resources would be spared. The television stations and their experts would go wild with discussion and speculation.

As Janet opened the door of the van, she realized that she had no confirmation of the identity of the dead person. She only had the word of the young policeman. What if he was mistaken? She had been swept by the event and had not paid attention to crucial fundamentals. She had believed the apprentice's utterance that it was Santiago. But that was insufficient, she needed more.

No corroboration meant no article. Neither Boris nor any other editor in his right mind would accept it. But if the

16

Daily did publish her article, it would be her big break. She had to return to the crime scene to get confirmation. Just as she opened the van door, she saw a piece of paper on the driver's seat. She leaned over to pick it up.

"Get in and start driving." Janet gasped and stepped back. As she swung into a run, she realized that the voice was a familiar one. She took a deep breath and turned back toward the van.

"You scared me half to death." She climbed in and sat down.

"Don't turn around." Janet tilted the rear view mirror. Even in the darkness, she could see the outline of Rosie's round face. She pushed in the clutch and turned the key.

"Did you get everything you need?"

"Is it Jose Santiago?"

"Yes." Rosie's voice was flat, devoid of emotion.

The affirmation was the green light Janet needed. But she did not feel relief, only a tightening knot in her stomach.

"Start driving. Drop me off somewhere near Centraal."

*Some place with hundreds of people milling around so I won't be noticed;* Janet read between the lines. Seven minutes later they were within fifty yards of the train station.

"What else can you tell me?"

"Nothing." Rosie pushed the passenger seat forward and climbed out. She kept walking and disappeared into the crowd as the van made a u-turn.

Janet's foot pressed down on the accelerator, she had to work fast. The typing would begin as soon as she got home. She had already profiled Santiago and would use a lot of the same material. She might have just enough time to make the early edition.

The drive home seemed to take even longer. Waiting at traffic lights, the impatience gave way to a heavy heart. She felt sad about Santiago's death and the manner in which he had died.

Once home, Janet went directly to the dining table. If printed, the article would be her first big hard news story. She hoped she was the only one delivering it to the Daily.

*At least let it be the first one.* If the editor liked it, she could be asked to continue writing on the topic. With an on-going investigation, it would mean weeks or even months of work.

Janet could not ignore the pangs of guilt – she worried about her career while a great man lay in a pool of blood.

»«

Janet sketched an upside down tree and wrote a W next to each of the branches. A bold H stood above the root. She remembered Professor Turner's unrelenting mantra of the journalistic code. The image of his owl-like face was vivid, it bobbed each time he stressed the five Ws and the H.

She had been able to account for the *What* and *Where*. The *When* would have to be an estimate. The *Who* had been confirmed to her satisfaction and hopefully to the editors'. The *How* was apparent. The *Why* was the big question mark. It would be a long time, months, maybe years before that question could be answered.

If at all.

After an hour of writing, Janet felt the article was acceptable. *Can I afford another rewrite?* She looked up at the clock. No, she did not have enough time. She had to give Boris a heads up, they both needed a half hour to get to the offices of the Daily. Not everyone would think the article as high quality writing but if she hoped to meet deadline for the morning edition, she had to deliver it very soon. What was the deadline? Three in the morning? Four? She would soon find out.

The phone kept ringing, one, two, three. *Come on Boris*; she urged silently. Boris the bear, they called him. Her editor personified the gruff and scruffy image of the newspaper man of the thirties in the black-and-white movies. If Boris' demeanour was meant to be intimidating, it worked on most people. Janet was affected by it at first but barely noticed it anymore.

She wondered how he would act at three in the morning.

"Yeah?" The impatient tone answered her question.

"I've just finished a story." Boris did not care for pleasantries. It was a waste of time; he had once declared. He wanted his facts straight off the bat.

"We need to meet at the office Boris." *I hope this is how it's done.* She had never called an editor in the middle of the night before. "Jose Santiago has been murdered."

There was silence. Boris was digesting the bombshell Janet had just dropped.

She knew she had his attention.

"Fill me in at the office." The line went dead.

Janet picked up the two envelopes. In case she had not been able to get hold of Boris, she had addressed the packages to him and one of his assistant editors.

The four minutes' wait in her boss's office seemed endless. Boris walked in looking even more unkempt than usual. She heard him mumble something which she guessed to be, 'good morning'.

Janet's hand shook as she gave him the envelope. Both kept their coats on as they sat across from each other. Janet twirled the pencil as she watched her boss's furrowed brow and pursed lips.

Once, he looked up at her with a question in his eyes. He seemed to ask; 'How did you hear about it?'

"A friend." She knew that he knew she was not about to say anymore.

"Corroboration?"

"Yes. A young policeman at the scene."

He turned the page. "Time of death?"

"Shortly before eleven in the night. But that's not official."

Boris nodded. "That won't happen till midday, at the earliest."

He read the article again from beginning to end. He then leaned back in his chair and held up the sheaf of paper. "Great work Janet."

She held back her excitement and said simply, "Thanks."

The article was now in the editor's hands. If he and the copy editors worked fast, it would soon be on its way to the morning edition.

Janet had not seen such a wide grin on the otherwise scowling face of Boris the bear.

# CHAPTER 3

Janet bolted into a sitting position. *That police siren is horribly shrill.* Where were the police cars? She squinted in the darkness and looked down to see herself on the living room sofa. *Was it a dream?* The noise did not stop. As she became more aware, she realized it was not a siren but the alarm clock going off.

Janet tried to stand up but tripped on the blanket which had slid down to the floor. She straggled toward the bedroom, stepping over crumpled up pieces of paper, rejects of her writing the night before. The palm of her hand came down on the clock, finally stopping the cacophony.

Kneeling before the night stand, she stared at the clock. What had to be done that she had set the alarm? It must have been something important. She picked up the notepad. Yes, there it was; *CALL THE DAILY*; written in bold letters and underlined.

*Yes, the article*; her shoulders slumped as she recalled the events of the previous night. The Santiago shooting in an Amsterdam parking lot. A cold blooded assassination.

*Assassination*?

She had not used the word before, neither in the article nor in her thoughts. A chill ran down her back. She remembered the blood soaked clothes, the shattered face. She clutched her stomach and dropped down on the bed.

"The European Daily." An unfamiliar female voice was at the other end.

"My name is Janet Simmons. May I speak to Boris please?"

"Oh Miss Simmons." The voice chirped excitedly. "He is not yet in. But there is a message waiting for you. From Mr. Davidson."

*Gareth Davidson?* The General Manager had something to say to her?

Word about her had reached the higher ups. "What is the message?" Janet's words sounded matter of fact but her pulse raced.

"Let me see." She heard the rustle of paper. "It says; Good job, see you on Thursday."

She had hoped for more but for now, Janet had to be satisfied with the brief compliment and an invitation to meet the chief of the publication.

Her body ached for more sleep. She looked longingly at the bed. However, she had made no arrangement for the dogs and needed to drive to the mansion. She stood up and stretched. As tired as she was, she knew the fresh sea breeze would invigorate her body and mind. It always did.

She arrived a half hour past her usual time. The dogs began yelping as if to let her know she was late.

The cool morning air had the effect she hoped. The cobwebs gradually abated. But being alert only accentuated the painful memories of the previous night.

*How do I handle this?* She kept asking. Her work from the previous night gave her the recognition she craved. Yet, the excitement of the article on page one was completely deflated by the sadness at the demise of a man with promise.

>«

Janet hesitated. There was no cheery welcome, no invitation to morning coffee. Surely, the housekeeper was working today? She decided to go inside to check.

The table at the bay window had newspapers spread all over it. Maurice Flanders sat reading while Mrs. Steen stared at the wall.

"Mrs. Steen?" Janet spoke softly, uncertain what to say on such a sad day.

"Did you hear?" The housekeeper waved the newspaper.

Janet nodded and walked over to join them. Different publications covered the table. She picked up the *Courant*. The headline was the most dramatic she had seen thus far; *A dark day for The Netherlands*.

Her own headline was much more subdued, *Prominent Dutch citizen killed*. She had looked forward to sharing with Mrs. Steen the biggest accomplishment of her career.

*This isn't the time;* she decided. Mrs. Steen gestured animatedly while Flanders sat across from her, listening and nodding in agreement.

Mrs. Steen and Flanders had come together, sharing the one thing they had most in common, the love and pride of their country. How sad and angry they looked; Janet listened as she slowly made her departure.

There had been no mention of the upcoming party. Santiago's murder had side-lined its preparation. That dismal event would overshadow all others, if only for a brief period.

23

Life had a way of moving on.

Janet's eyes welled up thinking of the time when her world had come crashing. She had recovered and life had indeed moved on.

# CHAPTER 4

Blowing out the eleven candles was Janet's happiest childhood memory. She recalled the final year of her life with both her parents.

The family was middle class, like most others in the neighbourhood. She had everything any child could wish for. She loved her mother and adored her father.

The bomb hit a few days after the birthday party, when Janet's parents announced that they were getting a divorce. She was in shock. Her parents made repeated assurances that they loved her and *that* would not change. But the world as Janet had known it, had come crashing.

After the break up, Janet was raised by her mother. It was a lonely time. Janet saw her father during regular, scheduled visits. She could not wait for the holidays to be with him. In the years that followed, he remarried. A new family did not help close the chasm between Janet and her father. As time went on, the visits became more infrequent until one day when they stopped altogether.

When Janet was thirteen, barely two years after the breakup, her mother met and married an American, Alexander Rutherford. The couple seemed happy but Janet resented Alex moving into their lives. A year later, the new family moved from England to Alex's home in Vermont. Janet was becoming increasingly discontent and restless. Her father had become even more distant and she felt lost, not being able to turn to him.

Janet knew her mother was in a good place and made an effort to get along with Alex. She could never love him, at least not like a father. He was nothing like her beloved Papa nor did he endear himself to her.

Something about her stepfather troubled Janet. One day she would find out.

Janet survived high school without major mishaps. When it was time for college, she was determined to study in a place far away. As far from her stepfather as possible.

At university, Janet became a much calmer and happier person. She had little desire to return to live with her mother. Her visits home were always filled with tension. Janet decided to stay away.

During one summer, she decided to find out about Alex. She began with the areas where Alex had declared he had lived.

Despite suspicions about Alex, Janet had not been prepared for the sordid story which unravelled.

Alex's surname had not always been Rutherford. It had changed from Reid. Before that, Richards. Janet kept digging. She tried not to lose sight of her studies and only barely managed to keep Alex's story from becoming an obsession.

Several months had passed before she unearthed his telling past. There was more to Alex than just different surnames. He had been convicted of fraud and had served a prison sentence. Janet was not shocked; the discovery explained a lot of odd things she had felt about him.

At the next opportunity, Janet broke the news to her mother. To her surprise, there were no tears, hysterics or anger.

*She must've known all along;* Janet thought with sadness. Her mother's silence was tacit acknowledgement.

Shortly thereafter, her mother divorced Alex. Janet felt unhappy about having caused this pain but at the same time, relieved for her mother's sake.

In the process, Janet had learned some things about herself; her stubbornness in not accepting things at their face value; her realization that her instinctive suspicion of Alex from the very beginning had proven prophetic.

Most of all, Janet felt justified in her search for the truth. She had paid attention to her hunch. Most importantly, she had not ignored the nagging little voice.

# CHAPTER 5

*Where are you Boris?* Janet's fingers rapped on the table. The day was a very important one and she had not been able to speak to her editor.

*I'll just have to track him down.* On such a busy day, the only way to catch Boris was in the narrow window between meetings. Janet gave up on waiting for his telephone call and drove to the offices of the European Daily.

The door to Boris's office was shut. His secretary Alice stood in the outer office, with her back to Janet.

"Hello Alice. Is Boris in?"

"Oh, hello there Janet." Alice turned around, her eyebrows raised. "Yes he is. He's been in conference with Mr. Davidson for well over an hour." She paused for Janet to speak, then continued, "some news, eh?"

*I was there, remember?*

"Yes." Janet said simply. "When can I see him?"

"Let me see." Alice ran her finger down the calendar. "He's booked just about the entire afternoon."

*You don't understand.* Janet tried not to glare at Alice. *It's my article they're talking about.*

"I'll just wait here." She walked to the small sitting area.

Alice smiled sweetly, "Yes, of course."

Janet shifted to get comfortable on the lumpy sofa. *Now that I'm here, what am I going to say to him?* What was it that she wanted? More money? A permanent position?

She began jotting down the talking points. She had to be clear with the demands; Boris had little patience for beating about the bush. *Clear but not unyielding.*

The morning edition was still in her hand. She unfolded it carefully and read the article again. How many times had she read it already?

Boris had complained about the lack of time to get to the morning edition. He had to have thrown his weight around. Janet had heard of his ability to move mountains in seemingly impossible situations.

She ran her fingers over the by-line. *"Prominent Dutch citizen killed - By Janet Simmons."* Her first article on page one of the Daily. It felt unreal. She still could not believe it.

Positioning the pen carefully at the top, she signed her name. Without a doubt, the article would be displayed prominently in her mother's living room.

*Should I send a copy to my father? No*; she acknowledge sadly. Her father was lost to her. He had been out of her life for more than a decade.

A familiar grunt interrupted her thoughts. Boris stood by the open door, his grin wider than before. Next to him was General Manager Davidson, exiting the meeting.

"Good to see you Miss Simmons." Davidson took a few steps in her direction.

*Have we met?* Janet stood up to take his outstretched hand.

"Well done Miss Simmons."

*So now you want to shake my hand.*

Janet checked herself and smiled as she said, "Thank you."

"For a foreigner, you get around pretty well." Davidson was still smiling and waving as he disappeared around the doorway into the corridor.

Janet followed Boris into his office. The door shut behind her and she was now alone with her editor. It was the time to make the sales pitch.

"Here's the deal Janet." Boris spoke before she had a chance to begin. "You were the first one with the report. The work was excellent. And since you've done some background work on Santiago, we're giving you the follow-on story. I should say stories."

What did she just hear? Assigned articles? They were what she had been wanting for the past two years. Was she imagining it? No, this was for real.

Janet's time had finally arrived.

As she walked past news-stands, one bold headline jumped out. *Prominent Dutch citizen killed.* It was in full view.

As she stood staring at the words, horrific images of the night flashed through her mind; flashing lights, white overalls and shuffling feet.

A blood soaked torso on the ground.

Gloom descended once again on Janet Simmons.

»«

*I must call Rosie;* standing before a phone booth, Janet looked at her watch. How long had she been walking? She had hoped to leave the painful images behind as she moved away from the offices of The Daily. It was of no use.

Regardless of her mood, she had to thank her friend. Janet stepped into the phone booth and dialled Rosie's number at home. Her mother answered. Rosie was already at the station; she said.

That meant Rosie would not be able to speak freely at work. *I must let her know.* She should have done it sooner. She had waited too long already.

Janet dialled the Amstelveen precinct office and asked for police officer Rosalinda Hopman.

"Good morning, you're speaking with Agent Hopman."

"Good morning, my name is Valeria van der Veen." Janet altered her voice. *I hope you remember our code name.* The last time Janet used 'Valeria van der Veen' was almost a year ago.

"Excuse me Madam, is this an urgent matter?" Rosie's tone implied she knew the voice was Janet's.

"No, I have questions about..."

The sentence was cut short. "We are very busy at this time Madam. Can you call in the afternoon, after 2pm?" It was a cue Rosie could not or did not want to speak.

Janet understood that to mean she ought to be home by then to receive a call.

The telephone rang at 2:01.

"Hello Janet. Read your story, great job."

"Thank you Rosie. Couldn't have done it..." *without your tip*; Janet skipped saying the words, it was safer that way. "Sad business, isn't it?"

"Yes. Sad day in Holland."

Was there more information? *Should I press her?* It was as though the question was anticipated.

"Listen, I can't tell you anymore. At this point you probably know as much as I do."

"I understand."

"When things quiet down a bit, we have to have a toast to your front page article, eh?"

"Yes, that would be nice. Thanks once again."

Janet stared at the phone as she hung up. The buzz was over. It was quiet.

It was anticlimactic.

# CHAPTER 6

Balancing the camera in one hand and the umbrella in the other, Janet stomped her feet to shake off the clumps of mud stubbornly clinging to her boots. The paved path of the cemetery was reserved for family members and dignitaries attending Santiago's memorial service. The press had to remain at a distance, behind ropes on the grassy area.

Janet tried to get a look at the faces attending the service. Between umbrellas, hats and hooded raincoats, she had been unable to recognize a single person so far.

The attendees who had already arrived, stood at the bottom of the church steps with their backs to the press. Janet nudged her way to a narrow space along the cordon. Leaning over the rope, she was able to see arriving mourners walking up the path.

*That I recognize*; Janet stiffened. A familiar fragrance floated up the path. Even with the drizzle and humid air, she knew the scent of that perfume. Immediately she pulled back, not wanting to be seen.

With a broad rimmed black hat and oversized sun glasses, the person's features were not clearly visible. But Janet knew the face. Arm in arm with her husband, Sheri walked with her head slightly bent.

Janet remained partly hidden. She would do well not to be seen by either of the Van Reefs. Especially Lars. Eye contact with him was particularly uncomfortable.

Their presence at the service was unexpected. *Why should I be surprised?* She questioned. Perhaps Santiago and the Van Reefs had been acquaintances, even friends.

Somehow, such an alliance seemed improbable. *But why not?* After all, Sheri in her position came across many an important person. Janet concluded that there was nothing surprising about the Van Reefs' presence at the funeral.

Santiago had been on the road to occupy the highest office in the land. It made perfect sense that they would have cultivated his friendship.

»«

"It's good to see you sweetheart." The hug was warm and welcoming.

"It's been a busy three weeks. I missed our chats Mrs. Steen."

*I miss the coffee sessions with you but I really like being busy at the Daily.*

The Santiago affair had not allowed Janet much free time. Her writing was featured every day in The European Daily. Except for the first week, the articles had moved away from page one. Nonetheless, she was writing and paid well for it.

Still, Janet did not give up the job of walking the dogs. The check from Sheri was steady and good; not something she could rely on at the newspaper.

"It feels like years since I saw you last." Mrs. Steen's importance in her life came as a surprise to Janet.

The stories of the Steen grandchildren sounded vaguely familiar. Still, Janet sat listening, content to be in the housekeeper's company.

*Does she know Sheri attended the memorial service?* Janet wondered. Was Mrs. Steen aware of Van Reefs' association with Santiago? Why had that not surfaced in conversations before?

*Should I mention seeing them at the cemetery? No*; she decided. It was none of her business. Besides, they had talked enough about the Santiago affair. It would only bring down the mood.

*Better to talk about something light.* Janet brought up the upcoming Van Reef event. "So, how is the preparation for the party?"

"You are on the staff list for June 19th, yeah?" Mrs. Steen waved the pad at Janet for confirmation. She then walked to the counter and pulled out a sheet of paper from the top drawer.

Janet needed no explanation; she had seen the official looking piece of paper before. It was a confidentiality agreement. The staff hired to work at the party were required to sign it to keep private conversations from being splattered across tabloids.

When Janet first met Mrs. Van Reef, she had downplayed her primary career of a reporter. If any of that conversation was forgotten, it was not the no-nonsense instruction from Sheri.

*Everything you hear about us will remain behind these walls.*

# CHAPTER 7

The knocking kept getting louder. *Patience, patience, whoever you are*; Janet glanced at the clock as she walked to the door. Eight thirty in the morning; who wanted to see her at such an early hour? The rapping stopped just as she slid the latch. She saw the back of a retreating man as she opened the door. In the dark hallway, she did not recognize the person.

"Hey." She called out to him.

The man turned around. "Hello."

Janet's frown turned into a smile. Her neighbour William stood holding a bouquet of flowers. "Happy Birthday."

"You remembered." The annoyance of the morning calm being interrupted had become a welcome diversion.

"Of course. Besides, the only way to see you is to show up at your door." William followed Janet into the kitchen. "So, which is it? Twenty seven, twenty eight?"

Janet smiled. "Only because you are my favourite neighbour, I'll tell you." *Well, you really are the only one I know in the building.* "Thirty four." She pointed to the strands of grey above the right temple. "See?"

"You look great." William leaned on the counter and smiled.

*Of course you'd say that;* she flashed a smile.

"It's good to see you Wil. How have you been?" The noises

from below told her he was alive but Janet rarely saw him.

"Janet, I thought you kept tabs on me. We are only separated by my ceiling and your floor." His broad grin brightened the otherwise lazy eyes.

"When you're not playing music, you are quiet like a mouse."

*And that music keeps me up nights;* Janet bit her lip.

They moved to the balcony with their coffee cups. William sat quietly as Janet tried to fill the awkward silence with chatter. It was as she had realized during their first encounter. What they had in common was the building in which they both lived and not much else.

"I say," William reached into his shirt pocket, "how would you like to celebrate your birthday with a free trip to the Rijksmuseum?" He waved what appeared to be two tickets.

"That would be perfect."

*It'll break the monotony.* Each day was beginning to look like the next; police briefings, Santiago updates and trips to the mansion and the Daily.

Today was going to be different; a museum outing with William and dinner date with Ryan.

Ryan and William, how different they were. Ryan was steady, practical and predictable. William on the other hand had a relaxed, almost a lazy manner about him. He was the artist, spontaneous and the opposite of the meticulous planner Ryan was.

*Practical and predictable*; how tedious that sounded. *Don't*; she chided herself to stop complaining. Ryan was dependable and committed. She ought to be content.

"So, what time shall we leave?" William chirped.

Janet was relieved by the interruption, it helped get rid of her negative thoughts.

>><<

"Well, where shall we begin?" Janet pulled out the museum guidebook. "Shall we follow the suggested path?"

"I want to show you *The Night Watch* first." William was leading the way even before she had finished the sentence.

They arrived just as a large group converged before the Rembrandt exhibit. Their guide held up his flag and waited.

"This might last a while." William whispered. "Let's go to the front."

Janet nodded and the two nudged their way through the crowd to the red silk rope cordoning off the painting.

"It's massive" Janet whispered as she scanned the canvas from side to side.

A lot was packed into the scene. How life-like the characters were. How the rays selectively highlighted one or two of the figures. Janet was in awe of the masterpiece.

"Was it worth the trip?"

She jumped at the sound of William's voice. He stood next to her and yet for a brief time, she had been far away, all alone.

"Impressive." She turned to him.

The tour group had already moved on. *So soon?* How many years did Rembrandt require for this painting? How much time did the average visitor spend in front of it? She checked the time, William and she had been gazing at the Night Watch for twelve minutes.

A group of school children was now moving their way.

"Time for the next one?" She pointed in the direction of the chattering voices. William took her elbow and the two hastened to the next hall.

They walked from painting to painting, from hall to hall.

"You like these family scenes, don't you?" William whispered as they stood before a winter landscape by Avercamp.

"I do. It's a snapshot of life back then." She shared her thoughts. "A day frozen in time."

"Life was probably quite difficult. We're looking at it with nostalgia and thinking how wonderful things were."

William's lazy demeanour belied a serious side. *I like you;* she thought but said aloud, "You surprise me Wil."

Two more hours went by. Janet sat down on a bench and massaged her aching feet.

"Ready to call it a day?" William sat down next to her.

"Almost. I want to see one painting again. You know that equestrian scene?"

"The one with the sand dunes?"

She nodded. Soon, they stood before the *Morning ride on the beach.* The scene was peaceful, serene and elegant.

"You know, this could be where I walk the dogs." She pointed to the female equestrian. "Although, I'm usually wearing jeans and not riding a horse."

William's soft laugh echoed around the high ceilings.

Janet made a mental note, *Morning ride on the beach by Anton Mauve.*

# CHAPTER 8

*Pretty darn good;* Janet smiled fastening the cameo brooch on the collar. She took one last look at the outfit; the customary long black skirt and a white blouse. It was the one she had purchased for the first of the Van Reef parties.

*Quarter to six;* she checked the time as the van turned the last corner. Six o'clock was the specified time; the party was to begin at eight.

The gate was already open. A man in dark clothes gestured with his hand. Was he waving her in or telling her to leave? She stopped to confirm before driving onto the property. As the man moved closer, she realized that he was not the regular guard.

"Name." The face was unsmiling.

"Janet Simmons."

His index finger ran down the list on the clipboard. He nodded and pointed to the backyard.

"Thank you." Janet smiled but he had moved on.

Janet bristled at his brusque manner. She looked up to say something but his eyes were trained on the car behind. He was already walking toward the next visitor to the mansion. Annoyed but feeling the pressure to begin work, Janet put the van in gear and charged toward the backyard.

The brightly lit kitchen was already a beehive of activity.

Platters were lined up on the large work table in the centre. The hostess and the housekeeper sat at the nook and appeared to be going over a check-list.

"Good evening Mrs. Van Reef, Mrs. Steen." Janet announced herself.

The hostess turned to her and flashed a smile.

Sheri was even more stunning than Janet had ever seen before. Still, something was not right. The look in Sheri's eyes did not seem to match the radiant smile. Janet had seen that look before. Was it sorrow? No, that could not be.

What were the eyes betraying?

Stress; that was it; Janet concluded. Stress of hosting such an elegant party. After all, the soiree would be the talk of the town for days to come.

The event had to be the perfect party given by the perfect couple.

At ten minutes past seven, the staff assembled in the kitchen for final instructions.

"But most of all," Sheri concluded as she surveyed the faces, "be very attentive to the guests." Her dress swirled as she glided out of the kitchen.

*Be attentive, cater to their every whim*; she seemed to be saying.

At eight twenty, the doorbell rang. By nine, the living room was buzzing. Janet recognized several people, some faces familiar because they were on television regularly. His honourable Lord Mayor of Amsterdam, Florian Coleman, the politician.

Was that tall man a Royal? The attire was in accordance but

he was definitely not first string. Claiming royal connection by distant relatives was all too common.

Once, when Janet looked up at Lars, she could not help thinking how good he looked. Perhaps the gushing descriptions were not off the mark. Mr. Van Reef was indeed very handsome. *Handsome and regal*; Janet remembered the compliment in the Great Homes magazine.

The striking of the antique clock reverberated throughout the house. Janet counted eleven. The frenzy had tapered off and the party had settled down to a relaxed pace. Janet sat down at the kitchen table, removed her shoes and began massaging her right foot.

"Mevrouw Simmons." She looked up at a young server walking into the kitchen from the living room. "You are wanted in there." He pointed in the direction of the staircase.

She walked into the living room and saw a woman bending down and examining her cream coloured dress. Even from a few feet away, Janet could see the red wine spilled on it.

Mrs. Van Reef stood next to the guest and turned as Janet approached. "Janet, could you take Mrs. Martin up to the dressing room and give her a hand?"

The guest was already walking toward the steps.

"Yes, of course." Janet walked quickly and caught up with her. *I hope I'll know what to do;* she walked past Mrs. Martin and led her to the master suite on the upper level.

An array of items was placed next to towels on the dresser. Janet looked through and picked up the stain remover.

"I think this is what you need." She handed Mrs. Martin the spray bottle and a towel.

"Mrs. Van Reef thinks of everything. She is the perfect

hostess." The woman smiled awkwardly, embarrassed at having brought attention to herself. "Thank you young lady. Sorry for the bother."

"Not at all." Janet smiled. For someone who appeared distinguished and important, Mrs. Martin sounded completely unspoilt.

"I'll be in the corridor if you need me." The door made a soft thud as Janet closed it and stepped out of the room.

In the hallway, she noticed a variety of objects adorning the walls. Even door frames looked ornate, like bits and pieces out of Greek history. She remembered the description in the magazine; *Essence of elegance.*

*Gaudy and pretentious;* is how Ryan described it when Janet showed him the article.

*I know that door.* Lars' office was across the hallway from the master bedroom. She recalled the brief tour of the house on her first day at the mansion.

"Oh, we do not go in there." The housekeeper had sounded as though the office were not a mere room but the Sanctum Sanctorum. "Except for Mr. Flanders, of course."

The statement was telling. It had underscored Maurice Flanders' undisputed importance in the Van Reef world.

Mrs. Martin was still in the dressing room. She had not called out to Janet. *Should I check on her? No.* She thought of the lady's face flushed with embarrassment.

Janet walked to the end of the corridor and looked out the window. The front yard was packed with shiny vehicles. *There's the charming guard;* she saw the dark figure pacing near the gate. Did he just look up? She recoiled. *Just my imagination.* Still, she thought it was better to be away from

46

the window.

Janet walked back and paused at the office door. It was open halfway. She leaned in for a glimpse. No lights were on but the evening glow of the long summer days illuminated the room sufficiently.

The office was large, occupying more than half the length of the house. Janet stepped closer. The space was an unexpected combination of working and lounging areas. The office furniture did not seem unusual; desks, chairs and cabinets. In contrast, the sitting area was plush, furnished with burgundy coloured leather sofas. Behind the larger of the two sofas was a bar, lining the back wall of the room. Two of the bar stools were pulled out and looked as though they had been used recently.

Janet scanned the room. The furniture felt discordant, with a mix of practical pieces and items of grandeur. Elegantly framed paintings stood out on the otherwise plain walls. The room was very unlike a typical office. *That's no surprise;* Janet thought. *Nothing about this house is typical.*

As her eyes traversed the walls, they stopped on one painting. Why was it so familiar? She leaned further for a better look. She began to remember. The painting was very similar to one she had seen somewhere else. Where? In a museum? She pictured the hall in which it was displayed. Yes. She could see it. The painting was the one hanging on the second floor in the west wing of the Rijksmuseum. How could she have forgotten? She had returned for a second look at the end of the day, after already having spent a long time admiring it.

The clacking of high heels on the hardwood floor made Janet lurch out of the office doorway. She moved quickly to the top of the stairwell.

Mrs. Martin emerged from the bedroom. "Dear, you are waiting for me. Thank you." She patted Janet on the shoulder. They walked side by side down the staircase and into the living room.

The rest of the evening felt easy. Janet relaxed in the kitchen and sampled the canapés. She knew the gourmet food was not the sort she would be eating any time soon.

Some guests were still present when the caterer's staff filed out. Janet waited until five minutes past two a.m., put on her coat and went to the edge of the living room. A few couples still remained and appeared very relaxed.

Janet saw Mrs. Martin waving and walked to her. The guest stood up and held out her hand, "Good night sweetheart. Thanks for your help."

"Good night Mrs. Martin. Good night Mrs. Van Reef." Janet held out her hand to Sheri but to her surprise, the hostess stood up and kissed her on both cheeks. "Thank you for your help tonight Janet. And for staying so late."

The appreciation was genuine. Janet saw it in the large blue eyes. Throughout the evening, Sheri had been warm toward her. Perhaps there was friendship in the air.

*Don't be silly.* Janet dismissed the thought immediately.

She did not inhabit the same sphere as the Van Reefs.

»«

Janet settled herself at the table. She had lost many hours and needed to focus on the articles. Distractions such as the party were a pleasant break from routine but she reminded herself that her primary career was that of a journalist.

After a half a day of writing, she examined her work. *Not bad;* she thought. It could use some refining but she was restless. She needed a change. She arranged the sheets of paper into a tidy pile.

Perhaps making dinner would provide the change. The array of food the previous night had inspired her to try something other than her staples. Flipping through the pages of the cook book, she settled on a stew. It seemed simple but was already stretching the bounds of her cooking talents.

*Wouldn't it be nice to share the meal with someone?* Should she ask William? He would be a good dinner companion, pleasant and easy going. What would Ryan think? But William was simply a friendly neighbour. Surely, it was not improper. She walked down the narrow stairwell to the third floor.

"Hey pretty neighbour." William greeted her with his lazy smile. Janet could not recall seeing any other expression on his face.

William's reaction to the dinner invitation was lively. "I'd love to." He scooped her up in his arms. Even at 5'5", Janet felt like a small person.

"Let me at least bring some wine."

She waited while he disappeared around the kitchen counter. She looked around the living room. There was no mistaking the fact that it was William's music studio, office and the space where he spent all of his time.

William listened with interest about Janet's day and her articles on Jose Santiago.

As the evening wore on, conversation turned to intimate matters. Janet's childhood, her distance from her father, her mother's unfortunate association with Alex. *No, no*; her mind screamed; that part of her life was too unpleasant to revisit.

49

She changed the subject. "Do you think there could be two identical masterpieces?"

"You mean paintings?"

"Yes. What would you think if you saw a painting just like one you might have seen in a museum?"

"Come on Janet. There must be a million sunflower paintings like Van Gogh's." He laughed. "You see copies all the time."

"I suppose." She said, resigned.

*The one in the mansion might have been a print.* From the distance where she stood and with fading light, Janet could not even be certain that the framed painting in Van Reef's office was the *Morning ride on the beach.*

»«

"Hello!" Janet walked into a quiet kitchen in the mansion.

The only noise came from the noisy refrigerator. She surveyed the uncluttered workspace and the dark, cold oven. Mrs. Steen was still not back at work.

As she turned around to leave, she saw the white sleeved arm of Maurice Flanders.

"Good morning Miss Simmons. If you are looking for Mrs. Steen, she has taken a few days off."

"I imagine she's quite tired after the party." She waved and walked out of the kitchen without striking up a conversation.

*Mrs. Steen must be exhausted.* Why did she continue to work at her age? Janet knew the answer. At seventy one years of age, the housekeeper's loyalty to Sheri kept her going. She had once complained that it was increasingly difficult to continue working. Her daughter had been urging her to quit her job. With the children grown, fewer bills to pay, she could retire very comfortably. But Mrs. Steen wanted to work.

She wanted to work for Sheri.

As a housekeeper, she had a major role in running the household. That was not the only reason why she insisted on coming every day, cooking and baking for the family.

Janet recalled the only time Mrs. Steen spoke of a painful, personal subject.

The first of the Steen grandchildren had a developmental disability. Sheri had taken it upon herself to find treatments, mainstream and alternate. Being the celebrity she was, Sheri had access to many resources unavailable or unknown to the average person. What the treatments were, Mrs. Steen did not elaborate. But it did not matter, there was a satisfactory ending.

Sheri had been a pillar of strength during a difficult time in Mrs. Steen's life. She had been a friend in need.

Since that conversation, Janet knew and understood the trust Mrs. Steen and Sheri had in one another. She understood the housekeeper's unquestioned loyalty to the Van Reefs.

*Why not visit Mrs. Steen?* Janet thought impulsively. A week felt like a long time without seeing her.

The little town of Leimuiden was only a slight detour from her way home. At a roadside florist along the way, she stopped and picked up a bouquet of bright pink daisies.

She drove past the "Welcome to Leimuiden" plaque, looking for street names. Four minutes later, she was parking the van in front of the door with the largest red, white and blue Dutch flag. The small brick house at the end of a row of houses looked like a doll house. The gateposts with violets felt cheerful and welcoming.

*Ah, the quintessential Dutch house;* Janet smiled, looking up at the hoist beam and step gable.

The gate made a grinding sound as Janet pushed it open.

A tall man peeling off garden gloves answered the door bell.

"Mr. Steen?"

"Yes?"

"I'm Janet Simmons. Just thought I'd stop in and check on Mrs. Steen."

"Come in. Come in." The look of suspicion disappeared.

"Ah, schatje, it's good to see you." The housekeeper looked diminutive next her husband.

"Well, I had to get a cup of your coffee one way or another." Janet joked. "I hope I'm not intruding."

"Oh no darling. I'm so glad you took the time to come see me." The old lady chattered excitedly as she poured coffee.

The two women inquired after each other's well-being. Janet discovered that she did not have much to say. It was as most mornings in the mansion were. The housekeeper chattered while Janet listened and interjected every once in a while.

A half hour passed. "I must be getting along."

"I'm sure you have much work to do Janet. Thank you for coming by."

"Thanks for the coffee." The time was well spent but Janet was anxious to leave.

*It's still early;* she looked at the clock as she put the van in gear. *The article's in good shape, maybe I could go wandering.* Freelancing had its advantages.

*Amsterdam?* It was a great city to visit on any day. Perhaps a trip to the museum. Perhaps another look at that painting?

The previous evening with William had her thinking about art again. William was the one who had brought her to the museum the last time. As Janet waited in the ticket line, she mulled over some of the paintings she had enjoyed during her last visit. How would she remember them? Would her impressions be the same?

Those other paintings would have to wait. This time, Janet was interested only in one painting. Not ten minutes had passed when she found herself standing before the serene landscape. Yet again, she had been drawn to Mauve's magical scene.

It was as though the dunes called out to her.

Minutes ticked as she looked at it, up, down and sideways. Was it not the same painting in Lars Van Reef's office? But how could it be in two places at once? She shook her head. No, that was not possible. But here it was, just like the one she had seen on the night of the party. Of course, it could have been a print reproduction. She had been too far away and the light was not sufficient to see the difference.

Perhaps she could look at it up close someday. She might have another opportunity to be in the Van Reef office.

Janet left the museum but the *Morning ride on the beach* did not leave her.

»«

*Yes, today is Thursday;* the frown deepened; *what is the matter with me?* Janet kept asking. All she was doing was going to look at a work by Anton Mauve.

The cause of the jitters was not the painting itself, rather its location, Lars van Reef's office. *Sanctum sanctorum* is how she had referred to it in jest. Later in the day, she would be in that room, the entry to which was reserved for a privileged few.

Something else was tugging at her. Why was she doing this? What exactly was the purpose of the visit? What did she hope to accomplish?

*I'm making too much of this;* she shook her head. The truth was, she liked works by Anton Mauve. Her interest in this particular painting was simple, academic curiosity.

She hoped Mrs. Steen had cleared it with Sheri. The housekeeper had said as much on the phone but she was becoming forgetful. Did she get the day right?

*I wished I'd asked Sheri myself.* When Janet came for the dogs in the mornings, Mrs. Van Reef was already at the television station. Janet decided it was easier to make her request through the housekeeper.

"Thursday morning's the best time." Mrs. Steen had suggested. "Mr. Van Reef goes golfing every single Thursday."

Arriving at the late morning hour, Janet noticed the house was devoid of activity. The only light came from the kitchen. Janet walked in to find the housekeeper wrapping up her work.

Janet posed her question immediately, "Did you ask Mrs.

Van Reef?"

"Ask her what?"

*Oh dear, just I suspected;* the elderly lady was becoming more forgetful each day. "About my taking a look at the painting upstairs."

"Oh that, yes." Mrs. Steen nodded, "Madam said it was fine."

Janet walked to the edge of the kitchen and looked around the living room. The house was still. Now was definitely the time to go upstairs. The sooner she was done with it, the better.

"Go on." The housekeeper motioned toward the stairs and returned to wiping the table.

Janet moved quickly and made her way to the second level. She paused outside the office. The door was ajar. She nudged it open and waited. Hearing nothing, she took a step closer.

Her eyes swept across the large space. The office contained many creature comforts. She was not surprised that whenever Lars was home, he spent little time elsewhere in the house.

From left to right, her eyes travelled to each of the four frames. She leaned into the narrow entryway, from where she had seen the landscape on the night of the party.

The painting was on the far wall, the distance too great for her to see clearly. She took several steps into the middle of the room. The dunes, the North Sea and the horse were clearly discernible. The painting was breathtaking, just as the one in the museum was.

Were the two works alike? Or did they only resemble each other? Janet moved closer till she was inches from the frame.

She peered at the different parts of the canvas. The painting was definitely identical to the one in the Rijksmuseum. There was no doubt in Janet's mind. This too looked like an original. She examined the signature. It was clearly the Mauve scribble she had begun to recognize.

The two paintings were identical masterpieces.

How could that be? Why would an artist paint two of a kind? *There must be a million Van Gogh sunflowers;* she recalled William's comment.

Janet was lost in her world and completely oblivious to the sound of approaching footsteps.

"What are you doing here?"

Startled, she whirled around and found herself looking at a pair of unsmiling eyes, those of Lars Van Reef.

Janet could hear her heart pound. *Say something. Anything.* But words did not come.

"I said, what are you doing in my office?" The tone remained even but the expression turned from unsmiling to cold.

Janet struggled to get out the words, "I had seen these paintings during the party." She pointed to the Mauve and the frame next to it. "They are so beautiful. I," she paused, "I just wanted another look."

*I want to get out of here;* Janet was desperate to leave but Van Reef stood between the doorway and her.

*He doesn't believe me.* Aloud she said, "I cleared it with Mrs. Van Reef."

*I hope Mrs. Steen was not mistaken.* Janet was now overcome with doubt. Maybe the housekeeper forgot about having asked Sheri. Perhaps she had the day wrong.

Without saying another word, Lars waved his hand in a dismissive manner and walked past her to the desk.

Janet paused to apologize before leaving. With his back to her, Lars was leafing through the papers in his hand and seemed to have forgotten about her.

She turned around and stepped out of the room. Fighting the urge to run, she walked softly to the end of the corridor and down the steps.

Once in the kitchen, Janet re-lived the moment she came face-to-face with Lars. It was awkward then. But now, she felt invisible. He had brushed her aside like an insignificant fly. He had not given her a second look.

The kitchen was quiet. The housekeeper was nowhere to be seen. There was no time for goodbyes. Janet had to leave, in case Van Reef came downstairs. She could not bear another encounter. A shiver ran down her back as she recalled the expression on his face. It was such a hard look.

She shifted restlessly in her seat during the drive home. The confrontation had left her feeling miserable. She told herself it was overblown in her mind. Lars had probably forgotten about it already.

Still, Janet wished she could take back those few precious moments.

# CHAPTER 9

Santiago, Santiago and more Santiago; Janet had been at the article all day. The murder was not solved but the story continued to be covered. With little new information from the investigation team, the writing on the subject was becoming repetitive and tedious.

*I need to get out.* The walls of the attic apartment were closing in. Janet needed to get away, at least for a few days.

Forecast called for sunny weather for several days. The islands up North would be a pleasant retreat. She reached for the phone to call Ryan but stopped. Was it too soon? She cradled the receiver in her hand. *What would he think of my initiating a weekend away?*

She told herself it was all right. After all, they had been together quite some time. They even spent a short holiday taking in the sights of Rome. Ryan was the only man in her life. This was not improper.

Where did she want the relationship to go? Was this the real thing? If it was, should she be asking herself such questions?

Ryan sounded pleased at the invitation. Surprised but pleased. *I'll make the arrangements;* Janet offered.

She was still thinking of Ryan's cheerful voice after she hung up the phone. He was nice. He liked her. So why all the questions?

Was it because she had spent time with William? *No, that's silly;* she chided herself. William was just a neighbour, a passer-by. She had known Ryan for almost six months now. He was a straight arrow.

Why then the trepidation?

*I know why;* Janet's jaws clenched, recalling the time in her life when she had paid attention to alarm bells going off in her head. Her premonition had led to the discovery of her step father Alex's sordid past.

Was the same nagging voice telling her something about Ryan? *No*; she decided. Her guard was up and it was simply telling her to be careful. Yes, she had something special with Ryan. He was the one.

And time would tell.

# CHAPTER 10

Marjan led Janet to the kitchen.

"Can I pour you some wine?" She pointed to the chair.

"Yes, thanks." Janet smiled. "I really appreciate this Marjan."

"Ah, it's nothing. I know what you did for my brother."

Janet recalled the time when Marjan's brother Rob arrived at the university. Being the senior student, Janet had taken him under her wing during the first few months.

"You know, the last time Rob and I spoke was New Year's day." Janet had been concerned about Rob's reaction to her calling after a long time and only when she needed something.

She had been desperate to find someone to solve the riddle of the two masterpieces. She wanted to ask Rob for an introduction to his sister Marjan, who had studied art.

"No worries Janet." Marjan handed Janet a glass. "Rob was happy he could help."

Janet felt grateful. Marjan was her chance to find out about the Mauve.

"So, I understand you work in Amsterdam." Even as she spoke, Janet formulated the questions she was about to ask.

"Yes. I work at a gallery in the Jordaan. A small one."

Marjan smiled awkwardly.

Was she embarrassed about her job? Janet wondered. Was working in a gallery considered less than modest achievement? Was the ambition of her peers to be employed by renowned museums?

"That must be interesting."

The woman across the table from her shrugged but said nothing. This was not going to be easy.

"I have one or two questions." Janet pushed. "I've been reading about art, going to museums." She kept talking, hoping to draw Marjan into the conversation.

"Books teach some things but don't have all the answers." Marjan smiled. She seemed to be opening up to Janet. "What do you want to know?"

"I've been commissioned by my paper to write about the Dutch Masters and the Golden Age."

*It's a harmless white lie.* Mentioning the paper gave Janet a cover. Sometimes it got people to talk but in many cases made them avoid her.

Marjan did not comment.

*Good, no negative reaction*; Janet continued. "Some artists have made an impression on me." Was the time ripe to bring up the real issue? "There is this one painting."

*Should I mention which one? No, not just yet.* "It was beautiful. Then I thought I saw it somewhere else."

"What was this painting?"

"It's the..." She paused.

*I'll have to keep it general. She mustn't think I'm obsessing about this.*

"It's in my notes." Janet reached for her bag. "Is it possible I could have seen two identical paintings?"

"Yes sure. You find copies all the time. Our gallery even carries copies of some popular works." Marjan said matter-of-factly.

"But made by someone else?"

"Yeah, usually some budding artist. It's legitimate, we sell it under their name not the original artist's. No funny business here." Marjan laughed.

That was a good sign, Marjan was relaxed. *This chat might go a bit longer yet.* Sensing Marjan's mood when they began, Janet had feared the meeting would be brief.

"Copies yes." Now was the time, Janet decided. "But these were originals, by the same artist. At least I think they were, judging by the signature."

"Well, artists like some scenes and keep doing it." Marjan no longer needed prodding, "It's possible that his work resulted in a series."

"These two were exactly alike."

"They might have seemed that way. Take another look at them both."

Marjan was not getting it. Janet kept her impatience in check.

"Small time artists make a living selling copies of masterpieces." Marjan continued with her take. "Many people enjoy owning a Van Gogh or a Picasso but can never afford the real thing. Knowingly, they pay good money for a copy by another artist."

This was not working, Janet changed the tactic, "If you saw them, do you think you would be able to tell them apart?"

*What are you doing?* Janet could not believe the words she had uttered. Why would she go back to Van Reef's office and risk another encounter with him? The last one was still fresh in her mind. Why would she subject herself to the torture?

Janet had to know about that painting. She had to find the explanation.

She would do it differently this time, ask Sheri herself and make absolutely certain Lars was not home.

Her thoughts were interrupted by a soft murmur.

"I suppose I could."

Even though Marjan sounded half hearted, she had not declined. That was a start.

*Hurry before she changes her mind;* Janet added quickly, "Would you have time? It might take a couple of hours."

They were going to need more time than that but Janet had to get Marjan to agree.

"I have to check my calendar."

That was almost a commitment. Janet rushed to close the loop. "Great. I'll get back to you with details."

"Now tell me about this painting."

"Yes, of course." Janet flipped the pages of the notebook. "It's an oil by Anton Mauve called *Morning Ride on the Beach.*"

"I might have seen it but don't remember."

Janet described the scene and the painting's location in the west wing of the Rijksmuseum.

"I'll get there when I have some free time." The polite smile re-emerged.

Marjan did not share Janet's curiosity. That was disappointing. But the Mauve was Janet's preoccupation and not a priority for someone else.

Curiosity? What began as academic interest was now verging on obsession.

》《

*She doesn't want to do it and hopes I'll forget.*

Janet had not heard from Marjan for more than a week. She tried to put the matter aside and returned to the typewriter.

The phone rang at noon, Marjan was calling. Janet could not help thinking it was probably at Rob's insistence.

"I took a good look at the Mauve in the museum. This one's particularly lovely. I had seen other Mauves, ones with farm animals and such. *The Morning Ride* is very elegant."

"I thought so too." Janet knew what Marjan was about ask.

"Where's the other one?" Marjan's voice carried an eagerness Janet had not heard before.

*Now she wants to know.*

"It's in a private residence." Janet wanted to lock in the commitment. "Are you free on Thursday morning? I'll check with the owner and let you know."

There would be no loose ends this time. She would ask Sheri personally. She would make absolutely certain Lars was gone.

"Coming Thursday is out." There was a rustle of paper.

*I have to sweeten the pot;* Janet added quickly, "A week

65

later? How about a quick look first and lunch afterwards? My treat."

"That'll work."

"Perfect. I'll call as soon as I know."

Janet walked slowly to the sofa. *Why am I doing this?* She asked. *Why am I risking another brush with him?*

After the painful encounter with Lars, Janet had sworn never to go near the upstairs office. But she had to. The painting's real identity had to be confirmed.

Why was this important?

Why could she not let go of it?

»«

Janet had already been to the mansion once when she came for the dogs. She returned for a meeting with Sheri.

"What can I do for you Janet?" Sheri smiled warmly.

"Sheri, I'm fascinated with some of the beautiful paintings upstairs, in your husband's office."

"Yes. You asked to look at them some time back."

This was the confirmation yet again that Sheri knew about her previous visit and had cleared it on her husband's behalf. Janet felt relieved. There must have been some mistake about the day. Or Lars van Reef had simply changed his mind about golf.

Sheri did not seem to know of the confrontation. Had her husband not mentioned it?

In her mind, Janet had blown it out of proportion. It was of little significance to Lars and he had probably forgotten about it right away.

"The paintings are beautiful," Janet repeated, "I mentioned them to a friend. She's a real art buff. Now she would like to have a look."

It was all true. However, was Janet lying by omission? Should she mention the awkward run-in with Lars?

Sheri probably knew but thought nothing of it. "Yes, of course." She waved her hand. "No need to be so formal Janet. Do you have a day in mind?"

"A week from Thursday?"

"I'll see if Lars is away that morning and leave a word with Mrs. Steen."

Janet winced; she did not need a repeat performance if the housekeeper forgot.

"Better yet, I'll leave a note for you. You know Mrs. Steen forgets sometimes."

"Yes I know." Janet chuckled with relief.

Sheri's casual air was a surprise. Lars van Reef's office had been painted to her as an unapproachable bastion. Sheri did not appear to attach the same importance to it.

»«

Marjan arrived at ten past ten on Thursday morning.

Janet pointed to the van. "We'll take mine. I know the way and it'll be faster."

"Okay." Marjan did not object.

"I'll drive out. You park in my spot."

Janet waited for her to settle into the passenger seat. "Thanks for taking the time."

"No problem." Marjan smiled but her eyes were dull.

*She has second thoughts.* Janet could not help thinking Marjan regretted agreeing to something for which she had neither the time nor the interest.

Marjan's silence continued during the drive. *Maybe this wasn't such a good idea.* However, they were on their way and it did not make sense to call it off. After an uncomfortable twenty minutes on the road, Janet was leading Marjan into the mansion.

Noises emanated from the pantry. Janet announced their arrival.

"Hello Mrs. Steen," she shouted, "here I am with my friend Marjan."

Calling her a friend was a stretch but introducing her as an acquaintance felt rude.

The housekeeper appeared from around the corridor.

"Good morning to you both. How about some coffee schatje?"

"Thanks but we're in a bit of a hurry. Marjan needs to get back to work."

*She looks as if she'd rather be anywhere but here.*

"Going to look at the paintings?"

Mrs. Steen had been informed by Mrs. Van Reef. Janet had her confirmation in the note Sheri had left for her. During the drive, Janet had decided that if neither Sheri nor the housekeeper was present, they would not go upstairs. She did not want to do it without either of the women present to back her up.

"Is it okay to go upstairs now?" *Check and double check;* Janet could not be too cautious.

"I heard Mr. Van Reef leave." The elderly woman walked to the window and peered through the glass. "Only blue skies today. He'll be busy for a few hours."

Janet nudged Marjan into the living room. Her pulse quickened as they walked up the steps. The door to the office was not locked.

"This way." The two walked to the far wall. "What a shame it's tucked away in such an unceremonious location."

Marjan pulled out a magnifying glass from her purse. She began examining the painting in narrow strips from top to bottom and worked through every inch of the canvas. She then slid the magnifying glass a few times over the signature.

After several minutes, she spoke. "I'm as intrigued as you." Her face was knotted in a frown. "It appears to be a perfect twin to the one in the museum."

"That's what I told you, remember?"

Marjan nodded. "Your observation was spot on."

Finally, Janet had her confirmation. Still, many questions nagged her. But she could discuss those somewhere else, away from here.

She had the one answer she sought.

"OK, let's go." Janet was ready to leave but found herself addressing the back of Marjan's head. Marjan's attention had moved to the painting next to the Mauve.

"Oh, you want to look at the other paintings." Janet glanced at her watch. Another few minutes would not be a problem. After all, Marjan had taken time out of her day to do Janet this favour.

"I'll be over there." Janet walked to the door. Her eyes

shifted back and forth between the corridor and the wall clock.

A gasp made her turn to find Marjan beckoning.

"What is it?" Janet whispered.

Marjan's eyes were wide. "Come here."

Janet walked back into the room.

"This is a Chagall Janet." Marjan pointed to the painting before her.

"And?" Janet moved closer.

"This is a work by Marc Chagall. It's called The Blue House. It's such a classic." On Marjan's face was an intensity Janet had not seen before.

"What about it?"

It was as if Marjan did not hear the question. Minutes ticked by. The grandfather clock in the living room bonged eleven times.

They had been upstairs close to a half hour, it was time to leave. Even though Janet had Mrs. Van Reef's clearance, running into Lars again was bad news.

Or worse.

"We have to leave." Janet's voice carried urgency but Marjan did not budge. "Let's go." Janet grabbed Marjan's arm and led her out of the room and down the steps.

They picked up their belongings and went to the van without taking leave of Mrs. Steen.

As Janet fished the key out of the purse, the gates opened for someone. A car drove in. Janet could not see it but the soft purr of the engine was not unfamiliar.

She held her breath. The vehicle stopped under the portico. A few seconds of quiet were followed by the slam of the front door.

Janet took a deep breath and turned the key.

"Are we waiting for something?" Marjan had not said a word since they left the upstairs office.

"Oh, nothing really." Janet hoped the quiver in her voice was not noticed.

She drove out of the mansion gently to keep the noise down. As soon as the van was at the end of the block, Janet's foot came down on the accelerator.

"You know, I wrote a paper on Chagall in college." Marjan began without prompting.

*Now she's in a talkative mood.* Marjan's chatter was welcome because Janet did not feel like conversing. Besides, she felt too rattled to sound cohesive. *The less she notices how nervous I am, the better.*

"I can't be one hundred percent sure," Marjan continued, "but *The Blue House* in there is very much like the original."

In addition to the Mauve, an original Chagall hung in Lars' office.

Marjan described the nuances of the painting. "It has all the characteristics of an original Janet." Her voice was at a higher pitch. "If it is a copy, it's a damned good one."

The mystery had migrated from the Mauve to the Chagall.

Janet fell silent. Confusion swirled in her mind. *The Morning ride on the beach* in the museum, the same painting in the Van Reef house.

How could a painting be in two places at once?

71

Why were the paintings tucked away in an obscure corner? Why were they not displayed in a prominent place where they would be noticed and receive praise from guests?

"I'm no expert." Marjan's voice interrupted Janet's thoughts. "I'm thinking now maybe they're copies. Perfect copies." She turned to Janet. "Do you think this Mr. Van Reef was duped into buying fakes?"

"Maybe he was." Janet did not believe her own words.

*Lars van Reef deceived? Not in a million years.*

'Duped' was a notion as far removed from Lars Van Reef as anyone could imagine.

# CHAPTER 11

A large crowd had already assembled in the conference room. *Damn, I thought I was early.* Janet nudged her way to the front. Being 5'5" among the world's tallest people had some disadvantages.

The Santiago murder had been the major news for weeks. Was there a new development today? She stood with the pad ready in her hand.

A sudden surge in the noise level suggested the spokesman had arrived.

"Make way to pass. Please."

Just as she had done, someone fought his way through the crowd to the podium.

"Good morning ladies and gentlemen. Thank you for coming."

Janet listened to the statement. The sentences she heard were long but lacking in new information. The crowd murmured restlessly.

"Please ladies and gentlemen. Every single lead in the case is being followed." He stressed that the investigation was indeed going full speed. "The case is our highest priority. We are not sparing any resource."

"Blah, blah, blah." Someone muttered.

"Does the murder appear to be a contract killing?" A reporter asked.

A hush fell across the room.

The spokesman hesitated for a second but did not answer the question.

"Do you agree that the murder was execution style?" The voice persisted.

The spokesman did not look up but began gathering his papers. The crowd's murmur grew to a loud hum and drowned the officer's effort to thank everyone for attending.

The networks had already speculated on the execution style killing. The talk on the streets was no different. This was the first time the sentiment was expressed during a police press conference.

The spokesman had hesitated when the question was thrown at him. Was that a tacit affirmation of a contract killing?

The realization sent chills down Janet's spine.

>><<

"Your Santiago article's very good." Ryan waved the paper.

*He's just being polite.*

"Are there things you know that didn't make it to the paper?" He persisted.

Ryan's interest seemed genuine. Janet wanted to speak on the subject but something else was tugging at her. The matter of original masterpieces hanging on the walls of the Van Reefs' office.

She wanted to know Ryan's opinion. "By the way, I spent a morning with Marjan recently."

"Yes, Rob's sister. I remember you went to her house."

74

"That evening I had talked about some art at Sheri's house." Janet broached the subject lightly. "Marjan wanted to see it."

"I see." Ryan nodded obligingly.

Was that politeness once again? *Should I go on?* She gave it another try. "They have a famous Chagall and Marjan thinks it's authentic."

"Why not?" His brow creased.

"There's another lovely painting in there. I could have sworn I had seen it in the Rijksmuseum."

"Janet." Ryan grimaced. "Why are you preoccupied with what's in the Van Reef house? Who cares?"

Janet decided not to argue the point. Ryan was right.

She ought not to be wasting time with what went on in the Van Reef household.

»«

The Santiago investigative team was tight lipped. It meant they had nothing new to go on. Or they were very close to a resolution.

The Director of Internal Security had made crime fighting his personal mission. Santiago posed a serious threat to criminals. Scores of people could be wishing him gone and the nature of the murder carried a chilling message.

*Don't mess with us.*

The elimination had been executed cleanly and with little trace.

*Don't get in our way.*

The message of reprisal had been sent.

The shrill ringing of the telephone jarred Janet from her

thoughts.

"Hey there Janet." Marjan was on the line.

"Hi Marjan. Nice to hear from you." Janet was glad Marjan called. She had hoped for more insights on the two paintings.

"I've done some quick checking." The voice was strangely dull. "I'm afraid I haven't really uncovered anything."

"Oh." Janet sighed.

Marjan had nothing exciting to report. "I looked up phone numbers of major museums and auction houses. Give them a call if you have time."

*If you have time;* that really meant *I don't have time for this nonsense.*

"Ask about recent sales. If you get them talking and if you're lucky, someone might let slip some information."

Janet began scribbling down names and numbers; Chagall museum in Nice, auction houses in New York and London. She recognized the names Sotheby's and Christie's.

"Thanks for this information." The lack of any new leads was anticlimactic.

"I may have one more piece of news which might interest you. A guy I went to college with is an administrator at the Rijksmuseum."

"Really?" Janet brightened.

"His name is Marco Haarlemmer. He's been at the museum four or five years."

Marco Haarlemmer; Janet committed the name to memory. Things were looking up.

"Why didn't you tell me about him before?"

"Well, I didn't really know him that well. Besides, I'm not in touch with the college crowd so I had to ask around."

"This is good news." Janet could not wait to hang up and establish contact with Mr. Haarlemmer.

"I think he'll know all the angles Janet. I hear he's doing quite well."

"Thank you so much."

This was too good. Marco might just be the person who could shed light on all her questions.

He might be the one to unlock the mystery of the *Morning Ride on The Beach*.

# CHAPTER 12

The museum cafeteria was crowded with jostling lunchtime throngs. The air was thick with smells of food. The noise of clacking silverware and chattering voices reverberated through the high ceilings.

Janet hovered near the entryway, wishing she had come at another, quieter time. But the meeting was as Marco Haarlemmer had requested. Why the cafeteria? She wondered. Why could they not have met in his office?

Janet surveyed the dining area and chose a table in the least crowded part of the room. With her back to the wall, she had a clear view of the entrance. She had been assured Marco was easy to spot.

"Trust me, you can't miss him." Marjan had gone on to describe him; six feet two, thirty-ish, with reddish blond hair.

A man wearing a dark blue suit made his way through the wall of people. A badge pinned on his left breast pocket suggested he was an employee.

There was no mistaking Marco.

The man scanned the crowd and started toward Janet as he caught sight of her waving.

"Good afternoon. I am Marco Haarlemmer." He held out his hand. "You must be Janet Simmons?"

Janet was looking at the most striking pair of eyes she had

ever seen.

"Yes. Thanks for seeing me at such short notice Mr. Haarlemmer."

"Call me Marco please." He had an easy smile. "Sorry about meeting here. Our offices are being painted. Mine is a mess."

"It doesn't matter really."

"Not the best time, is it?" He looked around the crowded floor. "But it's the only time I have today."

"I understand." She had asked to meet him soon, today if possible.

"Can I get you some coffee before we start?"

"No. Thank you." He was amiable and charming.

"Okay, let's get started, I have about a half hour. How can I help?"

He was a man whose time she could not waste.

"Did Marjan tell you anything?" How much did he know already?

"Not really. I got a message through a mutual friend." The smile was disarming.

Nothing had been given away so far. Janet had rehearsed different approaches and decided to use the newspaper as a lead-in. It was always a good cover.

"I'm doing an article for my newspaper, The European Daily. The theme is Dutch Masters and the Golden Age."

"Surely, you can find that in any book." Marco waved in the direction the museum gift shop.

She had to come to the point or would soon find an impatient

Marco. "The paper also wants coverage of other aspects such as, theft, forgery etc. The dark side, if you will."

Marco's eyes rested on hers. She felt as though they were seeing right through her. Perhaps her cover story had not been convincing.

She need not have worried. Marco spoke without further prompting.

"You have aptly called it the dark side Janet. You can imagine our feelings on the matter. As museum officials, that is our absolute worst nightmare. Not just the Rijksmuseum but any museum in the world."

Speaking about art came easily to Marco. He was probably equally well versed in economics or politics. He seemed just that sort of a person.

"You see," he continued, "the general public does not perceive theft or forgery as grievous. These stories make entertaining news."

*True*; Janet agreed silently. People were amused rather than sympathetic. With their own struggles, what did they care about a painting, something so far removed from their everyday lives?

"It's perceived as a victimless crime." The intensity in Marco's eyes was noticeable. "But there are victims. The artist, the museums, the collector who pays enormous sums of money."

Janet had been listening without interrupting, captivated by his every word. She slid her wrist under the table and checked the watch. The half hour had elapsed, she had scarcely noticed it. She had to ask now, the meeting would end soon.

"Have any paintings from here gone missing?"

Marco's eyes did not leave her face. "We have been more fortunate than most." The smile radiated satisfaction. "The Rijksmuseum has not been a victim in recent decades."

"Decades?" That was a long time. "Nothing bad has happened in all those years?"

"We have the best of security and surveillance Janet." He beamed.

"Impressive." It was all she could say.

Marco checked his watch. It was a signal the meeting was coming to an end. "I do have to get back to work."

The chairs scraped as they stood up. Janet realized just then that during their conversation, the crowd around her had faded out of focus. She had barely heard the loud noises which were grating when she first entered the cafeteria.

"I've really enjoyed our chat Janet."

"So have I." The arresting blue eyes held her gaze.

"Let me know if you think of other questions." He smiled as he held out his hand. "But another time. Okay?"

Janet's eyes followed the slender figure weave its way through the crowd.

The past forty five minutes had been fascinating. However, she was leaving the museum without the answer she sought. Had she wasted a valuable opportunity? Perhaps she should have posed the question of the two identical masterpieces.

*No*; she decided; it was too much for the first meeting.

Something else bothered her. What was it? She pictured the easy smile.

*No, that can't be.*

Marco had offered to meet her again. Was the feeling mutual?

*Don't be a fool.*

Marco had been agreeable but was simply doing an old friend a favour.

She felt certain about one thing. *He* was the person to answer her questions. As assistant director of Rijksmuseum, he had to know a lot if not everything.

»«

"Marjan, I just finished the meeting with Marco." Janet did not wait till she was home and called Marjan from the museum pay phone.

"How was it?"

"Good but there wasn't enough time for everything." She realized now that nothing relating to the painting was discussed. "Marco was helpful."

"He's good, isn't he?"

"Yes, just as you said."

"I knew you'd find what you wanted."

"Well, I haven't. At least not yet. But he certainly knows what he's talking about."

"He was the star in our class. And not just when it came to grades." Marjan's laughter trailed her comment.

*Yes, I believe that.* Janet could still see the blue eyes and the easy smile.

However, she still had no answers. "I think I want to come

right out and ask him about the Mauve. What do you think?"

"Why not? The answer can be yes, no or I don't know. It costs nothing to ask, yeah?"

Marjan was right; there was no harm in asking. Besides, her concerns might even get Marco to look into it. Janet felt charged. She might finally learn the truth about the painting.

Janet could not help wondering if the elation she felt was about unlocking the mystery or the anticipation of seeing Marco Haarlemmer again.

»«

*Today marks a week since our meeting.*

Janet waited to reconnect with Marco. The delay was calculated. Even though the pull of the two Mauves was unrelenting, she deliberately held back.

A week had since passed and the time was right to put the matter to bed.

"Yes, I'd be happy to answer your questions." Marco had sounded interested. "Let's meet at the pub on the far side of the museum square." He suggested an evening. This way they would not be rushed.

Janet arrived fifteen minutes early. The building with the pub was as Marco had described, blue-grey exterior with red awnings.

Standing inside the doorway, her eyes washed over the interior. Marco had not arrived yet. She walked down the narrow space along the bar to the last booth.

Janet fervently hoped Marco had the facts on the painting. Finally she would put this matter to bed. What was she feeling? Anticipation? Anxiety? Excitement?

Swirling the drink in her hand, Janet reviewed the questions. Sometimes actual conversations did not follow rehearsed ones. Janet hoped this was not one of those times and that she would leave with some answers.

Marco glided through the door, at exactly seven o'clock. His broad smile seemed to brighten the dark pub.

"Hello again." As he sat down, Marco signalled to the barman for a drink.

"Well Janet, you've had a week to mull it over." He asked as cheerfully. "Now what do you think of this business?"

Janet held off till the waiter set the glass down and left. "I want thank you again for meeting me."

"It's my pleasure." Marco raised the glass. "Glad to be of help."

"I have thought about how serious this whole business is." Without any urging from Janet, he began. "It is crime, but hugely fascinating. And it's not a twentieth century phenomenon. It's been going on for ages."

He loved art and words flowed effortlessly. When he paused for a sip, Janet knew she had to mention her finding.

"I think I've seen the same original painting in two places."

"Oh really?" His interest was genuine. "Which painting? And where?"

The time was not ripe to bring up names or places. "Let me check my notes."

"Come now, you must remember the painting."

Marco was sharp. Janet had to drop the act. "Of course, it was a pretty landscape. I'm rather curious, how can there be two of the same?" *Better not sound so sure;* she added casually, "At least to my untrained eyes they look alike."

"Which ones?" Marco's tone was tinged with impatience.

*I can't beat about the bush any longer.*

"The artist is Anton Mauve and the work is 'Morning ride on the beach'." She pointed to the museum building through the window. "I recall seeing it in the west wing, second floor."

Janet had just dropped the bomb. Her pulse raced. This was it. What was Marco's reaction? She watched his face.

Marco sipped his drink leisurely.

*Come on, say something.* She could not wait, "Has there been a theft or forgery in the Rijksmuseum?"

The blue eyes twinkled. "If there was Janet, you know more than I do."

She averted her eyes to avoid Marco's probing look. "I feel rather silly." The smile was forced. "I guess my imagination ran amok." She laughed, hoping to sound light hearted.

Marco held up the glass; "Here's to your active imagination." The disarming smile was back.

Janet's shoulders relaxed. *But this might be the last opportunity.* She decided to ask one last question. "Have there been any incidents at all in the Rijksmuseum?"

"No, there hasn't been a serious threat in the last twenty years or so." Marco leaned closer. "And my dear friend, you are not crazy. It's quite likely you saw what you thought were identical paintings. I can assure you right here that the Rijksmuseum is still the proud owner of *the one*."

"Oh." Janet smiled but her face did not conceal the disappointment.

"By the way Janet," Marco held her hands in his. "We pay serious attention to the grapevine. As a journalist you might hear stories." He reached in his wallet for a business card. "Do call if you have some information."

He motioned for the bill. The meeting was over. This one had lasted close to an hour. Still, after two discussions, Janet felt she had heard a lot but learned little. She had been unable to draw any conclusion.

Perhaps it was time to ignore the entire matter. It had been an amusing little mystery but she had a life to live.

The *Morning ride on the beach* had been too much of a distraction already.

# CHAPTER 13

*Ten weeks to the day;* Janet tapped the calendar. More than two months had gone by but Santiago's murder remained unsolved.

What was going on? She felt puzzled at the lack of progress. After the first month, the daily police briefings had slowed to once a week. Now they were held sporadically.

Of late, the investigation team had nothing new to announce but speculation in the media continued. Fingers pointed as far as South America. Where was all that coming from?

Janet's own writing on Santiago had become infrequent. She had exhausted all the material she had collected for the election articles. It was now a matter of keeping her ear to the ground and waiting for news to break.

Did Rosie have anything? They had not met since the night of the murder. That was a fleeting exchange of words and not a real meeting. Once or twice, Janet had tried but her friend had not been available. She had to give it another go. It was worth a try.

The evening began as it usually did; *I've missed you; what have you been up to? Hope you are well.*

Rosie seemed preoccupied. "Is your mother okay?" Janet probed.

"Yes. Getting old but all right."

*Does she want to tell me about the investigation?* Janet had many questions but held back. She wanted the friendship to continue without special favours from Rosie.

"Now, about the Santiago murder." Within minutes of sitting down, Rosie brought up the subject without prompting.

Rosie did have something to tell her. Janet pulled the chair closer. Just then a couple walked in their direction, choosing the table next to theirs.

Rosie jerked her head toward an isolated table. The two picked up their drinks and walked to the far corner of the bar.

"What news?" Janet asked as they sat down.

Rosie shook her head. "There just isn't enough hard evidence. God knows they're trying to piece it together. Whoever did it was very thorough and hasn't left any trails. A very clean job."

That sounded very much like the police mantra Janet had come to expect. But Rosie knew more that she was leading on.

"What about the South American connection?"

Rosie shook her head. "That was some time ago." She leaned forward, "new leads are pointing to right here Janet." Her index finger tapped the table as if showing Janet the ground below.

"In The Netherlands?" The information was more than Janet had hoped for.

"That's right, close to home."

*Come on Rose, give me a name.*

Rosie shook her head as if responding to Janet's silent request. "So far, they've run up against brick walls. They get close. And then nothing."

The lack of news was anticlimactic. From Rosie's manner, Janet was convinced her friend was going to divulge crucial information. That was not the case. Still, Rosie had one vital piece of news.

The one who ordered the hit was close to home.

# CHAPTER 14

*Ten more minutes.* Janet pulled the covers over her head. *Just a little bit longer.* But the long list of chores would not let her fall back to sleep. She swung her feet to the floor and sat at the edge of the bed. Her body ached from lack of rest; she had not gone to bed till the small hours of the morning.

Janet scrambled to the balcony, counting on the cool air to clear the cobwebs. Only a few seconds later, the clean morning feeling became contaminated with cigarette smoke wafting from below.

She began to retreat but was stopped by a greeting from her neighbour.

"Morning Janet."

She leaned on the railing to see William looking up lazily, not making an attempt to get up off the chair.

"Good morning Wil."

The greetings were enough of an exchange; Janet was not in a chatty mood. It was a relief that William seemed even less inclined.

She arrived at the Van Reef home only fifteen minutes late. *The dogs are going to be impatient.* She parked the van and stepped out.

The backyard was strangely quiet. As she looked around to see where the collies were, a familiar voice shouted her name. Janet followed Mrs. Steen into the kitchen.

Something was wrong. There were none of the usual kisses. The housekeeper wore a strange expression, her face was flushed. She stopped at the work table, not saying much.

"Mrs. Steen, what's the matter?"

The frown deepened. "Schatje," she paused. "I've been asked to tell you something."

"What is it?"

"You don't need to come here to work anymore. The family has made other arrangements for the dogs."

"I see." So they did not need her anymore.

That was not really a problem; she did not need the additional income. But the suddenness was a surprise.

"Rather a quick decision, don't you think?" Janet felt irritated. Not because of the short notice but because of being informed by the housekeeper and not Sheri.

Mrs. Steen shook her head; "I don't know child. That's all they told me and didn't say why."

*Who were 'they'?* The housekeeper looked as though she was about to cry.

"Mrs. Steen, don't worry. It's not a problem, really." The job had become a little more than a friendly commitment. "You know I'm doing okay at the paper."

"I know." In the Steen household, Janet's coverage of the Santiago murder had turned her into a minor celebrity.

Both women were quiet for a few minutes. Janet did not need explanations. Her time was up. She had no desire to stay where she was not wanted.

She picked up her keys. "I hope to see you." She gave Mrs. Steen a reassuring smile.

"Me too child. I shall miss you."

The housekeeper grabbed Janet's arm as she walked to the door. "But tell me." She seemed to be searching for words. "Did you say something to Madam? Make her cross?"

"Of course not Mrs. Steen." Janet put her arm around the old lady who seemed more upset than she herself was. "Don't worry. Okay?"

"You come and visit me sometime, eh?"

Suddenly, Janet wanted to get out of the mansion, she no longer belonged there.

*I never did belong here.*

The housekeeper shoved something in Janet's hand. *The last care package.* Janet smiled despite her irritation.

"Take care liefje."

*Child, liefje, schatje, so many terms of endearment in such a short time.*

The morning walks with the dogs and coffee sessions with Mrs. Steen had become a daily ritual. How much a part of her life they had become.

Rocky and Coco were not in their pen. It was sad to not say farewell. Janet looked at their empty home and climbed into the van. She drove out of the compound wondering what had transpired.

*The hell with it.* She stepped hard on the accelerator. Sheri had not even said a proper goodbye. Instead, she had palmed off the responsibility on the housekeeper.

*I thought she and I had a connection*; Janet reflected with sadness. Sheri had always been friendly toward her. Was that fake? Was it just Sheri's television mask?

The more Janet thought about it the more she fumed. It was not the money. She wished Sheri had spoken to her personally. Anything less was an insult.

The stairs to her fourth floor apartment felt strenuous. She tossed the backpack on the floor and sank into the sofa. Her feelings were muddled. Confusion, irritation. Most of all anger, for having been relieved without as much as a 'thank you'. Sadness that she had put so much stock into her relationship with her employer.

Janet remembered the little paper bag. Looking in, she saw neatly arranged baked goodies on a flower patterned plate.

For a brief moment the hurt lost its sting.

# CHAPTER 15

Sparrows landed on the bird feeder, nibbled at the seeds and flew away. Other birds followed. This went on as Janet sat on the sofa watching. How simple their lives seemed. She on the other hand, sat there contemplating the day, her mind cluttered with uninvited thoughts.

As much as she wished it, the Mauve did not leave her. Some days went by without the painting crossing her mind. Then suddenly, she would be reminded of the *Morning Ride* and could not stop thinking about it.

Today was such a day. What did sparrows have to do with that painting?

Whatever the association, it did not matter. *I must find out.* Janet stood up. *I have to know.*

Marjan had mentioned another name. Who was that person? She picked up the notebook and flipped the pages. There it was; *Oudekerk*. He once owned the gallery where Marjan now worked.

"He is considered something of a painter himself." Janet recalled Marjan's admiring description of the elderly Mr. Oudekerk. "He set up the gallery during the late fifties. In the years that followed, he was thought of as quite the art expert."

"This is great news." Oudekerk had moved up in Janet's estimation. "He might know about the Mauve and such things."

"Definitely. He was even a consultant to museums and law enforcement agencies."

"In what way?"

"He provided expertise, you know, for investigations of theft or forgeries."

Why had Marjan held back this information? "You didn't mention him before." Janet's voice had not concealed the irritation.

"Well," Marjan had explained, "these days he leads a quiet life. I hear he's the caretaker of an old windmill."

Marjan's deliberate omission of Oudekerk's name was not malicious. He sounded like a recluse who no longer welcomed contact with the outside world.

Janet wondered if she could persuade him to meet her. Surely, his love for art had not faded?

The more Janet thought about Oudekerk, the more she wanted to meet him.

*I must find him;* she walked to the phone and dialled the number.

"Yes?" The gruff voice sounded hostile.

"Hello Mr. Oudekerk. My name is Janet Simmons."

"Have we met?"

*This is not a good start.* "You don't know me but a friend, Marjan, who works at your gallery, suggested I speak to you."

"She did. Did she?" The tone had not softened. "What is this about?"

*This is going to be more difficult than I thought.*

Janet chose her words carefully. "I have questions about a certain work of art Mr. Oudekerk." *I should come to the point before he cuts me off,* she added quickly. "I think I might have seen two identical paintings. One in the Rijksmuseum and one somewhere else."

She heard nothing for a few seconds, then the clearing of throat.

"Well. Let me see, how about ten o'clock tomorrow?"

*This man is actually interested in talking to me? I don't need to explain?*

"Thank you. I'll be there at ten."

"Do you know how to find me?"

"No Sir. I understand you live in a windmill."

"Yes. Do you have a pen?"

Name: *De Avondster*, Janet began scribbling.

Oudekerk was now decidedly more cheerful than when the conversation began. Or was she imagining it?

Or was it just wishful thinking?

»«

In the flat Dutch countryside, the windmill was visible from a long distance. Janet did not need a street address. There was no mistaking Oudekerk's residence.

A chest-high gate marked the start of the property. Janet turned off the van and stepped out to open the gate. As she undid the latch, she noticed that the gate had no fence connected to it. She smiled, thinking it was a left-over artefact.

A small wooden sign shaped like an arrow pointed to the windmill. *De Avondster*; the name read; *Anno 1658*.

Despite driving the van slowly, the rock laden uneven path caused the vehicle to rattle violently.

The windmill which had seemed remote and small, grew larger and larger as the van moved closer to it.

As she stepped off on to the ground, the structure before her looked gigantic. With the strong winds, the blades rotated at high speed. With every turn, the sails came swooping down like a giant bird flapping its wings. *Thwok, thwok;* the boom of the sails drowned out any noise in the immediate vicinity.

Oudekerk could not have heard her drive up. It was time to announce herself. Janet took a few steps toward the door but stopped. An uneasy feeling was brewing within her.

What on Earth was she doing here? Why was she doing this? Why was she spending time and energy on a matter which was inconsequential in her life?

She recalled Ryan's reaction tinged with irritation. He was right. What began as simple curiosity now verged on obsession.

Of course, she could turn around and leave as quickly as she came. *But I'm already here*. If she left now, she would always wonder if Oudekerk had the answer. It would haunt her forever.

She had to give the puzzle one last look.

The gravel crunched beneath her shoes as she walked to the front door. Strands of the thatched wall became coarser as she moved closer.

Two wooden shoes hung on either side of the entrance. They each had a small flowering plant in the heel. A pair of wooden clogs on the step looked well-worn and still wet from recent use.

As she stood before the front door, she searched for a doorbell. There was none. Instead, a pull chord tied to a brass bell dangled through a rusty loop. She tugged at the rope. Surprised by the loud bong, she moved back, stepping off the step.

"Miss Simmons?" The same gruff voice sounded from above. A white haired man leaned out of a window half way up the wall. "I will come down shortly. Go in and make yourself comfortable."

"Good morning." Janet greeted him and waited.

"Go on." He gestured for her to go in.

The door felt heavy and resistant. She pushed hard and stepped inside. The dark interior did not allow her to see much. She waited, not certain where to go. As her eyes began to adjust, she saw furniture to her left, took several steps and sat on the chair.

The room was circular, with a column shaped like a mushroom stalk at the centre of it. Hugging the column was a narrow staircase, curving its way to the upper level. The steps were nothing more than open wooden slats. A rope dangled from above for support.

The level where she sat was one continuous, ring-like space. Further into the windmill, on the left, was a very small kitchen.

The *thwok, thwok* sounds became less frequent. The windmill blades slowed down and came to a stop. The deep boom of the rotating sails had given way to an eerie quiet.

A minute later, Janet heard footsteps. They became louder.

She stood up as feet descended the wooden slats.

"Good morning, good morning."

Janet was shaking the callused hand of a tall, burly man. "I must say I don't get such pretty visitors often." A kindly face smiled at her.

Ouderkerk was much gentler in person.

"Thank you for taking the time to see me."

"The pleasure is mine." He motioned for her to follow him into the kitchen. "Have you been inside one of these before?"

"No." Janet shook her head.

"I should show you around then." He filled the kettle from the tap.

"I would love to see the inner workings of the windmill." She paused, "If you have the time."

"Time I do have my dear, especially when it comes to *De Avondster.*"

That was the name carved on the wooden sign at the entrance. *De Avondster. The Evening Star.*

"The windmill could not have a more perfect name."

"You are quite right my dear." Oudekerk smiled as he led Janet to the front door. They went outside and stopped where the blades could be seen clearly.

He pointed to the top structure, "We have many different kinds of windmills here in Holland." He beamed. "This one is called a *bovenkruier* or a top turner. This is a typical mill used to drain the low lying land which we call polders."

On the side of the mill was a screw-like mechanism. Janet

peered at the huge piece of metal which lay at an angle. "It's called the Archimedes screw." Oudekerk explained. "The wide blades push the water upwards, into the canal. This is basically how the polder is drained."

"This way." He walked toward the front of the structure. As Janet caught up, he turned to face her. "So, what is it you wanted to see me about?"

This was her chance. The carefully rehearsed questions escaped Janet. She said bluntly, "I want to ask you about two identical paintings."

"Who is the artist?"

Janet flinched at his probing stare. *He's testing me. He's trying to decide what my motives are.*

"Anton Mauve." she replied.

"I see." He returned to the windmill. "You notice how the blades are tied up? In this case like a cross? This means I am taking a break."

Was that the end of the Mauve discussion? Janet felt confused. Should she continue talking about the painting? *No*; she decided. She would let Oudekerk take the lead. At least for a short while.

He continued the description; each resting position of the blades had its significance; short rest, long rest, celebration or mourning.

"You know," His eyes twinkled mischievously, "during the war, we used these positions as codes, to send special signals."

*De Avondster is such a part of his life. As art must have been at one time.*

"Tell me where you saw these paintings." He said pushing open the door. They had circled the windmill and were back at the entrance.

He was still interested. Janet's spirits lifted. "The first one's in the Rijksmuseum. Its title is 'Morning Ride on the Beach'."

"I see." Once again the eyes searched her face.

Without another word he pointed to the second level and walked to the narrow steps.

Oudekerk was the one driving the conversation. That much was clear to Janet. She had to be patient and wait for her chances.

She clung tightly to the rope as she walked up the wooden slats. "The other painting is in a private residence."

Oudekerk stood at the top of the steps and held out his hand to pull her up the final, steep part.

She stood on the second level which was narrower than the first. It contained sleeping arrangements; single bed, a writing table and a lamp. The bed seemed much too small for the large man.

"Simple isn't it? But it's all I need."

A part of the floor was wedged off like a piece of a pie. It was packed tightly with shelves, an easel and two bins.

"Ah, the painter's corner." Oudekerk's eyes twinkled. "I still like to think I'm an artist."

Among the clutter was a black and white photo in a plain frame.

"My late wife and I."

Janet glanced sideways and saw him looking wistfully at the photo.

"Speaking of artists," he steered the conversation, "this discovery of yours, it's quite recent?"

Janet now knew he believed her. He was not suggesting that she was mistaken or asking her to justify her theory.

She felt relieved. "My conclusion was gradual, over a couple of months." She looked directly at him. "Do you believe what I'm saying?"

"Yes. I know you have studied it. You wouldn't be here otherwise." He turned back toward the steps and pointed downstairs. "Let's talk over a cup of tea."

»«

"Thank you." Janet smiled at the cup handed to her by Oudekerk. The fine china seemed out of place in his large, rough hands.

"These are only for special occasions." He grinned as he poured the tea. "Now, young lady, tell me all about these Mauves."

"I am convinced they are identical but I can't really find out much more. Any kind of history or background." She paused wondering whether to mention Marco. "I also talked to someone at the museum."

"And who is this person?"

"His name is Marco Haarlemmer. We had an interesting discussion but I didn't really discover anything."

Oudekerk said nothing.

Janet did not want to lose the momentum. "Are you familiar with this particular painting? It's called the 'Morning ride on the beach'."

He nodded. "I have seen it. Once or twice."

"Did you know if there was another one just like it?"

"Hmm," he paused, "that could mean many things."

"You mean copies?"

"Copies, imitations, call it what you will. But you tell me the two are identical."

"I'm positive. I looked at them more than once and compared the signatures. They were both by Mauve."

Oudekerk fell silent. Janet examined the weather beaten face. What was he thinking?

"I can see you have become suspicious Janet. You are thinking that perhaps one of them is a counterfeit?"

He was echoing her thoughts. She had alluded to her suspicion in different ways but had not used the word counterfeit.

Janet no longer felt foolish about her preoccupation. "What other explanation can there be?"

"I'm beginning to think so too." His eyes were serious, even sad. "Unfortunate as it is, bootlegging in art is indeed big. Even world class museums are not immune."

Janet wondered what his role had been in the past. "I understand you were a consultant to Interpol."

"That was my other life." He leaned forward. "Now, this friend of yours at the museum."

*He is not my friend.* Janet flushed remembering Marco's piercing blue eyes.

"I have no doubt he is competent. But he just may not know. With thousands of pieces housed in such a large museum, it is impossible for an official to be knowledgeable about even ten percent of the works, much less the entire collection.

"A switch of a museum painting is not inconceivable but not likely in a place like the Rijksmuseum. But out of the question? No." He shook his head. "Nothing in this business surprises me."

For the first time since her involvement with Anton Mauve, Janet felt vindicated.

"Now, let's see what can be done."

Was he suggesting taking action? Janet was taken aback. She had come to Oudekerk with no expectation but his decisive reaction came as a surprise.

"I can talk to the museum curator."

She gasped. "You know Director Zalm?"

*This is unbelievable.* She had tried but was unable to get an interview with the curator. When she decided to meet with Oudekerk, she did not think he would take her seriously, much less raise an alarm.

He smiled at her shocked expression. "You see Janet, I've been around a long time and have come to know many people." He smiled. "Yes, I know Leonard Zalm quite well."

Things were moving fast, Janet's pulse raced.

"And don't worry, whatever we talk about will be in the strictest of confidence."

"So it's not a public inquest?"

"Not at this stage. We have to do our own investigation quietly."

"I wish I had some pictures but I don't."

Taking a photo of the second Mauve had crossed Janet's mind. But using a camera in the Van Reef mansion would be crossing the line.

What if the museum director demanded to know where the painting was? She felt a knot in her stomach.

"Mr. Oudekerk, do I have to tell you..." she paused.

"Who owns the second one?" He had anticipated her concerns. "No. At least not right away. Besides, we have to be cautious and not cause a scandal."

Yes, she remembered Marco's words; *bad publicity could be damaging to the museum.*

"Who knows?" Oudekerk continued his slow, rambling speech, "The museum's Mauve might well prove to be the real one and we will be finished with this matter."

Conversation slowed. The host picked up the tea cups. Janet wanted to stay but the visit seemed to have come to a close.

"Thank you so much for your time." She gathered up her bag and her coat. "And for listening to me."

"It has been very interesting. And Janet, be careful to whom you mention this." The smiling eyes betrayed a warning.

Janet drove home feeling relieved. She had unburdened her worries on a pair of knowing and sympathetic ears.

The relief was short lived as she remembered Oudekerk's parting words.

*Watch your step.*

# CHAPTER 16

"Hello *mi Reyna*, how about dinner tonight?" Ryan's term of endearment sounded clumsy but the dinner invitation was tempting.

Two weeks had passed since their last meeting. Janet had been distracted but knew time spent together was important. If she was not attentive, the relationship was in danger of derailing.

"Same place as the last time?"

"Perfect."

She liked the Ethiopian restaurant at the edge of the semi-circle that is Amsterdam. The food was always tasty, the service familiar and friendly.

Janet arrived first, by public transportation. They were to drive together to Janet's place after dinner.

She chose a table near the window and sat facing the door. She did not wait long. Ryan showed up promptly as Janet knew he would. Punctuality was something she could count on from Ryan. He was dependable and predictable.

*Too predictable.*

Janet smiled broadly and erased the frown.

"Good day at work?" As was often the case, conversation began with work.

So much had happened. Janet wondered whether to mention her dismissal from the Van Reef household. It could wait; she decided. Even though it gnawed at her, there was no hurry to bring up the topic.

Midway through dinner, she sprang the news. "By the way, I no longer work for the Van Reefs." She said, suppressing lingering resentment and trying to sound casual. "It appears they don't need a dog walker."

*Well, not me anyway*. She left out the details, still unable to explain the manner in which she was terminated.

"This means you don't have to get up at the crack of dawn anymore." Ryan did not appear to think it severe.

Another matter plagued her thoughts. She hesitated once again. *I should be able to talk to him about it*. If the relationship was going anywhere, she hoped he would be interested in all things important in her life.

"Remember the acquaintance of Marjan I mentioned?"

"The college friend?" Ryan referred to Marco.

Janet hoped her face did not turn red. "No. The elderly gentleman." She added quickly. "He actually lives in a windmill. A working polder mill with proper living facilities."

She smiled recalling the agreeable morning spent in Oudekerk's company. She described the way de Avondster's interior was arranged.

"Has he always lived there?" Ryan's interest seemed real.

"No, only in the last eight years or so. As a caretaker."

"What did he do before?"

"Many years ago he owned the gallery where Marjan now

works."

Janet watched Ryan's face. What was his reaction? She recalled how an earlier conversation about the *Mauve* had ended abruptly. Ryan had sounded annoyed. She was too preoccupied with it; he had said.

"Gallery? That must mean it has something to do with the painting." His eyes twinkled.

His amused smile was a relief. "Yes of course, the *Mauve* was reason for the meeting."

Encouraged by his nod, she continued; "Anyway, he heard my concerns and said he would look into the matter."

Janet's account was a deliberate understatement. Oudekerk was giving it a lot more than a look but she did not elaborate. She had herself been feeling uneasy about the all consuming involvement.

She decided to steer the conversation toward a safer subject, Ryan's work. "Everything okay at work?"

He talked about the latest corporate issue. To Janet, it sounded like all the other issues except with different names and places.

Ryan was still talking about it as they left the restaurant.

"The plan's still on? You're coming to my place?"

"Of course." He held the passenger door open.

Ryan's car exited the parking lot but swerved as another car on the street raced in their direction. The wheels screeched as Ryan stepped hard on the breaks.

"Damn." He swore. "Where the hell did he come from?"

The other car slowed and stopped a few feet in front. The

driver stepped out, turned around, looked at them and got back in the car without saying a word.

"An apology would have been nice." Ryan muttered. He then turned to Janet, "Sorry I screamed. I'm okay now."

"It doesn't matter. At least there wasn't an accident."

They headed South, out of Amsterdam. Neither said much during the journey.

All through the drive, Janet wondered whether to mention her discussions with Marco Haarlemmer. *No*; she decided. Marco was simply one of several people with whom she discussed the painting. Why bring up his name now? There was no point to it.

Or was there?

Janet wished she knew what her own feelings were.

# CHAPTER 17

*That didn't take too long*; Janet gathered up the sheets of paper.

*Prinsjesdag*; the first sentence read; *the ceremonial inauguration of the Parliament by the Monarch.*

Janet described the sunny September day, the gilded coach, the marching bands and the outfits the Royals wore on that day and in the years past.

Such soft news stories were uncomplicated and entertaining. Janet herself enjoyed covering the event. It was no secret that the public had an insatiable appetite for information on the Royals. The European Daily's readership seemed to devour any and all news relating to European blue bloods.

*Better hurry and get dinner started.* It was nearly dark. She looked up at the clock, it was not even five. Autumn was changing into winter, dusk fell earlier each day.

She slid the sheaf of paper into an envelope, already addressed and waiting to be delivered. She stood up and walked to the kitchen but stopped when the doorbell rang.

*He's here already?* Ryan was not expected for another hour.

She turned around, walked to the front door and opened it. An unsmiling Ryan stood before her.

He stepped in and shut the door behind him.

*Not even a hello?* Ryan was not one for elaborate greetings but at least a smile would have been nice. Still, there he was, wanting to spend the evening with her.

"You're early." Janet threw her arms around him.

"Later." Ryan separated her hands from around his neck.

*Did he have a bad day?* Perhaps dinner together was not such a good idea.

"What's the matter?" She watched him dart to the sliding balcony door and look all around the backyard.

Something was really wrong. She had never seen him this agitated.

"What is it?" She repeated the question.

"Let me show you something." Still frowning, Ryan took her hand and led her to the second bedroom.

Situated on the front part of the building, the room faced the street. The two walked around the narrow bed to the window.

"Here, look." He motioned to the street below.

Janet pushed the curtain to the side and scanned the scene. What was upsetting him? She searched but saw nothing out of the ordinary. It was as most evenings were, children kicking the ball around and commuters walking home from the train station.

"I don't understand. What you are trying to show me?" She looked up and saw Ryan's knotted brow.

"Look to your left. What do you see where Veldweg crosses the street?"

Janet saw nothing remarkable. Two people walked on Veldweg with their dogs and were moving in the direction of the open fields.

114

"That car, the dark blue one, does it look familiar?" Ryan moved aside to allow her more room.

She opened the window and leaned out. "Not really. It could have been any of a dozen cars I've seen this week."

"Janet, it was the Renault that nearly crashed into us at the restaurant parking lot."

Was that the car that nearly hit them? Details such as the colour or the make failed her memory.

Ryan stared for another thirty seconds. "I suppose there are many dark blue Renaults in the city."

He continued looking up and down the street. Janet did not think he would leave the window. Whatever bothered him could be discussed in the kitchen.

She drew the curtains close. "Come on. I have to start cooking."

Ryan left the window but the worried look did not leave his face. Why did the car below bother him so? It was ordinary looking, the most common kind of car she could imagine.

"You're right." He shrugged. "It's just a coincidence. The city's full of blue Renaults."

Dinner proceeded with little conversation. Even as they turned in, Ryan seemed preoccupied.

What was bothering him? Was it really that car? Or was it something else?

Was there something Ryan was not telling her?

»«

Janet awoke before daybreak. No alarm had been set. She had no police briefings to attend, no dogs to walk. There was no rush to jump out of bed. She pulled the covers over her shoulders and closed her eyes.

Sleeping in felt like the ultimate luxury but Janet missed walking the collies. They had been a part of her life for close to three years. She missed her visits to the mansion and the morning coffee ritual with Mrs. Steen.

*There's no point in looking back*; she told herself. *The only way is forward.* She recalled her grandfather's words and wondered if he was actually able to live by that rule.

Moving forward was easier said than done.

Ryan stirred when she kissed him good morning. He would be gone to work by the time she returned. She wished she could stay but had to drop the article off at the office.

Even at seven o'clock, most cars had not left the parking lot. Janet needed a few tries to reverse the van out of the space which was too narrow for the large vehicle. As she waited to turn left out of the driveway, something familiar jumped out at her.

Directly in front, across the street was a navy blue car. Janet studied it. Was that the one Ryan talked about? Was it the car in Amsterdam which nearly collided with Ryan's?

Someone sat in the driver seat. She squinted. Was it the same driver? Sunlight glinting on the windows made it impossible to see the person behind the wheel.

She rubbed her forehead. The pounding in her temples became more intense.

*This is ridiculous;* she told herself. Ryan's suspicions were having an effect on her. She knew she could not be wary of every single Renault which crossed her path.

As she drove away, she told herself it was nothing. Still, she could not rid herself of the uneasy feeling.

She checked the rear-view mirror repeatedly. It was draining. Finally, after driving through several crowded city blocks, she breathed a sigh of relief.

No blue Renault was following her.

Nothing remarkable was happening.

»«

Errands had been run, articles were written; Janet stood up and stretched. It had been a busy day so far but she felt like doing something. She needed a diversion.

Perhaps it was time for a visit to Mrs. Steen. The thought lifted her spirits. She would spend an hour or two with a dear old friend. It was early afternoon and if Mrs. Steen kept to her schedule, she would be home by now.

Mrs. Steen had a look of delight as she answered the door. She led her visitor into the kitchen and began filling the coffee filter.

Janet felt the anxieties melt away.

"My morning coffee at the mansion is not the same without you schat." Mrs. Steen's eyes were sad. "Now tell me. What have you been doing with your time?"

"You do know I have a real job?" Janet joked lightly. "I did, all these years."

The small talk continued. Janet knew her unceremonious departure would come up before long. The chit chat lasted only ten minutes.

"Now, tell me Janet, what happened in the mansion?"

"I wish I knew." She herself had been trying understand it.

"It was all so sudden." The tut-tuts were loud. "Now child, don't be upset with what I'm going to ask."

Janet knew probing questions would be coming her way.

"That day, when you were upstairs, did you take something?"

"Mrs. Steen, you know I wouldn't do such a thing." Janet frowned. Even the suggestion was stinging.

"I know you Janet and I know that you would not have done anything like that. But I had to hear it from you." She leaned across and patted Janet's hand. "I think they made a big mistake."

Janet suddenly had a sinking feeling. "Is that what they are saying? That I stole something?"

Mrs. Steen said nothing. The accusations were crushing but Janet felt comfort in knowing she had Mrs. Steen's trust.

The incident did not come up again during the rest of the conversation.

Janet left with a heavy heart. The image of her as a thief being perpetuated in the Van Reef household suddenly wiped out any fondness she felt for the place.

# CHAPTER 18

Janet fumbled with the keys. The telephone was already on its third ring. She unlocked the door, walked in and dropped the bags on the floor. Four, five. She picked up the receiver on the sixth ring.

Oudekerk was at the other end. Her heart raced.

He made no announcements. The lack of news was disappointing. There was not even a mention of the Mauve; only an exchange of pleasantries.

Then came the surprise invitation to visit de Avondster for dinner.

Janet beamed. Oudekerk had initiated contact. He was someone whom she initially perceived as hostile. That same person was inviting her to dinner now.

She wanted to show her appreciation. "Would you like me to cook dinner Mr. Oudekerk?"

"This is even better than I had hoped. I would love that Janet." The offer was accepted without argument.

Janet felt strangely charged at the thought of an evening with Oudekerk. Armed with dinner ingredients, she headed out to the windmill.

The uneven access road made the van feel even older; it was time to trade it in for another vehicle, something newer and smaller.

That would have to wait. The generous pay by the Van Reefs was gone. Her exposure at The Daily was better but the income was not great or steady.

As she drove closer to de Avondster, it seemed even more awe inspiring than when she had first seen it. The windmill was indeed huge but she wondered how much of the marvel had to do with the man inside.

They greeted each other like old friends. Oudekerk had traded his overalls for a dress shirt and corduroy slacks.

"Janet, do you know why I called you?" He asked as Janet unpacked the groceries on the kitchen table.

"I was hoping you had some news." She had been wondering all day.

"I have information that might interest you." He poured wine and handed her a glass.

"Prost." They toasted.

"Here's an update," Oudekerk spoke in his slow, unhurried manner, "you remember I was going to talk to director Zalm about your concerns?"

*Yes, yes*; she nodded, urging silently; *please hurry up with it*.

"Well, we inspected the Mauve which is in the museum." He leaned closer, "Are you ready for this?"

Janet's pulse quickened. She wanted to shout *hurry up* but she said simply, "Yes."

"The museum painting is not the original."

She stared. Her mind was a flurry of thoughts but she could not think of a thing to say. Finally, after weeks of suspicions and conjecture, this fact had been established.

The conclusion was what she had imagined but did not dare to express aloud. She had not expected this. She gazed at Oudekerk, trying to absorb the words just uttered.

"*Not* the original?" She spoke after sometime, her voice barely above a whisper. "I don't know what to say. I have been preoccupied with this for such a long time. But now, I just can't believe it."

"When I first learned of this, I too had the same reaction as you."

"But how?" Janet shook her head as if to shake loose the million thoughts running through her mind. "This has happened so fast. It was only a week ago that we talked about this."

During that meeting, Janet had felt that Oudekerk's interest was genuine. However, she had not felt that he was that alarmed to act so swiftly. That too surprised her.

"I was able to do it because of Zalm. He's a childhood friend of mine. When I broached the subject, he listened." He paused as if to make sense of everything that happened. "He must not think me a crazy old fool." His laugh boomed.

Oudekerk's face then turned serious, "With such cases, speed is of the essence."

He explained that the two men had moved quickly to have the painting authenticated. It had been kept quiet, only a select few were privy to the information.

"So it isn't public knowledge?"

"We like to keep these things under wraps initially. We must prevent the original from taking flight. Once it disappears underground, all bets are off."

"And the museum doesn't need negative publicity." Janet

remembered Marco Haarlemmer's words about public opinion.

Would Marco know about this development? Was he important enough to be among the privileged few? *No*; she concluded. He had not taken instant action as Zalm had.

Marco had come across like someone with authority. Was that a mere act?

"We've talked everyday on the phone and met three times already." Oudekerk explained.

The inspection had been conducted at the museum after closing hours, when most of the staff had left. The guards on duty were long time, reliable employees. Zalm and Oudekerk had summoned two of the best experts on whose discretion they could rely.

"They worked several hours into the night. I drank coffee and waited."

"How long did it take?"

"Oh, till about two in the morning. The initial examination was visual. Then they applied and re-applied their tests." He continued. "The two worked independently so they didn't influence one another.

"The painting is a copy, a good one at that. It was done quite recently, no more than four or five years ago." Oudekerk leaned forward. "Get this Janet, the frame is the original one."

"That means only the canvas was switched."

He nodded.

"So what happens now?"

"That is the question. Where do we go from here? The

trustees are meeting soon. My guess is, they will authorize more tests, make it official.

"Assuming that does not change the result, there is now a much more burdensome task. The museum has to launch an operation to track down the original."

Janet froze.

Sooner or later, the Van Reef name would have to be revealed.

"Something worries Zalm and me even more." Oudekerk kept talking. "If this has gone unnoticed, how many more are there? When did this switch actually take place?" Gloom seemed to descend on him. "This could be the tip of the iceberg."

Janet suddenly felt nervous. Would they want to talk to her? She could be drawn deeper into it, more than she wanted.

"Did Mr. Zalm ask how you came by this information?"

"Yes but I have not revealed your name. You realize there will be questions for you."

"I suppose that's inevitable."

Both sat still for a few minutes. The mood had turned sombre. Janet stood up and walked to the stove. She had lost her appetite but wanted to keep her promise of cooking dinner.

She remained quiet through the meal. Oudekerk praised the food and seemed to relish every mouthful.

When they finished, the conversation reverted to the painting.

"So you worked on such cases in the past?"

"Quite a few." Oudekerk stared into space. "It is a daunting scenario when a fake is first discovered.

"The challenge of ferreting out the original feels impossible." The frown persisted. "Investigators are knowledgeable and have immense resources but the underworld is always two steps ahead of them.

"In this case however," he turned to face her, "we might know where it is?"

Janet weighed whether to reveal the whereabouts of the second Mauve painting.

*Yes*; she decided; *now is the time.*

"After all you've done, I feel I should tell you where I saw the other one."

"Only if you want to. When the investigation begins, the authorities will want to question you but you could choose to be anonymous. For now, I could speak on your behalf."

So, there was an option. Janet's spirits lifted. Her name could be concealed. She was safe.

*Safe from what?* She wondered. *Why am I so afraid?*

She could not explain it but she did feel frightened. "Okay, until then we have to keep this between us." She waited for his acknowledgement.

"It's at the home of the Van Reefs."

"Hmm." Surprisingly, his face showed no reaction.

"Do you know the Van Reefs?"

"I know of them." Oudekerk nodded but did not add anything.

Finally, after several seconds, he spoke. "This is delicate

Janet."

She could only guess his thoughts. The Van Reefs were a high profile couple. The family name had been known for generations. Lars and Sheri were well connected and enjoyed friendships with influential people.

How did one go about examining the painting owned by such people?

It was as though Oudekerk heard her question. "I suppose the museum could just ask them and hope for cooperation."

He appeared to be thinking aloud; "They have to establish if that is indeed the original. We need proof. Without it..." His sentence trailed off.

Oudekerk knew of the Van Reefs but had not made any comment on them. How much did he know about the family? Surely, he could not have escaped the ubiquitous stories in the newspapers.

More questions arose than were answered but Janet was glad the fact had been established. For the first time in months, she no longer worried about the painting. She had pursued her suspicions and aired them. She had come forward.

*'You were instrumental.'*

She beamed at Oudekerk's compliment.

*But what about the Daily? Surely, Boris would like a front page story.*

"Mr. Oudekerk, you know I work for a newspaper."

"I was expecting you to bring that up Janet." He looked directly into her eyes. "I feel strongly that you should not write about it. At least not yet. It's too sensitive."

"All right."

*Still, shouldn't I tell Boris?* It could be kept under wraps until the time was right.

"Perhaps you could work some deal with the museum." Once again Oudekerk seemed to have anticipated her concerns. "But you should not talk about it."

She nodded, knowing this was probably the most critical phase. The less known about the counterfeit, the better.

In a way it was a relief that her involvement was finished. At least for the moment. In a few weeks, she could negotiate exclusive rights with Zalm and the museum. Soon, she would have an article on page one. Once again.

"I look forward to a good ending." She said as she shook her host's hand.

"We had some good discussions, didn't we?" He patted her shoulder. "But Janet, you must be very careful."

The parting warning left her nervous and yet she felt oddly at peace. The gnawing doubts of the recent weeks had evaporated. Doubts about the painting, about her preoccupation and priorities.

Most of all doubts about herself.

The drive was easy and the roads lonely at the late hour, except for one other car.

# Chapter 19

Ryan walked in at 4 o'clock, two hours earlier than expected.

"Hey gorgeous!" His voice was exuberant but his furrowed brow said something else.

"Hello to you too." Janet was puzzled by the contrast.

As he put his arms around her, Ryan whispered, "Don't say anything important. Just talk about this and that."

He rambled on about traffic, weather and asked about dinner.

*This again? What's going on?* Janet was bursting with questions but went along.

"Can you believe the rain we had today?"

Ryan nodded for her to keep talking, walked to the stereo cabinet and turned on the radio.

He then led her to the sofa and the two sat down. Janet could barely hear him above the loud music.

"I know you think I've gone crazy." He took her hand in his. "I think there is something strange going on."

"Is someone outside?" She pointed to the front of the building.

"I'm not sure." He rubbed his chin. He seemed to be struggling for words. "Maybe I'm paranoid but I feel the blue Renault was no coincidence.

"I saw the curly haired guy again. The one who was at the wheel when we had the near collision in Amsterdam. That was no fluke. I've seen that same guy driving the same car a few times now."

Janet sat listening, not knowing what to make of it.

"Does he live around here?" He spoke rapidly. "Have you seen him before?"

"No."

Ryan leaned closer. "I don't want to frighten you but you might be watched. And listened to."

What did he mean 'listened to'? Who wanted to know?

Was the curly haired man waiting in the street? Or was he in the corridor? Were they at the door listening?

A chill ran down her back.

She knew why Ryan had turned on the radio full blast. "I don't get it." Her shoulders slumped.

"I didn't tell you before because I hoped I was mistaken. I've seen the same Renault and same man a few times now. Seeing the car parked on your street the other day made me suspicious. Until we know differently, we have to be on guard."

It explained Ryan's erratic behaviour during the past several days. He did not want to frighten her unduly. He was looking out for her, protecting her.

"Can you describe this man?"

"5'10", tanned, has a stocky build. He looks like a boxer. He was wearing a black leather jacket the few times I saw him."

Janet sat still. The images from the night in Amsterdam

flashed through her mind. She could now picture the face framed by curly hair.

"Ryan," Janet's voice trembled. "He is a guard at the mansion."

Ryan said nothing for a few seconds. "Those were Van Reef's men." He nodded as if he suddenly understood.

Janet put her head down on her hands and stared at the floor. What had they just discovered? What did it all mean?

She did not know how long she sat on the sofa. A loud noise jarred her from thoughts. She looked up to see Ryan at the table. He had knocked over a candlestick and was examining the bottom of it. She could only guess what he was looking for, hidden microphones.

"You think I've seen too many spy movies?" Ryan tried to lighten the mood.

Neither laughed.

Ryan walked back to the sofa, knelt on the floor and leaned on the armrest. "I think I'd like to have the flat checked by a professional. Is that okay?"

Janet nodded. What choice did she have?

"I'll arrange it."

Hours went by. Janet could not fall asleep. She lay in bed and stared at the ceiling. She tried not to think of Van Reefs' men or hidden microphones. But it was useless.

*It'll seem better in the morning;* she told herself.

*It must.* She repeated silently. *It must.*

»«

*The chapter is closed.*

That is what Janet had said to herself after the evening with Oudekerk. The matter was out of her hands. She had congratulated herself.

Was this a new chapter?

At 2 pm., the bug sweeper arrived. Janet tried to work but found it impossible to concentrate. The entire episode seemed unreal.

What suddenly happened to her life?

The technician worked through the house and the balcony. After two hours, he announced he was finished.

"You can relax now Miss, I didn't find anything." He handed her the paperwork. "Would you sign here please? The invoice will be sent to," He peered at the name, "Mr. Parks."

Ryan was picking up the four figure tab.

*Love works in strange ways.* Janet smiled despite the maelstrom brewing within her.

# CHAPTER 20

Janet awoke to the clear blue skies of an autumn day. The good weather put her in the mood for an outing. Perhaps she could take a drive out and visit Mr. Oudekerk. She had not made an appointment but decided to go there anyway. If he was away, she would just stroll around and enjoy the scenery.

The windmill's blades were tied in an X position. That meant a pause, she recalled Oudekerk's explanation. He could be away. She parked the van and stepped out.

The noise of the vehicle on the gravel drew Oudekerk out to the front yard.

"Hello." Janet shouted.

"How nice to see you Janet." He leaned the rake on the wall and peeled off the garden gloves.

He waved her towards him and together they walked to the garden. Gathering up the tools and pointing to the shrubs, he said, "I think I'm a better painter than a gardener." Both laughed. "Darjeeling tea awaits my dear, let's go inside."

Sipping the dark brew at the kitchen table, Janet wondered if she should bring up the events of the past few days.

*I have to*. She needed to talk to him about it. He understood the situation better than anyone else.

"I think my place is being watched. My friend Ryan is

convinced someone is keeping tabs on me."

Oudekerk's smile disappeared. "That is not good. Are you sure Janet?"

She nodded. "We both noticed it over the last week."

"Do you know who it is?"

"I have an idea." She shrugged. "Whoever it is, I really hope they quickly lose interest in me. It's making me edgy and I'm not sleeping too well."

"That's not good. I don't like that you are living alone. Can you stay with friends?"

"Ryan is with me on most days now. I'm taking whatever precautions I can." She gave him a brief account of the bug sweeper's report.

"Any word on the painting?" Janet needed the distraction. Talking about being followed or looking for listening devices was wearing her down.

"Nothing dramatic has happened yet. The authentication is being performed by a company in Amsterdam. The museum has used their services in the past.

"One day, you and I should visit these people. They will explain the techniques used. It is very interesting."

Janet nodded mechanically. "I'm sure it's fascinating." She wanted to know but at the moment felt drained.

"Zalm has announced it within the museum as routine checking. It's a normal preventative measure in museums. Several other paintings have been randomly selected. Hopefully it won't give rise to talk about the *Morning Ride on the Beach*."

"When will you know?"

"It will be some time yet. But both Zalm and I know what the outcome will be. Next comes the formal step in declaring the Mauve a counterfeit. Not something any of us is looking forward to." The deep sigh said it all.

The riddle of the two masterpieces had fascinated Janet for months. Now, this topic too was exhausting.

"Clear day today, eh?" Oudekerk had noticed the dullness in her eyes. "Nice change from the rain we've been having."

Talk of weather did not last long. Conversation reverted to the painting and its authenticity.

The *hows* and the *what ifs*.

How did one go about pursuing the original? If the painting was believed to be in the household of a family such as the Van Reefs, it was not an easy matter. Naturally, at first they would simply request to view the piece and avoid any confrontation.

"In all likelihood, within the next week a formal complaint will be filed with the police and an official investigation will follow.

"Now we wait." Those were calm words of wisdom from a man who had been in this situation a few times before.

The visit had not been cheerful. Discussions were either about the stolen Mauve or Janet being watched. Still, Janet liked being in the miller's company. She felt safe and comfortable.

*I mustn't overstay my welcome.* "I think I should leave you to your peace and quiet." She announced her departure.

"I'll let you know if there is any dramatic news."

The investigation was now official museum business but

unofficially, Oudekerk was very much in the loop.

Stepping out of the windmill and into the van, the secure feeling gave way to anxiety as Janet checked the rear view mirror.

»«

*I really want to see Mrs. Steen again.*

Janet missed her dear friend and needed to be in her comforting company. Mrs. Steen had been a part of her life for more than two years and had come to know her better than most members of her own family.

Janet set out for Leimuiden. Mrs. Steen was a creature of habit and at 2pm, home was where she would be after the daily trip to the market.

"Janet, *liefje*, I just got home."

"I see you are still keeping to the old schedule." Janet smiled with amusement.

"Come, let us take coffee outside."

Mrs. Steen's warm reception made Janet forget her worries, if only briefly. She listened as the host regaled her with stories of her grandchildren.

After the first round of coffee, Janet wondered if it was time to take the housekeeper into her confidence. She waited for a pause in the storytelling.

"Some odd things happened to me since I left the mansion."

"What do you mean child?"

"Several things. And I think they are all connected." Janet wondered how much to divulge. "I'm being followed wherever I go."

"Who wants to follow you?"

Two words, *Van* and *Reef* were on the tip of her tongue but Janet felt too nervous to make the allegation.

She took a deep breath. "They're eavesdropping as well. We had my place checked out last week."

"You mean bugs and such? And are you sure?"

"Yes. I didn't think so at first. Ryan and I have been paying attention. We're both quite certain."

"Have you found out who?"

Janet looked directly at Mrs. Steen. "One of the men is a guard at the mansion."

Mrs. Steen looked dumbfounded. "No, that cannot be." She shook her head in disbelief. "Janet, I hope you are wrong."

"I wish." Janet sighed.

"I feel so bad for you." Mrs. Steen stood up from her chair and walked to Janet. She put her arm around her guest. "But it may not be as bad as you think."

"But it is Mrs. Steen. It's keeping me up at night."

The elderly lady tried to make the situation seem less severe. "You know men, they go to such lengths to protect their business."

As Janet took leave, Mrs. Steen sounded a cautionary note. "Now, you be careful. Okay?"

The warning was one Janet was hearing again and again. She departed with mixed feelings.

Mrs. Steen's kind words had comforted her. The housekeeper had been sympathetic but had not asked many questions; what, where or who. If anything, she seemed eager to wrap

135

up the conversation.

Janet believed that Mrs. Steen knew a lot of what was going on in the mansion. The old lady was fond of Janet but her loyalty to the Van Reefs was unflinching.

She was sympathetic to Janet's pain but was not about to take sides.

# CHAPTER 21

"The careless repairman left the lights on again." Mrs. Steen muttered looking at the upstairs' windows.

The Van Reefs were away and the only explanation was the plumber whom Flanders had called in the day before.

"It's always something." She scowled remembering the messy footprints the handyman had left the previous time.

She unlocked the back door and turned on the lights. Suitcases? What were they doing down here? She walked over to the calendar on the wall. No, she had the day right, the family was still on holiday.

But they had returned. She recognized Mrs. Van Reef's grey and pink floral luggage. *Hope one of them didn't take ill.* She surveyed the kitchen as she hung her coat on the rack. Some dishes had been left on the table.

The family was definitely back. Sheri and Lars had returned home four days too early.

Perhaps the snow was not very good for skiing. It was not the first time they had changed their plans. Of course, this meant there would be more to do during the day. She had only come in to take inventory.

She pulled open the drawer and took out a pad of paper. It was time to make a list. The first task of the day would be baking the family's favourite red currant loaf.

Soft footsteps sounded from above. Someone was up. *I had better tidy up before they come down.* She picked up the plates from the kitchen table. Just as she placed them in the sink, she heard the flop, flop sound of bathroom slippers.

She turned around to see Sheri coming into the kitchen.

"Good morning." The lady of the house sounded half awake.

"Good morning Mrs. Van Reef. You are back already." She wondered if her statement sounded like a complaint. She added quickly. "I mean," she smiled, "I didn't expect you. But it is good to have you home."

She was puzzled by Sheri's half-hearted attempt at a smile.

"Yes, I'm back." The monotone matched the dull expression on her face.

Sheri walked to the table at the bay window and sat down. She stayed there, staring into space without saying anything.

The silence was uncomfortable. "I'll make some coffee." Mrs. Steen busied herself with the coffee machine.

"Thank you." The vacant expression did not change.

Sheri sat without saying a word while the coffee brewed.

"Here you go Mrs. Van Reef." As she poured coffee, Mrs. Steen watched her employer with concern.

"So what's been happening in the world?" Sheri asked feebly, attempting to make conversation. "You know I don't read the newspapers or turn on the television during my holiday."

The housekeeper nodded. She knew Sheri liked to be disconnected from the world when not working.

"Oh, nothing major has happened since you went away."

"How are the grandchildren?"

"They are fine." It was a subject close to her heart but Mrs. Steen did not elaborate. This was not a good time for stories of her family.

"By the way," Sheri poured herself a second cup. "Have you heard from Janet?"

"What?" Perhaps she had not heard the question correctly.

"I wondered if you had heard from Janet."

The comment came as a surprise. Mrs. Steen's employers had not explained why Janet was dismissed. She had wanted to know but it was not her place to ask. It was strange that Sheri was now asking about the employee she had fired.

"Janet came to visit me just the other day. She misses the dogs you know."

*And she is upset;* the old lady had much to say but held back.

"I hope she's all right."

Mrs. Steen looked at Sheri, puzzled. Her boss had fired Janet to begin with but now seemed concerned about her?

Sheri began to say something but seemed to change her mind.

Mrs. Steen looked on with alarm as she saw the large blue eyes well up.

»«

She floated down the church steps, one hand waving and the other tightly clutching her husband's arm. The dream could not get any better.

Sheri had become known as a beautiful, up and coming television personality. She was more than just a beauty; they said; she had smarts, played the violin and had, what was often termed, a sparkling personality.

She was described as a woman with the world in the palm of her hand. And now she had the heart of one of the most eligible bachelors in the country. Lars Van Reef was good looking, had a well known family name and was wealthy.

In the weeks leading up to the nuptials, tabloids were abound with accounts of his vast fortune. A villa in Italy, chalet in Switzerland, on and on it went. To those who valued fame and fortune, this was a match made in heaven.

Heaven is where Sheri felt she was. A great partner, loving family and friends. As a television professional, she never had to worry about a comfortable living and had not been swayed by Lars's wealth. And now they had their lives ahead, to celebrate, to plan and just to enjoy each other.

The first two or three years flew by. She was blissfully married and her career had taken off. The couple was regularly seen in the company of high society.

Sheri's thoughts would turn to children every now and then. She was not getting any younger. Lars did not seem to be in a hurry but was not adverse to the idea.

Soon their son Thomas arrived. He brought much joy to the household. Two years later, Karina. The family was complete.

Even in the first year of marriage, Sheri had felt the euphoria slipping away. *That's normal*; she told herself; *honeymoons don't last forever.*

Disillusion about her marriage seemed to intensify after the arrival of the children. *It will be better when they are a little older. It is all the stress of raising a young family*; she explained away the disenchantment time and again.

The high profile life became more intense. She was now an established television anchor and more sought after than ever. The public appearances and parties were exciting but maintaining the appearance of a happy wife was becoming a strain.

Years passed and the children were growing up. Sheri had more time than before and found herself feeling all alone. Lars was away a lot, tending to his businesses. When he was home, he seemed busy, spending hours on end in the office. Dinners often were not family affairs but included her husband's business associates. Sheri resented it but at least this was a way to get to spend time with the man she loved.

On the rare occasion when just the two of them dined, she felt an uncomfortable chasm.

Loneliness was giving way to sadness and resentment. What is the matter with me? She asked herself. She had a successful career, a beautiful home and a life that was the envy of most people.

*But where is my life partner? Where is my best friend?*

*Don't give in to clichés*; she would reprimand herself immediately.

One day she resolved to improve the relationship by becoming involved in the matters important to Lars, such as his business interests. She asked him if she could help in any way since she had more time on her hands. She received a polite 'no'. She persisted but it was clear Lars did not want her involved in his world.

Politely but firmly, he pushed her away.

Sheri's heart ached. Was there another woman? If anyone knew, it would be Maurice.

She confronted Maurice. Why was Lars away so much? Was there someone else in his life?

Maurice's response revealed nothing. He told her there was no other woman in Mr. Van Reef's life, absolutely. There was a lot going on with the different businesses; he said; it was perhaps preoccupation and nothing more.

Sheri had to be content with the explanation, even though she knew Maurice was covering for his boss.

The faithful ally would never betray Lars.

Sheri had to make the choice. Call it quits or remain married. But Thomas and Karina still needed her, she had to be strong. She pushed her resentment aside and began taking on more assignments, personally as well as in her profession.

In the years after the children had left home, doubts began to creep back in and take over. Her life, now with all its riches, was beyond anything she could have ever imagined. However, the void within her was worse than ever.

Sheri felt that she was at crossroads. Something had to change or she would fall apart. She made a decision to try and rekindle their relationship.

The ski trip was such an attempt. The two of them, alone, surrounded by the magic of the mountains. Something just might happen.

Only a few days into the holiday, Lars declared he would return. To attend to pressing business matters; he said.

Sheri knew something was amiss. In this day and age, most issues could be resolved from a long distance. Why the extreme urgency?

She had learned long ago not to bother him with too many questions. But she felt this was a different situation, she deserved to know.

"I have every right to know." The bottled up emotions came pouring out. "And if you can't be bothered, I will have to make some choices."

Sheri tried to control the trembling in her voice. Not keeping check of her anger would only make her seem weak. She wanted a discussion, not a shouting match.

The stare she received from Lars left her cold.

"Don't get any ideas Sheri." He walked to the door.

Those were not the comforting words she had hoped to hear.

"But I need you Lars. To be my partner, my friend."

He paused without turning back. "As Santiago was?"

"Santiago? What are you talking about?"

"Don't play innocent with me. I know you and he have been together."

Lars did not wait for an explanation. The door opened and slammed shut.

She listened with dread to the trailing footsteps.

*What is happening?* She wanted to scream. Why did Lars bring up Jose Santiago? It was true, she had spent time with Santiago. But it was in a professional capacity, in covering his candidacy for the Prime Minister's position.

What did Santiago have to do with the two of them? Their differences existed long before she ever knew the name.

*Now Santiago is dead.*

Sheri felt suffocated.

She fell sideways on to the bed and her body curled up in a ball. Tears began rolling down her cheeks. Soon the sobs became uncontrollable.

This was all a bad dream. She would soon wake up and see her husband walk through the door with open arms.

But Lars did not return.

Sheri spent a tortured night in the dark hotel room. Her life was becoming unravelled.

The following afternoon she flew home. Back at the mansion, she made up a story of not feeling well. It was far less painful than the truth.

"If you need a change, you come and see me. Okay?" The housekeeper's soft voice interrupted Sheri's thoughts. "You can stay with us if you wish."

Sheri nodded and stood up. As she walked out of the kitchen, Mrs. Steen watched helplessly when Sheri paused to wipe away the tears.

# CHAPTER 22

Janet threw off the covers. She had tossed and turned for hours but sleep had eluded her.

Oudekerk's words, *investigation, proof, delicate,* had invaded her thoughts throughout the night.

*Without proof there is no case.*

The thought was daunting. The museum needed proof that the Van Reefs owned the original. Getting that confirmation would not be easy. Asking the Van Reefs about the painting was tantamount to accusing them of illicit ownership.

It also meant Janet would be tagged as the one who made the discovery.

She felt a shiver down her back.

The uneasy encounter with Lars van Reef was fresh in her mind. She cringed, remembering the icy stare. His chilling expression on that unfortunate day had haunted her.

It still did.

She shook her head as if to rid herself of the troubling memory.

Her thoughts returned to the Mauve. If the painting in the mansion was an original, how did the Van Reefs come by it? Did they know it was an original?

Were they aware that the rightful owner was the

Rijksmuseum?

How would the museum go about resolving the issue? Would they approach Sheri or Lars directly?

That was possible only if Janet officially divulged the Van Reef name.

She recalled the moment when she mentioned the famous couple to Oudekerk. There was only a blank expression on his face. The lack of reaction was surprising, even puzzling.

Did Oudekerk know the Van Reefs? If he did, was he holding back his feelings?

Was Oudekerk concealing from Janet something about the famous couple?

# CHAPTER 23

Sheri stood before the mirror, adjusting the pin on her dress. She gave herself one last look and reached over for the yellow purse which matched her navy blue and yellow silk dress.

The phone rang. She hurried past the wardrobe to the secretary in the bedroom. Reaching to pick up the phone, she realized that the ringing was from Lars's office. That phone was on a separate line.

As Sheri walked back to the dressing table, she glanced at the clock. She would have to hurry to be on time for the monthly meeting with the station's vice president. Grabbing the purse, she stepped out on to the corridor.

Lars had his back to the hallway as he talked on the phone. Sheri decided he was too preoccupied to turn around for a goodbye.

The strain from the eruption during their vacation had eased but Sheri did not feel motivated to make an effort. She walked down the corridor without the habitual wave.

Something Lars said made her stop suddenly at the top of the steps.

"Yeah, about the Simmons girl, what I..."

Did she hear Lars correctly? Simmons?

She took a step back but a noisy seagull drowned out the rest of the sentence. What did her husband want with Janet?

She looked at her wristwatch. She would be late if she lingered any longer. But she had to know. Leaning on the office wall, she listened.

*No, that can't be.* Sheri felt faint and steadied herself on the banister.

»«

I really have to adjust the tone on that telephone; Janet ran to stop the shrill ringing.

"Good morning sweetheart." A cheery voice at the other end greeted her.

"Hello Mrs. Steen." Even though Janet did not like being dragged out of bed, the call was a welcome one.

"Janet. I know it's early but I called to say Mrs. Van Reef wants to meet with you."

"What? Are you sure?"

"Yes." The voice was impatient. "She talked to me an hour ago."

"Do you know why?"

"She didn't say. She asked that you come to her office. Maybe this morning?"

"I'll think about it."

Janet felt no desire to see Sheri. Why this interest in her now? *As soon as possible*; Mrs. Steen had insisted. Perhaps this was Sheri's way of making amends. To say 'Thank you' and bid a proper goodbye. But why the urgency?

*There's one way to find out.* She dialled the number on the notepad.

148

"Mrs. Van Reef's office."

"Janet Simmons here. I would like to speak with Mrs. Van Reef."

"Yes of course Miss Simmons. I'll get her on the line."

The secretary was fetching Sheri without questions about the nature of Janet's business.

The call was expected.

"Janet, this is Sheri. Thanks for getting in touch."

"I understand you want to speak to me." The words felt strained.

"Can you come by my work sometime?"

"I can but what's this about?"

"I'll explain in person Janet. It's complicated."

No hints, no introduction. It was all very strange.

Janet was suddenly curious, "Okay, which day is good for you?"

"Today, if you can." The urgency in the soft voice was unmistakable.

"What time?"

"Lunch time is probably best. I'm least likely to be interrupted then. Can you make it at one o'clock?"

"Yes, I can."

"Okay, I'll see you then. Bye the way, my office is on the third floor. I'll leave word at the lobby."

"Yes but can you tell me the..." Janet's question about the reason for her visit was cut short.

"Please Janet. I'll explain everything."

"All right, I'll see you shortly."

Janet stared at the phone. That was a strange conversation. It was urgent, there was no question. Whatever the information, it could not be conveyed over the phone.

She had to hurry, there was just enough time to shower and get to Hilversum by public transportation. Taking the van was faster but trains and buses would make it difficult for the men in the Renault to follow her.

If indeed they were following her.

Once on the bus, she took off her rain coat, folded it and put it in a shopping bag. She then put on a hat, scarf and glasses. The woman getting off the bus would look different than the one who had entered the bus.

Just in case someone was waiting at the other end.

She was relieved that the train station was crowded. Weaving her way down the steps through the mass of commuters and tourists, she hoped anyone following would not be able to keep up.

As she came out from the underground station, her eyes struggled to adjust to the brightness. Was there a tram or bus departing? She looked across the street. Just as the doors of number 6 began closing, she jumped in. She looked back and breathed a sigh that no one else had entered the tram behind her.

»«

"Thank you." Janet smiled at the man who escorted her to Sheri's office.

He nodded and shut the door softly behind him. Moments

later, she heard a familiar voice outside. Soon the door opened.

"It's good to see you Janet." Sheri held out her hand.

Janet wanted to skip the small talk and find the reason for the meeting.

*First you have to explain why you fired me.*

"Before we begin Mrs. Van Reef..."

"Oh, Sheri, please."

"Okay, Sheri. Can you tell me, why I was sent off without as much as a goodbye?"

Janet had suppressed the resentful feelings for some time. Now, re-living the episode, the anger came flooding back.

"I am so very sorry about that."

Janet was ready for a fight but was taken aback by the sadness in Sheri's eyes.

"I cannot tell you how sorry I am." Sheri repeated the apology. "The fact is, I only learned about that when I noticed you hadn't come in for a couple of days."

*She didn't know?*

Sheri was *not* the one who wanted her gone. Even stranger, she had no knowledge of the dismissal until after the fact.

Janet was no longer angry, only confused about what really happened.

"I am very grateful to you for caring for Rocky and Coco."

Janet regretted her angry tone earlier. "I'm sorry if I snapped at you."

Sheri waved her hand. "It doesn't matter." She looked

directly into Janet's eyes. "Do you trust me?"

Sheri's soft, almost vulnerable side was not something Janet had seen before. The resentment built up over the months evaporated.

"Of course I trust you."

Sheri continued, her gaze steady. "This is very important and I want you to be honest with me. Tell me if something happened in the house that I should know about. Something you might have heard or seen."

What did she mean? Was she asking about the painting? Janet remained quiet, not knowing what to say.

"Janet, this is just between you and me. Please tell me if you saw something strange in the house."

Janet was at a loss; how much to tell her, what to leave out.

Sheri must know something or they would not be having this conversation.

*Why is she asking me?* Why not Maurice? He was the one person who knew everything that went on in the household.

*But she is asking me; she thinks I know something the others don't.*

"Well." Janet paused.

She had to choose her words carefully and not throw out accusations. The woman she was talking to was after all, the wife of Lars van Reef.

Somehow, at the very moment, Sheri felt strangely like an ally.

"Do you remember some months ago, when I asked if I could look at some paintings in your house?"

"Yes, you had seen them when you took Mrs. Martin upstairs."

"One particular painting is by Anton Mauve." Janet waited for a reaction.

"Okay, go on." Sheri nodded.

"Before that evening," she continued, "I had seen one like it in the Rijksmuseum. The one in the museum is identical to one in your husband's office."

Sheri said nothing. She looked perplexed, as though she tried to understand what Janet had just said.

Did Sheri not know the painting's significance? How could she not? She was involved in all aspects of decorating the house.

*Or she just wants me to talk and tell her everything I know?*

"An acquaintance suggested that one of the two paintings might be a copy."

Had she said too much already?

"And?" Sheri prompted Janet to go on.

*How much do I tell her?* Janet fidgeted.

"Please Janet. I must know. Tell me everything."

Sheri was looking more and more like a bystander. Janet felt sorry for her. It was time to let her know.

"There's suspicion that the Mauve in the museum is fake."

"Dear God." Sheri turned pale. "And the one in our house?"

Janet held Sheri's gaze but said nothing.

"I can't believe this." The shock seemed genuine. "Who else knows about this?"

"A friend." Janet had Sheri's attention.

This was the opportunity to bring up the harassment by the mansion guards. "There's something else. It seems my curiosity has upset some people. I think I'm being followed. No, I know I'm being followed."

"Followed by whom?"

"By two men. I know one of them. He works as a guard at the mansion."

Sheri sat completely still. She appeared to be digesting all the facts laid before her. Her face showed neither shock nor anger, only a dull expression.

After a long pause, Sheri broke the silence. "Thanks for being honest with me. I needed to know." She reached over and touched Janet's hand. "I'm sorry about all this. I'll make this up to you. I promise."

Janet believed her. But what did that mean? Would she have Lars call off the dogs?

Janet's spirits lifted. Maybe this was the end of the harassment, anxiety and sleepless nights. May be she could go back to living a normal life.

Janet sensed that the woman before her wanted to tell her more. Sheri began to speak but seemed to change her mind. After a quiet minute, Janet felt there was nothing else to discuss. The meeting had come to a close.

As she walked Janet to the end of the corridor, Sheri chatted and smiled radiantly.

The public persona was back.

# CHAPTER 24

Janet awoke with a dull headache. *This is becoming an everyday occurrence;* she remarked unhappily.

The Mauve painting loomed large. Just when she thought she was done with the entire affair, it crept back in.

*I wish I had never set eyes on that painting*; she sat at the edge of the bed, rubbing her temples.

The phone interrupted the distressing thoughts.

"Good morning Janet." Mrs. Steen chirped.

What did she want at this hour? Her early morning calls were becoming a bad habit.

"Hello." Janet's tone was civil in spite of her irritation.

"Hello sweetheart. Did I wake you?"

"You did. What is it Mrs. Steen?"

"The collies don't have a sitter today. I was wondering if you would give me a hand?"

The housekeeper was filling in for the absentee dog walker. Janet knew the energetic collies were too much for the old lady. Besides, it would be fun to see Rocky and Coco.

"Okay. I need a little time to wake up and get dressed. I could be there in a half hour."

But where was 'there'? Not the mansion, surely. That would

be insane.

"No, no. Not here child. Come directly to the beach parking lot."

As Janet drove to Katwijk, she thought of how awkward the situation had become. She could no longer go to the place she had called her second home, for the better part of three years.

The dogs found Janet even before she spotted them.

"Hey guys." Janet gently pried the paws away.

She looked up to see Sheri and not the housekeeper.

"Good morning Sheri. This is a surprise." And yet, for some inexplicable reason, Janet was not surprised.

"How are you Janet?" The large sunglasses veiled the emotion.

They had not spoken since the meeting when Sheri had pressed her for details the Mauve painting. At the end of their meeting, she had promised to do something about the harassment. Janet did not know if much had changed. She had stopped looking.

That was the only way to maintain her sanity.

"The dogs adore you." Sheri threw the stick into the surf. "The girl is out this week. Mrs. Steen was going to walk them but it's a bit too much for her."

If Sheri was to walk the dogs, Janet's help was not needed. Why had neither of them called to let Janet know?

"By the way, Mrs. Steen packed some things for you. I'll get them."

Sheri walked to the car and open the rear door. She returned with a large shopping bag.

"Some of it is fresh from the oven."

"This huge bag?" Janet thought it was a little oversized for a few baked goods.

"There are one or two things from me."

Sheri was making amends. "Thanks." Janet smiled and took the bag.

As she drove home, Janet looked over at the bag on passenger seat. The smell of fresh bread filled the space. What else was in there? She slowed the van and stopped alongside the road.

A knitted wool scarf lay wrapped in soft tissue paper. *From Mrs. Steen;* she guessed. Next to it was a small teddy bear. Janet smiled at the tag which read; *From Rocky and Coco.*

*What's this?* A long, oblong cardboard box felt awkward as she pulled it out of the bag. She held it near the window for better light and opened the flaps on the side. The package within it was of a familiar shape.

Janet's hands shook as she slid out the long tube. Removing the plastic top and looking in, she stared at it in shock.

This was beyond belief. She reached into the tube but stopped. Her palms were wet with perspiration. As much as she wanted to find out for certain, she could not risk causing damage. She had to get home immediately.

Her hands were still trembling as she washed and dried them. She paused, took a deep breath and eased the package out of the tube.

Unrolling the paper, she gasped as she caught a glimpse of it.

In her hands, Janet held Anton Mauve's masterpiece,

*Morning Ride on the Beach.*

»«

The loud squawking of a seagull on the balcony snapped Janet out of her daze. She did not know how long she sat at the table, staring at the painting.

Her mind exploded with questions. Why had Sheri removed the painting from the mansion? Why had she given it to her?

It was certain to be missed. Would that not cause problems for Sheri?

*It's certainly going to complicate my life.* The pounding in her head became intense. How much worse could it get?

She knew the questions would not be answered any time soon. It was time to pack up the painting. Her hands recoiled as she went to roll it up. The canvas before her felt like a live grenade. The sooner she got rid of it, the better. Her unsteady fingers struggled to slide it back into the tube.

There was only one person to whom she could give the painting, Oudekerk. She placed the tube back in the shopping bag and headed out the door.

De Avondster's front door was open. Despite her recent familiarity with Oudekerk, Janet did not feel right simply walking in. When she reached for the bell chord, she noticed her trembling hand.

A minute later, Oudekerk appeared at the door.

"Good morning." Janet's voice was barely above a whisper.

"Is something the matter?" Oudekerk looked at her ashen face. "You should come in."

He led her inside and shut the door. The howling noise of the wind stopped, making the room feel calm.

The churning within her did not subside.

Without a word, she reached in her shopping bag and pulled out the cylindrical package.

Oudekerk took the tube, walked over to the kitchen table and set it down. Janet watched as he opened it and peered inside.

"What on Earth is this?" He spoke sharply and looked at Janet. "How did you get it?"

"It's a long story." She shrugged.

Oudekerk waited for an explanation.

"It's nothing illegal, I promise."

"I want to hear it. But first," he scowled, "we need to take care of this precious painting. The way it's packed, it could get damaged." He rubbed his chin. "I'll be right back."

Janet heard the rapid clomp, clomp of his wooden shoes up the slats on the mushroom-stem that was the windmill column. She had not seen the large man move that fast.

Her eyes returned to the tube. It was a relief; *she* was no longer the one carrying the grenade.

Oudekerk returned with two pieces of corrugated cardboard and placed the larger one on the table. He pulled on a pair of cotton gloves and his large hands slid the painting out of the tube with ease.

Janet held her breath as Oudekerk laid the painting flat and examined it with a magnifying glass. A few minutes passed before he spoke.

"It sure looks like the real thing." For the fourth or fifth time, he peered at the painter's scribble.

"I'm relieved to hear you say that Mr. Oudekerk."

"Janet," he looked up with a serious expression, "how did the Mauve come into *your* possession?"

"In a most unexpected way."

Janet described her morning meeting with Sheri. How, only the previous week, she had told Sheri about the identical masterpieces.

"The tale of the two Mauves, I called it." She laughed. The tension had begun to leave her body. "This canvas practically fell in my lap."

Janet spoke of her surprise at Sheri's unexpected presence on the beach. "There were no explanations, not even a mention of it. She just gave it to me along with a bunch of other things."

"That's quite something." Oudekerk stared into the distance.

He appeared to be coming to grips with the situation before him.

"I don't know what to make of it all." Janet felt dazed with the scenarios swirling in her head.

If this was the original, it meant a switch had taken place in the museum. But how? When?

"We have move fast." Oudekerk stood up but continued examining the Mauve. "Can you get some tape and packing material from upstairs? They are in a cupboard next to the easel."

Janet returned with the tape and padding material. She watched as he cushioned the canvas with layers of packing plastic and taped the two cardboard pieces together. It looked as if he was getting it ready for transport.

"You are planning to deliver it today?"

"Yes. But first I shall have to make a call."

"To director Zalm?" She guessed he would soon be talking to the museum's curator.

"Yes." Oudekerk walked to the phone. "I have to talk to him and only him. I need to know how to proceed."

He walked to the phone on the far side of the room. Janet tried but could not hear what was being said. At least a half hour passed before he returned to the kitchen table.

"It's arranged. But not as quickly as I wanted." Oudekerk frowned. "Leonard Zalm is in Rome. That's a little unfortunate. He will not return home till late tonight. So it'll have to be here till tomorrow."

"Oh." Janet sighed. "We have to wait till the morning then."

"At the earliest. Zalm will call me early and tell me when to meet him." He picked up the packing scraps off the kitchen table.

The hours were going to crawl very slowly till then. "I wish the painting could have been authenticated today."

"That makes two of us Janet. Three, counting the director. But not being here, he can't snap his fingers and make things happen."

"But what about someone else? His second in command?"

*What about Marco?*

"That is up to Leonard. He wants to be there in person. I imagine he doesn't trust anyone else to do it."

"What about the painting? Should we take it to the police?"

"I suggested that to him." He shook his head. "He's an odd bird, petrified of bad publicity. He wants me to hang on to it

161

till tomorrow morning."

"I hope the painting won't be missed."

If it was, a few hours could make all the difference.

"It *is* going to happen very soon Janet." Oudekerk put his arm around her. "We should put it away till then." He motioned for her to follow him.

Janet walked behind, helping Oudekerk balance the unwieldy package up the narrow slats.

On the second level, by the bed, he rolled up the area rug. Janet watched him pull out two floorboards skilfully.

"Give me a hand here."

The two slid the wrapped painting in the space below the floorboards.

"This by the way, is my safe." He grinned. "The painting will be protected here."

He replaced the floorboards and pulled the carpet back over the space. He adjusted the rug till its borders matched the fade lines.

"That's a weight off." Janet expressed her appreciation. "I'm glad you're taking care of it Mr. Oudekerk."

She felt giddy with relief as she ran up the steps to her attic apartment.

*Damn. I thought I turned everything off*; she grumbled, noticing that lights were left on in the living room as well as the kitchen.

# CHAPTER 25

The alarm screeched at six, earlier than had been the case for many weeks. Janet rubbed her eyes as she looked at the clock. What was the rush today? *Ah*; she remembered, a police briefing was scheduled at nine in the morning. She felt immediately alert, roused by the prospect of breaking news in the Santiago investigation.

She walked to the window and drew the curtains open. The sight of dark clouds was disappointing. Autumn days were already short and lack of sunshine did not help brighten her mood.

As she poured coffee, Janet almost missed the cup, distracted by the commotion on the street. Car doors slammed.

*That young couple across the street again;* she muttered to herself. They often argued loudly and openly. Their fights had sometimes wakened her in the middle of the night.

She walked to the second bedroom and looked out the window. It was not that couple but three teenagers waving their arms and shouting at each other. Janet strained to hear but could not discern enough to know what was happening.

Further up the road, two men stepped out of a car and looked up and down the street. The one gesturing looked vaguely familiar. *One of the neighbours;* she thought as she turned away.

Something made her look again. There was nothing unusual

about the man. He was bald and dressed in jeans and a rain jacket. Was he bald or was that a shaved head? Just as she asked herself where she had seen him, the face began to crystallize before her eyes. It belonged to the night guard at the mansion. She stared at the two men, wondering what they were doing on her street at such an early hour.

She watched them walk in the direction of her building. Their pace quickened and within a minute, the man with the shave head stood almost directly below her. Janet blinked and tried to comprehend.

*Why? Why?;* her mind screamed. Suddenly, the image of Sheri handing her the shopping bag flashed before her. It had been a day since, the painting was certain to be missed by now.

She remembered the feeling when she slid the Mauve out of the cardboard tube. How it felt like a live grenade in her hands. Janet was too shocked to think about how Sheri might have retrieved the painting. Or why. Whatever Sheri's reasons, her actions had grim consequences.

Now, Van Reef's men stood almost at her doorstep.

*Do they suspect I took it?* Janet clutched the curtain.

But how could they think that was even remotely possible? She no longer visited the Van Reef residence.

The men were after her. There was no doubt. She stared at them, paralyzed. She had to move, do something. But she felt frozen.

*Think, dammit, think.*

She grabbed the backpack on the sofa and headed for the door. She took two steps and stopped. They would be using the same staircase. Even if they could not come into the building, they would be waiting for her outside. It was hopeless.

*The balcony!*

The sliding door screeched as she opened it. She stepped out onto the balcony and slid the door closed. The only possible way out was the fire escape, down five flights on the dilapidated aluminium steps.

What if they were waiting for her in the backyard? She leaned slightly over the railing and looked down. Except for two cats, the garden looked undisturbed. The fire escape was the only option. She clutched the banister and tried not to think of the long trek to the bottom. She had to be quick, the men could come through her front door and be out on the balcony before she was safely down.

The metal felt slippery in the morning dampness. As she stopped to steady herself, she realized she was standing on the landing of the apartment one floor below, William's. In her panic, she had not thought of his place as a refuge. Surely, William would not mind if she stayed with him for a few minutes?

*Please be home*; she tapped rapidly on the glass.

William appeared with newspaper in hand. "What's going on?" She heard him say as he slid the door open.

She brushed past him, into the living room. "Close the door. Quick. And the curtains too."

"Janet, what's wrong? You're shaking. Let me get you a blanket."

"The door first, close it."

William complied but his brow remained knotted. Janet pulled him in to the kitchen, away from the balcony. She whispered, "Can I stay here for a little while?"

"Of course." He nodded and put his arm around her. "You can be here as long as you want. What's going on?"

"I have a problem. There are people looking for me." She was drawing short, irregular breaths.

"Who?"

"They, they..." The words stuck in her throat.

"My God, you're pale." William pointed to the sofa. "Sit down and get comfortable. Then we'll figure out what to do."

"No, not the sofa." She clutched his arm. "They might knock on your door. They were outside the building when I came down."

"Do you want to wait in the bedroom?" He led her to the bedroom and a chair by the bed. "You'll be safe here."

He pulled the blanket off the bed and wrapped it around her. "Do you want some coffee?" He whispered.

Janet shook her head.

"I'll stay with you here." He sat on the edge of the bed.

"No, Wil. Go back to your reading."

"Are you sure? You'll be okay here?"

"Yes." Janet acknowledged.

William looked at her with concern as he shut the door.

Through the missing slat in the panelled door, Janet saw him amble back to the living room. His outline disappeared around the corner. The sound of rustling paper suggested he was on the sofa reading the newspaper.

She went to the chair and sat down, sharing the space with unfolded laundry.

In the windowless room, the walls began closing in.

How long had she been sitting there? She checked her watch, only seven minutes had gone by. She stood up to open the door for air but stopped.

Were those footsteps she heard? A doorbell rang somewhere. It was followed by someone banging on a door. Soon the footsteps were directly above her. She realized where the movement of feet was.

Upstairs. Someone was in her apartment.

The noise from above continued. It sounded as though kitchen cupboards and drawers were being opened.

She froze when she heard the familiar squeak of the sliding door. They were now on the balcony looking for her. She hoped the morning mist covered any footprints she might have left. She sat with eyes closed and fists clenched. She could not even risk breathing.

The men had broken into her home.

They wanted to get something from her. Janet knew what it was.

Suddenly it went quiet.

"I think they're gone."

Janet jumped at the sound of a soft voice, William's. He had also heard the noise upstairs.

"Come and sit where you can be more comfortable. I'll get us some coffee." He held out his hand and led her to the kitchen. She looked up and was relieved to see that the curtains on the balcony door were fully drawn.

They sat on stools on either side of the kitchen counter. William was a picture of kindness, neither asking questions nor pushing for explanations.

Janet felt she owed him some answers. The time was now.

"I guess I better start talking." She smiled apologetically.

"Only if you want to."

"I am in trouble. It has to do with the Van Reefs."

"You walk their dogs, yes?"

"Not anymore. I haven't for a couple of months." She pointed to her place upstairs. "One of those men is a guard at the mansion. They think I have stolen something." She paused, expecting William to ask, what? But he waited without interrupting.

"I do have something of theirs." She saw him stiffen and hastened to add. "No Wil, it's not what you think. This thing, a painting, was given to me by Mrs. Van Reef. I swear."

William reached across the counter and patted her hand. "I believe..." his sentence was cut short by the sound of the doorbell.

Janet looked at him sharply. He held his finger to the lips and waved her towards the bedroom as walked to the front door. His hand stayed on the door handle till Janet was out of sight.

She heard the door open. "Yeah?" William's lazy drawl was faint but discernible.

A soft, male voice asked, "Oh, sorry to disturb you Sir. I hope we are at the right apartment. We are looking for Miss Simmons."

*Miss Simmons.* That removed any doubt. They were looking

for her.

"Who?" William's voice had a touch of irritation.

"Let me see, she lives in apartment forty four."

"This is thirty four."

"Oh, sorry." A second voice spoke. "Do you know Miss Simmons?"

"I don't know too many people here." William's calm voice did not waver.

"Our apologies again. We'll go up to forty four."

"Yeah, sure."

"Her family wants to get in touch with her. They think she's in some sort of trouble."

"I don't know man." William said lazily.

Still, the men did not leave.

"If you see her, you should let her know."

Janet heard herself being described; height, hair and the van she drove.

The voices thanked William for his time. "You can also call us if you see Miss Simmons."

Van Reef wanted her and would go to any lengths to get her. His men were sowing seeds of suspicion that she was in trouble, a criminal. The entire neighbourhood would now be on the lookout for her.

The feeling was overpowering.

The door slammed, William hummed as he made his way back. Janet heard clanging of pots and pans in the kitchen. She guessed he waited to be certain the men were not lingering in the corridor. Another five minutes ticked by.

Perhaps it was safe for her to come out. She walked to the door and looked through the gap. At the same time, William was walking toward the bedroom. Neither said anything as he led her back to the kitchen.

Janet stared at the grain on the counter top as minutes went by. William's tap on her shoulder snapped her out of her trance. He did not speak but the questions on his mind came through his eyes. He poured fresh coffee into two mugs and handed Janet one.

"I think it's time I told you the entire story." Janet took a sip and put down the mug. "I'll begin with the time you and I went to the Rijksmuseum. Remember the landscape painting I was drawn to?"

"Yes I remember, dunes and horses." William smiled. "We had to go all the way back to look at it again before leaving."

Keeping her voice low, Janet summarized the events of the past few months; the discovery of another painting like *Morning Ride on the Beach*; her own suspicions; subsequent confirmation by the museum that the painting they displayed was a fake.

Finally, Sheri handing Janet her husband's painting.

"She actually gave it to you?" William exclaimed.

"Imagine my shock when I saw it."

"So that's what the men are after?"

"It has to be. Why else would they be rummaging in my place."

*In my home;* the thought was distressing.

"So, the museum thinks Van Reef has the original."

170

"No, not yet. It's known only that the painting in the museum is a copy."

"I am astonished." William shook his head. "Okay, you made this discovery. But how did it get this far? Who convinced the museum to carry out an authentication?"

"I've made some good friends lately." Janet smiled a half smile. "I'll tell you about them another day."

"So, it looks like the Mauve has been missed. Why does Van Reef think you have it?"

Janet shrugged. "He saw me looking at it one morning. I was in his office where I wasn't supposed to be."

"That's hardly reason to suspect you. After all, you were working there many years."

"Yes. And I haven't been to the residence in a long time." She frowned. "There's something else that's odd. Why are they looking for the painting themselves? Why not just report it to the police?"

"Maybe they don't want publicity. You know, these rich people, they hide things from the tax man."

"I suppose." Janet sighed. "Anyway, that's the story Wil. Now, they are out there determined to get me."

"Didn't you think to go to the police?"

"I almost did, when I thought they were following me all the time. But something happened and the harassment stopped. At least I thought so and let it go. Wishful thinking maybe."

William came around the counter and gave her a hug. She felt comforted; his support could not have come at a better time.

"I should go to the authorities. I can't just be sitting around hoping the problem will go away." Something else had her worried. "If Lars is going this far to get a painting that belongs to him, think of what might happen if I file a complaint."

"I don't think you can deal with this on your own. You should go to the police. I'll go with you."

William was right, the situation was getting out of hand and she could not ignore it any longer. It was not likely the thugs would go away. Even if she took the painting back to Sheri and it were returned to Lars, there was no guarantee they would leave her alone. If nothing else, to teach her a lesson.

There was one other option. She could appeal to Sheri to set things right.

"Penny for your thoughts." William pressed gently.

She was lost in her world and had forgotten his presence only a few inches from her. He had not made a single noise but remained seated near her, patiently waiting for her to speak.

"You're right Wil. I need to go to the police. I've been very confused but there are few options."

She also needed a place to stay. She could move in with Ryan, of course. *Oh dear God, Ryan!* During the recent, anxiety filled hours, she had not even thought of Ryan. She had to let him know what happened. She would telephone him at noon when he broke for lunch.

"I wish I had never taken the Mauve from Sheri." Janet should have returned it but had been compelled by a sense of right and wrong.

Was it really a sense of justice or was it the excitement of solving the mystery?

All that was immaterial now. The entire affair was a twisted mess and she was in the thick of it, writhing and struggling to break free.

"That's it then, to the police I must." She stood up.

"Good Janet. Better sooner than later, it's not going to get any easier." William also stood up. "I'll drive you."

"No Wil. Those men might still be out there. We can't be seen together." William had told the men he did not know who Janet Simmons was.

"I'm not going to let you just walk out there alone."

Janet was warmed by his sincere concern.

"I'll ask my friend Rosie, she's with the police department."

Rosie was the best person now to help her navigate the tricky situation.

William's face relaxed; there was indeed someone who could help her. He handed Janet the phone.

"Rosie, I need your help." Janet began. "These guys, they are after me."

Confused words came pouring out. Rosie listened for a brief time and stopped Janet.

"Slow down Janet. One thing at a time. Now, let me get this right. There are two guys who are following you, correct?"

"Yes. And today they were in my place."

"How do you know?"

"I was downstairs with my neighbour William."

"Where are you now?"

"Still here with Wil."

"Are you safe there?"

"Yes. But terrified. I think they're still in the building."

"You stay put, all right? I'll come get you."

"Yes."

"Do not leave, do you understand?" Rosie's tone was firm as she hung up.

"I'm glad your friend will be here soon."

"Yes." Janet was not sure what she felt.

"While you're waiting, why don't you call Mrs. Van Reef?" William's question was surprising. "Maybe she can do something?"

She brightened at the thought. Sheri was possibly the one person who could set things right.

Janet dialled her number at the television station.

"Sheri van Reef." The tone was svelte but business-like.

"Hello Sheri, this is Janet speaking."

"Oh, Janet, how are you?" The voice softened.

"No too well I'm afraid." Janet held on to the hope that Sheri had answers.

"Hold on." There was sound of a chair being pushed, footsteps and door closing. "Okay, tell me." Sheri was back on the phone. "What is the matter?"

"This business," Janet took a deep breath, "it's gone from bad to worse." She described the harrowing morning.

"I am so sorry."

"I have no choice but to go to the police." Janet waited. Perhaps the powerful Mrs. Van Reef would offer to step in and do something.

There was only silence at the other end.

Sheri finally spoke. "I am truly sorry Janet." Once again there was a pause. "I'll see what I can do."

Janet heard no emotion; no alarm, no panic, just a polite offer of help.

Were the words just rhetoric?

Janet felt very let down. Very alone.

# CHAPTER 26

"How long has this been going on Janet?" Rosie sounded calm but looked worried.

"Weeks."

"Why didn't you talk to me before?"

"I wish I had but can't explain it." Janet felt relieved to be in Rosie's hands but embarrassed at being an inconvenience.

She began with the morning when the two men came looking for her. Hearing it all again churned up the anxieties. But soon the matter would be in police hands. The thought was encouraging.

Why then did Janet keep feeling as though she had done something wrong?

"We'll get you out of this mess."

Rosie's words were meant to be comforting but Janet still felt on edge. Her eyes darted from the windscreen to the side windows to see if the men lingered. There was not a hint of activity on the street. The eerie quiet sent shivers down Janet's spine.

"Can we get going?" She slid low on the seat and pulled the cap further down her forehead.

"Listen," Rosie leaned over and patted Janet's hand. "I know this hasn't been easy for you. But I'm here to help." She put the car in gear and began driving. "Now tell me everything."

Janet did not speak till they had left the neighbourhood. "It started a few months ago." She recalled the first sign, a near collision in the restaurant parking lot. "A car almost ran in to us in Amsterdam."

Over a period of days, she saw the two men and the blue Renault several times. "I brushed it aside at first." What at first appeared to be a coincidence, proved otherwise. "After a couple of weeks of this, Ryan and I were convinced I was being followed."

"They wanted to let you know they were following you."

The statement sent shivers. Rosie was right. If the men were just following her, they would not be seen. They wanted Janet to know they were there.

She recalled instances where she nearly came face to face with them. The panic she felt then and every time she drove out in her van.

After the near collision in Amsterdam, the driver had stepped out of the car. He had turned around and given them a look. He made sure he was seen. Van Reef's guards hovering outside her building had made no effort to conceal themselves.

Rosie's assessment was on the mark. "Yes, they wanted me to know." Janet spoke slowly, spelling out every word.

"Why didn't you talk to me about it?"

Janet wished she had. "At first, I thought Ryan was overreacting. And downright paranoid when he suggested checking for listening devices."

"And?"

"We found nothing." She added, "It seems to me, shortly after that their interest in me fizzled out."

"Until today?"

"I was petrified when I saw them this morning." At that moment when she looked out the window, the horror of those weeks had come flooding back.

"I thought of running down the fire escape and disappearing into the fields behind." She described her narrow escape from the apartment. "Luckily, William was home. They even knocked on his door." She sighed heavily. "They're telling people that I've done something wrong and am on the run."

Janet could almost hear the unspoken question; *what do they want from you?*

She answered. "They want a painting I have."

"A painting?" Rosie said sharply. "What's special about it?"

"It's an Anton Mauve original. It was in Lars van Reef's office."

Rosie winced.

"I know you're wondering why I have it." Janet hastened with the explanation, "Mrs. Van Reef gave me the painting." She shrugged. "Don't ask me why."

Rosie spoke with deliberation, "I think maybe you'd better not tell me anymore. I don't want to be privy to anything this sensitive."

Now Rosie looked scared.

The Van Reef name had that effect.

Both fell silent. A short while later, Rosie mumbled to herself, as if thinking aloud. "So they must have followed you all that time to harass you into giving them the painting."

The statement struck Janet like a bombshell.

The Mauve came into her possession only the previous day. But the harassment had begun months before then.

It all began the same week her job at the mansion had come abruptly to an end.

"What's the matter?" Rosie looked at Janet with concern. "You look pale. Do you want to get out for some fresh air?"

"No." Janet shook her head. "Let's get this over with."

The car slowed as they approached Amstelveen police station. Janet stepped out and stood facing the grey building. The nervousness returned with a vengeance.

What on Earth was she doing here?

The quiet existence she had known for three years had come to a grinding halt. Her life was crumbling. She did not even know why.

Now, she stood before a police building, about to file a complaint against one most powerful families in Holland.

"Rosie." She steadied herself by leaning on the car. "Do I have to mention where I saw the painting? I mean, names and places?"

In the same instant Janet asked the question, she knew the answer.

Rosie's voice turned serious. "You are going to the police because you fear for your life. It's not going help if you withhold information." She continued in the severe tone. "They will ask if you know who these people are. If you don't stick to facts, you'll trip yourself up." She put her arm around Janet. Her voice softened, "it's going to be all right."

Janet nodded reluctantly. The two women entered the

building and Rosie pointed to the waiting area. "Have a seat. I'll get the process started."

Janet took a few steps and looked around. Not a single seat was available. Twenty or thirty people hovered around, standing, sitting in chairs or leaning on windowsills.

Janet moved back to the entrance and stood by a plant. She kept her head down to avoid being seen. She scanned the faces in the waiting area. Did she know any of them? Or worse, did anyone recognize her?

No one seemed to take notice of her. They looked worried and seemed to be lost in their own miserable world.

Janet knew that feeling.

She wanted this to be over. She wanted the harassment and the accusation to end. She wanted it to stop.

Janet was tired of running.

Rosie returned five minutes later. "Let's go."

As they walked past the waiting area, Janet avoided eye contact with the others. It was enough that she was miserable. They did not have to see it.

Rosie opened the door to a room and waved Janet to the nearest chair. "Have a seat. Agent Maller from Criminal Investigations is on his way."

"Couldn't you do it?" Once again, Janet knew what the answer would be.

"I'm traffic police Janet." Rosie poured water into a glass and handed it to Janet. "Agent Maller is a good man. But I'll stick around if you like." She walked to the door, turned around and gave a reassuring nod. The door closed with a heavy thud.

Janet sipped the water but it only intensified the churning in her stomach. The windowless space left her feeling claustrophobic. She wanted to run out of the room and out of the building.

She stood up as the door opened. Rosie walked in with a man close behind. He appeared to be in his mid-forties.

"Agent Maller, this is Miss Simmons."

"Good day." The officer's address was courteous but his unfeeling eyes left Janet with a sense of dread.

She sat down without returning the greeting.

"Full name, address and date of birth please." His tone was without emotion and was matched by his expressionless face.

"What is your complaint?" He asked as he wrote down Janet's answers to his previous question.

"I'm being harassed."

"Yes, go on."

"Some months back, I began to notice two men following me. Sometimes they would be on the street outside my apartment."

"Do you know if they lived in your neighbourhood?"

"I don't think so."

"Hm." He continued scribbling.

"This morning they came into the building looking for me."

"They were in your place?"

"I slipped out before that and stayed with a neighbour."

"Do you know these men?" His voice had a mechanical tone.

"One of them is a guard where I worked before." Picturing the face with the shaved head made Janet shiver.

"And where was the place of your work?" She fidgeted and looked at Rosie.

She received a nod as if to say, "Do it."

"The home of the Van Reefs."

The officer's left eye seemed to twitch. He looked at his notes as if to review them.

Janet watched his face. She knew he was pausing for time. To regain his composure. The words she had just uttered had caused him to flinch.

The Van Reef name had struck its blow.

The deadpan face returned, Maller continued. "The men following you, did they say anything, make threats?"

"No." They did not need words to make her feel threatened.

"Do you have any reason to believe why they are pursuing you?"

"I think they believe I have taken something from the Van Reef house. But I have not."

*Does he believe me?* She searched for clues but his expression revealed nothing.

"And what could this item be?"

Rosie interjected. "Can I have a word with you?" The two police officers left the room.

*What could they be saying?* The pounding in Janet's head worsened. She was relieved that the door opened before her imagination was out of control.

"OK." Agent Maller sat down. "That last question, we will defer it for now."

The interrogation continued with specifics of when and where she had run into the two men; their physical descriptions; how they had rummaged through her apartment; the manner in which they approached William.

An hour later, the interview was terminated.

The officer led Janet to the hallway. "Do you have somewhere to stay?"

For the second time during the past hour, his face showed any expression. This time it appeared to be kindness.

"Yes, thank you. I have a few friends." She knew she would be staying with Ryan but did not want to drag his name into it.

"Please call us and give us your contact information." He waved the papers. "Until then we use Agent Hopman as the point of contact, yes?"

Rosie jumped in. "That's no problem Agent Maller."

She walked Janet to the front of the building. "Janet, why don't you stay at my place?"

"Thanks but I've imposed on you already."

Rosie's place was really her mother's house. Rosie had moved in to help when her father had taken ill. That was seven years ago.

"Are you going to be all right?" She pressed despite Janet's nod. "Let me drive you somewhere."

"No." Janet buttoned up her coat. "I'll call to let you know where I'm staying."

"Are you sure?" Rosie insisted.

"Yes, thank you. Right now I really need to be alone."

As she walked away, Janet looked back to see Rosie standing on the steps of the police station, still with a worried expression. Janet quickened her steps to be out her friend's line of sight.

She did not know how far she had walked when she noticed a few drops on her face. The afternoon sunshine was giving way to dark clouds. Soon the drizzle turned to rain. Janet saw a bus-stop a few hundred feet up the road and ran to it for shelter. Hoping the rain would let up soon, she sat down on the bench. The metal surface felt cold and damp but her aching feet were in need of relief.

Her entire being cried for relief. Already drained from the trauma of the morning, the police interrogation had made her revisit the entire episode in painful detail.

Janet was in desperate need of some reprieve.

»«

A sudden gust of wind blew the rain into the shelter. Janet sat up and looked around. It was dark.

How long had she been sitting here? She looked at the glowing dial on her wrist. Nearly three hours had gone by since she left Amstelveen police station.

She looked down to see her shoes soaked with rainwater. *I must get going*; she stood up.

*Go where?* She sank back down on the bench and tried to think. First, she had to sort out where to spend the night. Ryan of course. No, she could not go to him. They could be watching his place and nab her if she showed up anywhere near it.

185

William's perhaps. No, that was foolish. Being anywhere near her apartment building was completely out of the question.

She rubbed her forehead; what other options did she have? Could she seek refuge in the windmill? Yes, that was the answer. De Avondster would be a safe place to stay for a little while. She knew in her heart Oudekerk would want to help.

The hour was late, well past normal commuting hours. Buses would not run too much longer, there was not have enough time to reach the windmill's remote location by public transportation.

She looked up and down the street for a phone booth but saw none. Red and yellow neon signs in the distance looked encouraging. Perhaps she would find a phone there.

She began walking toward the flashing lights and broke into a run when she caught sight of the familiar brown cubicle, on the curb outside the all night filling station.

She dug in the bottom of her bag for loose change and fished out one Guilder, enough for a quick call to Oudekerk. She fiddled nervously with the chord as the phone at the other end kept ringing.

*Please, please be home;* it was the second time in the day she had pleaded for someone to be home. William in the morning and Oudekerk now.

*That was only this morning?* Hiding out in William's bedroom seemed days ago.

She jumped as she heard a click. Was someone outside the phone booth? She whirled around but realized the sound was coming from the other end of the phone line.

"Oudekerk here."

The miller's voice was pure magic.

"I am so glad you are home Mr. Oudekerk. Can you please come and get me?"

As Janet explained the reason, she did not know if her words were any less turbid than her chaotic thoughts.

She was nearly in tears when the large man stepped out of his very small Volkswagen.

# CHAPTER 27

"Ryan Parks speaking."

"Hey Ryan." The lazy voice at the other end announced it was William, Janet's neighbour.

"Hello William. This," Ryan paused, "this is a surprise. Janet has talked about you."

There was only silence on the line. Something was wrong. "Wil, speak up."

"Hasn't Janet been in touch with you today?"

"No."

"She left my place hours ago. I thought, I thought..." William did not finish the sentence.

Ryan felt his anxiety mounting. "I haven't heard from her. What's the matter?"

"Listen, it's complicated. How about we meet somewhere where we can talk?"

"What's going on Wil? Where is she?"

"She's safe Ryan. She was with me until her friend Rosie picked her up. You know the policewoman?"

"I'll call Janet right away."

"I don't think she'll be back in her apartment."

"I'll call Rosie then?"

"I already tried a couple of times but she wasn't there. You and I should meet and figure out what to do."

"Okay. Where are you?" Ryan asked calmly. He felt terrified but falling apart did not help in any way to find Janet.

"At home."

"I'll be right down."

"No Ryan, not here. Those guys might be on the lookout."

*Those guys.* William's vagaries made sense now.

Van Reef's men who had been following Janet were after her again. Ryan began to feel desperate. He tried to think of a meeting place, somewhere between the two of them so he did not have to wait long to find out.

"Wil, can you come to the Harvest café by the stadium?"

"I know it. I'll be there in ten minutes."

Ryan hung up feeling dazed. What exactly was going on? The situation was serious, there was no question. He had heard it in William's voice. Why had Janet not called?

He scribbled a note in bold letters; *HAVE TO GO* and left it on his desk. He was in no mood to explain to anyone why he had to leave. He avoided the elevator and ran down the five flights, hurried through the maze of vehicles in the parking lot and reached his car.

A door slammed, he looked over to see a beige sedan drive out of the parking lot. For a brief moment, images of the dark blue Renault danced before his eyes.

*Better not take the car*; he told himself and began running the half mile to the stadium.

He finally stopped in the café's doorway and looked over his shoulder. *Thank goodness.* No one was behind him. He paused to catch his breath.

Standing inside the café to let his eyes adjust, he searched for William. They had never met so how would he recognize him?

Only one man sat by himself at the bar. He had to be William. Ryan walked toward him, his eyes darting from face to face to see if he recognized other patrons.

"Hey Wil."

They were strangers but at this moment, William felt like an old friend.

"A beer, Sir?" The bartender wasted no time and was ready with his fingers on the tap.

"In a minute." Ryan brushed him off with a wave.

"I can't believe she hasn't called you." The anguished look was disturbing. William hesitated, then began speaking. "It's not good news."

In a low voice, he began with the morning, when Janet tapped on the sliding door to his balcony.

"She was in total panic man."

He described how terrified she had been, knowing those men were outside the building. She thought they would be knocking on her door soon.

"Did she say a man with curly hair?" Ryan remembered the very first time he had seen the man, when the Renault had nearly run into his car.

"She said she recognized one of them. In fact, the men came to my place too."

William described how they went from door to door looking for Janet; how they rummaged through Janet's apartment.

"We heard them up there." He shook his head. "This was too much for her. She knew she had to go to the police."

"Why didn't she telephone me?"

"She was terrified Ryan. She wasn't thinking straight. The only way she felt safe was to leave with the policewoman.

They left about two in the afternoon." He sat wringing his hands. "It's not good, man. She should have called by now."

"She must be staying with Rosie."

Ryan felt frightened for Janet's safety but comforted that she was in safe hands. But was she? She had to be. Otherwise Rosie would have called.

"God, I hope she's all right." Ryan's face began to show the desperation he felt inside.

"We should try Rosie again." William reached in his shirt pocket for the piece of paper on which Rosie had written down her telephone number. "Damn, I think it's still on my kitchen counter." He rifled through other pockets.

"I'll call the police station."

"I don't even know what Rosie's full name is. Let me go home and get it, won't be long."

"This is mine." Ryan wrote his telephone number on the cocktail napkin. "I'll wait... "

William was already on his way out.

Ryan had never missed Janet as he did now. He waited by the phone wishing he knew what in the world was going on.

»«

William tossed his keys on the kitchen counter and walked to the dining table. The notepad was just where he left it when he wrote down Rosie's telephone number. Ryan would be waiting for the information; he had to make the call right away.

William picked up the receiver but put it down when he heard a gentle knock on the door. He walked to the door wondering who it could be.

He looked through the keyhole. A face was looking directly back at him. They eyes looked familiar.

William pulled back when he realized to whom the eyes belonged. Standing on the other side of his door was one of the two men who had come looking for Janet.

He stood still, not knowing what to do.

Click. The door opened.

*Damn;* William cursed under his breath. Expecting to go out again, he had not locked the door behind him.

"And how is the beer at the stadium bar?" The affable eyes of the morning had gone cold.

"What?" William tried to collect his thoughts.

"You don't know about Janet Simmons, eh? And there you were having a drink with her boyfriend."

"Hey, I was at the bar having a beer."

"Sitting right next to Ryan Parks."

They had found him out. It was pointless to try to convince the man. The only thing left to do was get rid of him.

"I'm busy man. Please leave."

"Not until you tell us."

"I said get out." William said in a rigid voice.

That was when he saw a fist flying toward him.

»«

It was late, seven o'clock. He should have heard from Wil by now. Why had he not called?

Ryan dialled the number again. The phone kept ringing but William did not pick up. Another try, still no answer. The knot in Ryan's stomach tightened. Something was terribly wrong.

He gave up on the call. He had to go there and find out. Within minutes, Ryan was in his car, heading for Janet's apartment building.

The car slowed as it turned the corner onto Janet's street. *It'll be faster if I park directly in front. No*; he decided, that was not safe. He drove past the building examining the street for familiar faces. In the next block, he pulled the car over and parked.

Despite feeling restless and anxious, Ryan walked the two blocks at a normal pace. Running would only attract attention. Once inside the building, he ran up the three flights to the flat directly below Janet's.

He knocked and waited. No answer. He knocked again. Nothing. Perhaps William was on the balcony and could not hear. Ryan turned the handle. The door opened. He pushed it and went inside.

Ryan was wholly unprepared for what lay in store for him.

The living room was in shambles. He looked around, trying to understand what had happened.

Then he saw the forearm. He walked in its direction and

194

stopped. His legs seemed to be giving in. He leaned on the sofa and slowly sat down.

Ryan was looking at a bloodied and unrecognizable face.

The clothes were familiar; he had seen them only hours earlier. *No, no;* he screamed; *it can't be.*

The person lying before him was William.

"Wil. William." Ryan called his name softly. There was no movement or sound.

"Wil, it's me, Ryan." Still no answer.

*This is Wil. Isn't it?*

Yes, the man before him was William. But why was he on the floor? What was wrong with him? Was he ill?

*Oh, God. What do I do?*

*Call a doctor. Yes, I should call a doctor.*

"Hang on Wil. Everything will be fine, just hang on." There was no reaction.

The foul air was overpowering. The room swirled around as Ryan walked unsteadily, looking for the phone. It was buried under a pile of newspapers on the far end of the sofa.

His hands shook as he cradled the phone and dialled the emergency number. The calm voice at the other end wanted to know what the problem was. Ryan stammered incoherently.

"Sir, please slow down. What is the name of the street?"

"I don't know." Ryan had been at Janet's place a hundred times but could not remember name of the street.

"The address please, Sir." The voice urged. "Just take a deep breath and think of where you are."

"Er, Achterweg, number 126."

"Is it a single family house?"

"No, apartment building, fourth floor." No, that was Janet's. "I'm sorry, third floor, top of the steps."

"The emergency unit is on its way. What is the name of the person injured?"

"William, I don't know." His voice faltered. "Hurry, please."

He dropped the phone and returned to William. "They are on the way Wil. You'll be fine and I'll be right here with you." He kept talking, hoping it helped in some way.

Ryan did not know how long he sat on the floor. He looked up to see someone tapping him on the shoulder.

"Sir, would you please give us some room?"

Ryan moved away and sat on a dining chair. He could not see what the medical technicians were doing or hear what was being said.

Wil was in safe hands. He would be all right.

A man approached him. "We would like to contact the family. Do you know where they live?"

Ryan shook his head. He had only just met William. They were not acquainted until the afternoon but instantly William had felt like a friend.

Police arrived minutes after the ambulance. Their questions seemed endless.

Ryan outlined the afternoon. The two had met earlier in Harvest café. They left the bar and William was to call back with more information.

But the call never came.

Ryan told them he thought Janet had already been to the police. He ran through the events of her morning as told to him by William; Janet's flight and her subsequent visit to the police station.

"What is this Janet's connection to this man?" The policeman probed.

"They're neighbours. Janet lives upstairs in 44."

"You have to come with us to the station Mr. Parks."

"Okay, but can I first go with Wil to the hospital?"

The policemen exchanged glances.

A medic knelt beside Ryan, "Your friend Mr. Parks," he paused, "he is dead."

"Dead? No." Ryan shook his head. "We were just at the bar. He was drinking beer."

"I'm very sorry Sir."

The room went suddenly out of focus.

Ryan heard voices around him; someone was calling to him, "Mr. Parks. Ryan."

It was Wil, he was alive and well!

Ryan opened his eyes to see a man in white clothes leaning over him. No, it was not William. He looked around and saw himself lying on the sofa. Slowly, he sat up and swung his legs to the floor.

"How do you feel?"

Ryan stared at the face with the voice.

A policeman helped him up. "We will drive you to your

house. Tomorrow, when you are a little better, we will contact you."

The officer led him out of the building to a waiting police car.

»«

Ryan sat in his unlit living room, staring into the dark night. Tears streamed down his face.

Images of William's bloody face would not leave him. William was dead. He had lost his life trying to help Janet.

Ryan felt desperate. If he had gone to Wil's place a little sooner, this would not have happened. If Wil had remained at the bar, they would not have found him. Why did Wil have to go back home?

He went back to find Rosie's telephone number. Why did they not telephone the police from the café? Of course, they did not know her surname. But surely they could have located a policewoman whose first name was Rosie?

Now William was dead. He was only trying to help Janet.

And now Janet was missing. Why hadn't she called?

*What is happening? Where is she?*

Janet needed to know about William.

She needed to know the grave danger to her.

# CHAPTER 28

"Well." Oudekerk turned to Janet as he put the car in gear.

Completely drained, she could not muster enough energy to explain the reason for the call; why he had to pick her up at such a late hour; why she was stranded in a deserted part of the city.

Oudekerk noticed the vacuous look. "It can wait. First, we go home."

*Home*; the word sounded heavenly. Relieved at not having to explain, Janet leaned back on the headrest and closed her eyes.

"Welcome back to de Avondster."

Janet awoke to find Oudekerk holding the passenger door open. She stepped out and looked around.

She found herself standing at the foot of the windmill. Its blades looked like giant, outstretched arms welcoming her. Ouderkerk took her elbow and led her to the front door.

Once inside, surrounded by the windmill walls, Janet knew she was safe.

She followed Oudekerk to the kitchen table. A place setting for one still had a half-eaten meal. He had left his dinner unfinished, to rescue her.

The lingering aroma of food made Janet suddenly ravenous. She had subsisted much of the day on coffee and water.

"You look hungry."

Oudekerk wasted no time in dishing up a bowl of lamb stew. He pushed aside his bowl and sat quietly, watching her with concern.

Energy began seeping back into Janet's bones. She looked up to meet Oudekerk's eyes. "Thank you for the meal." Her eyes welled up. "And thank you for," she struggled to speak as she fought back the tears.

"I'm glad you are all right Janet." He reached over and patted her hand.

Janet spoke after a few seconds. "I think it's time I explained."

Explained! How many times she had done that already in one day. First William, then Rosie followed by the harrowing police interview.

Words came pouring out as she described her traumatic day. "It's not enough they go door to door looking for me. They are calling me a thief." Distress had turned into anger. "I'm sorry I sound so bitter." The chafing in her voice had surprised her.

"You have every right to be angry." Oudekerk nodded with understanding. "You are being forced to run from your own home."

"I *am* angry," she took a deep breath, trying to stay calm, "angry at Van Reef but worse, mad at myself for sticking my neck out."

"Janet, you did the right thing. We both know that."

The words sounded noble but lofty ideals did little to ease the pain and loneliness.

Suddenly she yearned for the security of her little attic apartment. The place she called home. But that was in the past. She could not go back there now.

"You are safe here." It was almost as though Oudekerk read her thoughts. "Now, you get a good night's rest and we'll sort things out in the morning."

"I would really like to get cleaned up."

Her body ached for a hot soak. She remembered the stand-alone bath tub in the only sleeping quarters, on the second level. During her first visit to the windmill, she had found the small space and its claw-footed tub rustic and romantic. Now it felt like a mere necessity.

Janet realized she had no clean clothes. She would have to ask Ryan to pick up a few things.

"Ryan!" She nearly shouted.

He had not been informed of what had happened. Perhaps William had given him an update. But neither William nor anyone else had knowledge of her current whereabouts.

"I need to call him."

"Over there." Oudekerk pointed to the small table across the room.

Janet ran to the phone and dialled Ryan's number. She let it ring but there was no answer. It was late, he was probably asleep. She hung up, disappointed. There was so much to tell Ryan.

*I have been so unfair,* she sighed. Those doubts and disappointments seemed so insignificant at the moment. *How could I have been so blind?*

She knew now what a good friend Ryan had been; how much

he cared about her; how much worry the past weeks had caused him.

Janet realized how much she needed him this very minute.

»«

Janet's phone call in the morning had put Ryan's mind somewhat at ease. He was sorry he was not by her side during her traumatic time but Janet and he would soon be reunited. He would be a source of comfort to her now.

With Oudekerk, she was safe. Even with all that she had been through, she had sounded relaxed on the phone.

Ryan had tried then but could not give her another piece of bad news. One so grave.

He had yet to tell her about William.

What exactly happened to William after he left Harvest café? How did it happen? What did they know? If they kept tabs on William, he was certain to be on their watch list.

Now, more than ever he needed to be cautious. Extremely cautious.

He looked at Janet's list of necessities; clothes, underwear, toiletries. He would have to visit at least two shops, maybe three.

Foremost on his mind was to arrange for a company car. He needed a vehicle other than his own. Everyone leaving the premises would be watched. The men would surely be on the lookout for him and his car.

He signed out a station wagon for just one day. It was needed only to deliver the items to Janet at the windmill.

And after that? His insides churned. Something needed to be done. *But what?*

He would be at the windmill in a few hours and they had to come up with a plan.

Ryan tried his best to concentrate on work but it was impossible. Thoughts of Janet on the run and images of William lying on the floor constantly invaded his thoughts.

*It's pointless.* He took the day off and set off on his chores.

Weaving in and out of inner city streets, Ryan took the longer route to the shopping area. Regularly checking the rear-view mirror and convinced it was safe, he drove into an underground garage and parked in a crowded section. He quickly fell in behind a family of five and followed them into the shopping mall.

Satisfied he had everything Janet needed, Ryan drove out of the parking garage, aware of faces and cars around him. He zigzagged repeatedly, knowing it was absolutely necessary. If he was careless, he could simply be leading Van Reef's men to the windmill. And to Janet.

Driving up the dirt track to de Avondster, the knot in Ryan's stomach tightened. How was Janet holding up? Such horrific things had happened to her just in the preceding forty eight hours.

Their peaceful existence had come to a grinding halt. Their quiet world was turned upside down.

Ryan winced, knowing he would soon be the bearer of the worst news of all, the sad and horrific end to William's life.

# CHAPTER 29

"The police say he was murdered." The short man in the brown shirt spoke.

"Mr. Linden, we just tried to shake him up a bit. You know, to tell us where the girl was." Bakker chattered nervously.

"The boyfriend called the authorities." Linden hissed. "I'm sure they have some idea of who was in the building."

The two men stood before him without saying anymore. The man across the table from them was half their size but his stare was unnerving. Bakker tried again to respond but quickly shifted his eyes to the window. Watching traffic on the shipping channel was a lot easier than facing Linden's steely gaze.

"You listen to me." They were forced to look at him. "We have to finish the job and finish it quickly."

He stood up and cracked his knuckles. They watched him walk to the windowsill and lean on it.

He delivered his instructions slowly and clearly. "You have two tasks. Number one, find the girl, number two, get back Mr. Van Reef's property."

"We are doing everything Mr. Linden."

"Use your head." His eyes narrowed. "The boss is getting impatient. This stupid thing is distracting from our business."

"We *are* searching boss." Bakker had to stress that he was on the case.

"Get in touch with everyone the girl knows." The man continued. "There can't be that many. She hasn't been here all her life. When you find her, tell her to hand it over. And let her know – another such move and she won't be alive to talk about it."

The men nodded, it seemed pointless to say anything.

"I want someone watching her place all the time. In fact, have someone move into the apartment. Sooner or later she is bound to come back for something."

Bakker nodded again.

"She works at a newspaper, The European Daily. Dig down there. Call and say you want to speak to her."

"We did Mr. Linden. Twice. But they said she wasn't in."

The man glowered at them for the useless interruption. "Use your fucking head." He barked. "Make up some story. Say you're her brother and came to visit but she didn't show up at the airport like planned. You're worried and want to know that she's okay."

"Yes Sir, we'll call the paper." Bakker mumbled and waited for a sign of dismissal.

"Get that goddamn painting back." The small man waved his hand towards the door. "And this time, don't fuck it up."

# CHAPTER 30

The dark interior of the windmill had Janet craving sunshine. She looked longingly at the rays streaming through the front window.

She walked to the door and reached the handle and paused. She wondered for a moment if stepping outside was too risky. No, she decided, opened the door and let the breeze caress her face.

The windmill blades cast faint a shadow on the ground. They were tied up in an X position which meant Oudekerk would not be running it any time soon. He had interrupted his daily routine to help her.

It was eerily quiet. Janet heeded the uneasy pangs and turned to go back in. Just as she shut the door, a car pulled into the yard.

She stood still as the crunching sound of the gravel became louder. Leaning toward the window and looking through the sheer curtains, she recognized Ryan's familiar gait.

Relieved, she flung the door open and took several quick steps.

"I'm so happy to see you." She threw her arms around him.

"Glad you're okay." With his unshaven face and crumpled shirt, Ryan's dishevelled appearance spoke volumes. Even as she felt comforted to be reunited with him, she was sad to see him weighted down.

"We're going to be fine Janet." The words were upbeat but the voice was strained.

As Oudekerk came to the door, Ryan shook his hand, looked at him briefly and turned away.

"Welcome." The host tried to make Ryan feel comfortable, "Any friend of Janet is a friend of mine."

Oudekerk's smile did not mask the tension. Janet knew how responsible he felt for her. Not only because she was now under his roof but also because of his own involvement in the Mauve affair.

*I wish I could wave a wand and make all this disappear*; she examined the faces of the two men.

Had she anticipated the fallout resulting from her curiosity, her actions would have been very different.

"Do sit down." Oudekerk pointed to the chairs as he poured coffee. A minute or two passed as they settled around the kitchen table. Ryan stared at his coffee.

Janet noticed that he had neither taken a sip nor said a word since the greeting outside.

Something was very wrong. "What is it?" She asked,

"I know you've been through a lot." Ryan's voice trembled. "But there is bad news."

Janet and Oudekerk waited for him to continue.

"William and I met yesterday afternoon. He wanted to tell me about, about..." Ryan stopped, his face contorted in pain. "They must have followed me or him. I don't know. But they got to him."

What was he saying? Janet did not comprehend the simple words.

Ryan struggled to speak. "William, he didn't make it."

"What do you mean?"

"He is dead Janet."

Janet was completely still.

"He's gone. They killed him."

The shock was overpowering. Janet sank lower into the chair.

Oudekerk took over, "Did you see Ryan? I mean were you there?"

"Yes. He was dead when paramedics arrived. That was only minutes after I got there."

"Was he alive when you saw him?"

"No. I thought he was alive. I kept talking to him." He shook his head. "It seems he had been dead for at least an hour."

"This is your neighbour?" Oudekerk turned to Janet. "The one you stayed with yesterday?"

Janet was silent. Dear, gentle William. He had shown such kindness. He did not deserve this. She felt defeated. Two people in her life had gone through a great deal of pain. One had paid with his life. It was her fault.

Gloom descended. No one said a word.

Oudekerk spoke after several minutes. "I think we can see what we are dealing with."

》《

Oudekerk made few references to the owners of the painting. Several occasions had presented themselves but to Janet's surprise, he had not mentioned the Van Reef name once.

He spoke instead of his extreme worry for Janet's safety. And that of her friends, which included himself. Janet's filing the complaint with the police had not really helped. If anything, it might have been detrimental; all three agreed.

They were up against a force which wielded tremendous influence and was more powerful than they could have imagined.

The Mauve which belonged to the Rijksmuseum was now in Oudekerk's possession. Lars van Reef was certain to have noticed its disappearance.

His own wife had passed the painting to Janet. Whatever her reasons, neither Oudekerk nor Janet understood them.

Since then, Oudekerk had anxiously awaited the return of Leonard Zalm, the director of Rijksmuseum. Zalm had been travelling in Italy and had urged that the matter be kept under wraps until he was back in Amsterdam to personally take charge of the investigation.

With a meeting scheduled for four o'clock, the end to the saga of the real Mauve was now within sight. In a few hours they would be leaving for the museum.

For Janet, the pain was unbearable. The sorrow of William's death, the stress of being on the run and now the agony of waiting were having their effect on her.

*I have to do something or I'll go mad*; Janet stood up.

"I'll fix us some lunch."

"Good thinking. We have about two hours before we have to leave. Janet, there are some late season vegetables out there." Oudekerk pointed to the garden.

Janet pushed open the window to look out. A cold draught burst through. It added to the chilling feeling consuming her.

"You're going to need this." Oudekerk handed her a basket.

Janet stepped out and walked to the garden. Searching through the overgrown shrubs, she began snipping off what remained of the summer vegetables.

Alone and away from Ryan and Oudekerk, the pain surfaced. She dropped to the ground. The sobs became uncontrollable. A few minutes went by. The tears ran dry but Janet felt empty. She sat on the ground, staring into the distance.

She stiffened, jarred by the rumbling sound of a large vehicle. It was perhaps the bread truck, she looked at her watch. No, it was too late in the day for bread delivery.

She walked to the edge of the bushes and leaned. What she saw was not a bread truck but a Land Rover. Her head jerked back at the sight of someone alighting the vehicle. A well-dressed man stepped down from the driver's side.

She turned back toward the garden. Whoever came to visit Oudekerk was not her business.

She struggled to add to the meagre selection of vegetables in the basket. So late in the growing season, the pickings were sparse. She would continue looking, Oudekerk's guests were still in the house and there was no need to rush back in.

The noises inside the windmill grew louder. Janet wanted to move closer and listen but the small voice in her head told her to 'leave it alone'.

Still, something drew her near. The frame of the window was just above her eye level. Janet balanced on a rock to get a good look. Her eyes adjusted to the darkness and she saw outlines of three men. One appeared to be wearing a sports coat and the other two were casually attired.

The well-dressed man stood in the middle of the living

space. The second man leaned on the central column. The third was by the door, hands clasped, as if ready to act on a command.

The man in the foreground was gesturing and appeared to be the only one talking. His back was turned to Janet. He faced Oudekerk, who stood a few feet into the living room from the kitchen.

Where was Ryan? Did he leave to allow them privacy? Janet could not see him.

*They must have let themselves in;* she surmised. Otherwise Oudekerk would be by the door and not close to the kitchen where he sat when she left. She stood on tiptoes to see the other men better. Even with only his outline visible to her, the size and shape of the man by the steps was familiar.

Janet's heart dropped when she realized who he was.

He was the same man who had been outside her apartment building just the morning before. Here he was, once again at an uncomfortably short distance from her.

Janet's mouth went dry. Van Reef's men had traced her to the windmill. They had caught up with her, in her very last refuge.

The voices continued. Janet leaned closer. The man's voice grew louder and Janet was able to hear some words.

"Mr. Oudekerk."

*They know each other?*

"Let me be blunt." He continued. "It's only a matter of time before..." the voice faded out of Janet's hearing. A few seconds on, the man shifted and she could hear him again. "You may as well tell us now."

The voice was vaguely familiar. It did not belong to anyone in the mansion. Who was he?

Oudekerk said something but Janet did not hear him.

The man now seemed to be shouting. "You stupid old man," The polite tone evaporated, "you'll be sorry."

He waved his hand. The guard moved from the steps and stood inches from Oudekerk.

"Hey, back off!" Ryan's shout emanated from the kitchen.

Janet could not see Ryan but saw the guard move toward him into the kitchen. What transpired was not clear to Janet but everything was quiet again.

Only for a brief period.

The man spoke, "I'm giving you one more chance."

Once again, Janet heard the faint growl of Oudekerk's voice.

"Tie him up." The man barked his order.

The guard carried something in his hand. It looked like coiled up rope. As if to make room, the man in the sports coat stepped back. As he did, Janet caught a glimpse of his face.

*That's impossible!* Her mind screamed as she recognized the profile. The man was Marco Haarlemmer.

*There must be some mistake.* The man resembled Marco but did not behave like him. He was not the museum official she had met, admired. She looked again. There was no question, he was Marco Haarlemmer.

No longer the suave, soft spoken art expert, this Marco was cold and callous.

"Do you want to give it up now?" He shouted.

As the second man's arm swung toward Oudekerk, Janet looked away. She could not hear the miller's voice now.

The noise stopped. Janet returned to the window and peered through the opening. The men had moved around and she got a look at Oudekerk. He sat in a chair, his head slumped to the side.

What have they done to him? Janet wished she could comfort her elderly friend. She knew she could not. She had to remain where she was, out of the men's sight.

Marco moved in the direction of the kitchen. *He is now going for Ryan.* The shouting continued; she heard the words, *Janet, painting.* Once, what Marco said made her cringe; *your girlfriend stole the painting.*

The noose was closing in. They had begun uncovering her circle of friends. So far they had made the connection to the three people with whom she associated, Ryan, William and Oudekerk.

Marco seemed louder and harsher with Ryan. There was no *Mr. This or Mr. That.* Janet felt her legs weaken with every punch Ryan received.

She would be next. *But they haven't told him where I am.* Despite the torture, Oudekerk and Ryan had not given away her whereabouts.

From the persisting violence, it was apparent Oudekerk had not given Marco what he demanded.

*Why is Marco here?* Janet kept asking. What was his role in all of this? What *was* the connection? The painting was Van Reef's and muscle man was in Van Reef's employ. But Marco?

Did he lift the original from the museum?

Janet felt jolted by the thought. Even suggesting such a thing felt immoral. But Marco had access and opportunity. The revelation explained many things that had baffled her. Slowly, the pieces of the puzzle began to fall into place.

One thing was clear, they were after the painting. Janet had upset the balance and they were after her.

Suddenly, the noise increased. The third man pulled Oudekerk up and let go of him briefly. Oudekerk fell, hit the chair and dropped to the floor. Janet stifled a gasp.

The man grabbed Oudekerk's shoulders. "Grab the ankles," he motioned to the muscle man. The two picked up the large man, carried and dragged the limp body out to the yard. He was being taken to the Land Rover.

Marco did not seem to know she was in the garden. Otherwise, he would have been there instantly. Ryan and Oudekerk had not given her away. They and protected her and now she could not even comfort them.

The men might suspect she was elsewhere on the property and come looking for her. Janet looked around for a way out.

She stopped. How could she flee when her friends were suffering? But what could she do? If she was caught, she would be also be tied up or worse, dead. Marco's animosity left her in no doubt.

Free from their clutches, she had a chance.

The men had been after her now for two days. From what she had witnessed, they would want to get their hands on her. By not going in to comfort Ryan and Oudekerk, she *could* stay alive. Somehow, somewhere, she would get help for her two dearest friends.

*I must escape;* Janet concluded.

The grassy knoll, on which the windmill was situated, tapered on the far side of the garden. Janet dropped down and crawled rapidly on all fours to the vegetable patch. She hoped the shrubs kept her from being seen. Within a minute of crawling in between the plants, she was on the edge of the slope.

*I have to do this.*

A leap down the side of the knoll and she would be out of sight. With sadness, she looked back at de Avondster. She was leaving Oudekerk and Ryan behind.

*No, I can't.* Janet felt wretched at the thought of abandoning her friends.

Noises at the front door made her turn. Peering between the branches, she saw a sudden burst of activity. Terror struck as someone appeared to be walking in her direction. She slid down over the edge of the garden and began running down the slope.

Frantically, she looked for the tall, grassy plants she thought lined the canal. But there were few bushes in which to conceal her 5'5" frame. She could see far and wide which meant she could easily be spotted in the open countryside. Desperately, she looked back. No, she could not go back up the mound.

Janet kept running. At least she could put some distance between herself and the men by the time they were in the garden. A few minutes later she arrived at a small foot bridge. It was a good place to hide; she decided.

The ground adjacent to the canal was uneven. She took a step and realized the grass had camouflaged a steep slant.

The marsh was slippery and her feet slid into the canal. The icy water soaked the shoes but cold feet were the least of her problems. A neighbour lost his life trying to help her and now, her dear friends had suffered beatings at the hands of the same men.

The frigid water was painful. *I simply have to keep going*, she repeated, *I must, I must.* She ducked her head below the low bridge and leaned on the supporting post. She would stay there and wait it out.

Janet's frantic breathing gradually returned to normal. A few minutes went by. Dreading what might be in store, she turned back and looked. No one had followed her down the hill. The outline of de Avondster was clear but she could not see any of the men.

A faint rumble made her look again. She could not see much from her low spot. The rumbling became weaker and finally faded away. *That's the Land Rover leaving.* The men were gone. She was safe.

The relief was instantly deflated. She thought of Oudekerk and Ryan, hurt and in pain.

She crawled out from under the low bridge and walked back along the canal. Pausing at the bottom of the mound, she wondered if the men might still be there. What if the noise she heard was from a vehicle somewhere else? But she had to find out.

Exhausted and barely able to walk, she dragged herself up the slope. The Land Rover was no longer parked on the gravel. The yard looked undisturbed. The basket was where she had left it.

She ran to the small window and looked in. Some pieces of furniture were out of place but there was no sign of

Oudekerk or Ryan.

The men had taken Oudekerk. She had seen him being dragged to the Land Rover. But where was Ryan? She walked to the front and nudged the door. It creaked as it opened. Hearing nothing, she stepped in and shut the door. She paused to see if there was someone inside.

There was only stillness.

"Ryan." She called out softly but heard nothing. His coat was where he left it, draped around the kitchen chair.

Janet was not prepared for it. She ran up the steps to the second level. It had been ransacked but Ryan was nowhere to be seen. The men had taken both. Janet felt crushed. *Please be alive*; she prayed. The alternative was unthinkable.

De Avondster had a deserted feel and Janet wanted to get out of there.

*Wait!* She said to herself. What about the painting? Did they find it? If the Mauve was still where Oudekerk had hidden it, they would keep him alive to find out.

Anxiously, Janet scurried to the side of the bed. The area rug had not been moved. She tugged at it fiercely, dragging it away from the two floorboards Oudekerk had pulled up. Slipping the index and middle fingers in the gap, she pulled on the plank. It was not nailed down and lifted easily.

Leaning and reaching with her left hand, Janet felt around in the space. The plastic wrapping rustled at her touch.

*The Mauve is here!* She cried silently; Marco had not found the painting. If he had, the men would have no further use for Oudekerk or Ryan. The two would be left behind, alive or dead.

But Marco did not have the painting. He would need

Oudekerk and Ryan to find out where it was. Or where *she* was.

That meant her friends were alive.

She stood staring at the package beneath the floor. What should she do about it? Should the painting be delivered to the museum? No, she decided, it was too risky. Especially if Van Reef's men lay in wait for her. They would get their hands on her and the Mauve.

For now, the windmill was the safest place for the painting. If they had not discovered it by now they were unlikely to find it again. Gently, she dropped the plank and pulled the carpet back over the space.

She ran down the steps, hoping to find the keys to Ryan's car. She picked up his coat off the chair and held it to her cheeks. Seconds ticked as she stood, coat still in her arms as if she held Ryan.

She had to get moving. She had to leave to try and help her friends. She went through the coat pockets and pulled out the keys. Ryan's car was her answer out of here. Going back out onto the yard, she paused, listening again for voices. There was no one.

She took a few quick steps toward the car and stopped. The front left tire was completely flat. She would have to take her chances and drive the car anyway. She gasped as she got closer and noticed the gash in the tire. She examined the other front tire. It too was slashed.

*I have to try.* She got into the car and turned the key. Click; nothing. She tried again. The car did not start.

The men had made certain the vehicle was unusable.

Janet's shoes felt like lead as she slowly made her way back

219

to the windmill. Driving away was out of the question. She could still call the offices at The Daily.

*I wish I had asked The Daily again for help.* Boris had told her simply to go to the police. She had hoped he would help her somehow, unofficially perhaps. But he had made it clear that the harassment was a police matter.

She would give The Daily another try. Receiver in hand and ready to dial, she noticed the neatly cut, loose end of the telephone cable dangling. The phone dropped from her hands. Never in her life had she felt this miserable.

# CHAPTER 31

Ryan sat at the kitchen table listening to Oudekerk's discourse on art. Words such as forgery and authentication had not been a part Ryan's everyday vocabulary but were now of much significance. The talk about the Mauve focused his attention and kept him from agonizing over William's death.

How could it have happened? He pictured the limp body and the bloody face. What horror William must have endured.

*I need air.* Ryan wanted to go outside but felt obligated to stay and converse with Oudekerk. The miller had been a friend in need. He had proved it at great inconvenience to himself.

Nonetheless, it was an effort to listen and Ryan found himself drifting off. He stared into space as the stories turned into background hum.

The noise of a vehicle jarred him awake. He saw Oudekerk rush to the kitchen window.

"Hmm." The miller frowned, "It's not the bread truck." He left the window to receive his visitor.

The door flung open even before Oudekerk was out of the kitchen. A man stepped in. Behind him, at the threshold was another.

The man in front was young and well dressed. As he took a few steps into the windmill, the second man followed him. A third person came into view. He stopped at the door.

Instantly Ryan recognized him. The knot in his stomach tightened.

Ryan had not forgotten that face. The man was the guard from the mansion who had been following Janet. After the near collision with the Renault in Amsterdam, Ryan had not forgotten the rigid face and eyes with no feeling.

They had found the trail to Janet. But how? Had *he* led them here? No, how was that possible? He had taken so many precautions, used the company car instead of his own. He had chosen a circuitous route to get to the windmill.

Ryan felt sick with fear. He could not to move. He continued sitting at the table, slowly turned his back to the men and pretended to study the piece of paper before him. Perhaps their visit would be brief and he would not come face to face with the guard.

"Mr. Oudekerk." The gentle tone matched the man's sophisticated appearance.

So, he was an acquaintance. A friend perhaps, because he had let himself in. Ryan's fear eased slightly. Still, the guard was in the room. Why was he with this man?

"What's the meaning of this Marco? How dare you barge into my house like this?"

*They are acquainted. But not in a friendly way.* Ryan tried to remember why the name Marco was familiar.

"I believe you have a painting that belongs to us."

Marco had not bothered with pleasantries or small talk. His tone had turned from polite to caustic.

"I have nothing that belongs to you." Oudekerk spoke in a

calm voice.

"Yeah you do." The cultured speech evaporated. "It is a Mauve work stolen by Janet Simmons, I believe you know her."

The man mentioned Janet. He knew about her. Did he say *stolen*?

"I'm telling you once again, I have nothing that is yours."

"We want the painting back." Marco ignored Oudekerk's assertion.

In his peripheral vision, Ryan saw someone walk up to Marco. They spoke in low voices and Ryan did not hear what was being said.

He stifled a gasp as Marco took a few steps into the kitchen. Ryan smelled the cologne as Marco leaned toward him. Marco then turned back to Oudekerk.

"And isn't this Janet's boyfriend?"

"Get out of my house Marco." Oudekerk's face was inches from Marco's.

"*He* delivered the painting, didn't he?" Marco spat out the words.

He stepped close to Ryan. "Where is she? Where is Janet?"

Ryan was forced to turn toward Marco. The icy stare was unnerving.

Ryan kept his tone even. "I don't know where she is. I came here looking for her." He hoped it sounded believable.

Marco turned back to Oudekerk. He placed a hand on Oudekerk's shoulder and looked straight at him.

"Give it up old man."

Oudekerk pushed the hand off his shoulder. "I'm calling the police."

"Don't even think about it." He motioned to the man behind him to move closer.

"I'm asking you one last time." Marco spoke with deliberation, "Where is the painting?"

He waited a few seconds for a response, then waved his hand.

Ryan looked on with disbelief as the man raised his arm to strike Oudekerk.

"Back off." Ryan lunged forward.

The man paused, turned toward Ryan and struck him with his fist. Ryan was pushed back by the blow, lost his balance and fell to the ground. He tried to get up but the man held him down.

Ryan swung his arms to break free. A fist flew toward him again. He felt a sharp pain on the side of his head.

There was a shuffle of feet and Oudekerk's voice.

"Ryan, can you hear me?"

Ryan opened his eyes. Initially fuzzy, the outlines of two men came into focus. He propped himself up and leaned against the chair. His vision was blurry but Marco's voice came through loud and clear.

"It's only a matter of time before we get to the painting. You may as well tell us now."

"Go to hell." Oudekerk growled.

"You stupid old man, you'll pay for this."

"Your grandfather is turning in his grave, you bastard."

Oudekerk was no longer composed.

Ryan clutched the edge of the table and pulled himself up to see Oudekerk getting punched in the stomach. The blow knocked the wind out of the old man, he teetered, grabbed the chair and dropped down with a thud.

Marco signalled to the men. "Tie them up."

The third man wound the rope around Oudekerk's wrists and ankles. The guard kept Oudekerk from falling off the chair and kept an eye on Ryan.

Ryan felt dizzy and weak. He watched helplessly as they bound the hands and feet of a man already weakened by the punches.

"I'll give you another chance." Marco glowered at Ryan. "Your girlfriend stole the painting and you know where it is."

"I, I don't even know where she is." Ryan stammered.

"Take care of him while I search." Marco signalled to the two men and left the kitchen.

Ryan's watched his own hands and feet being tied up. The two men waited while Marco rummaged upstairs. Ryan heard noises of cabinets being opened and things falling to the floor.

Ryan faded in and out. His head was throbbing. The smell of his own blood was sickening.

Where is Janet? Was she was still outside? If so, what she was doing? Was she aware of what was happening?

*Stay outside Janet.* He hoped she would not come into the windmill. He had seen Marco's fury directed at Oudekerk. He had felt their blows.

Marco was a madman. He was savagely angry at Janet and wanted to get his hands on her. Ryan dreaded to think what these men might do if they found her.

*Don't come in Janet;* Ryan tried not to think of her. He might say something inadvertently and give her away.

Not being able to move, his legs cramped up. His body was aching to stretch. How long had he been tied up? It felt like hours but the kitchen clock showed that only twenty minutes had elapsed.

The rummaging noise ceased. Marco returned to the first level. Ryan saw him say something to the two men. They nodded and walked to Oudekerk.

They undid the ropes around his ankles and pulled him up to a standing position. "Move." The man barked and let go. Oudekerk stumbled, hit the chair and fell to the ground.

"Grab the ankles." He motioned.

*Where are they taking him?* Ryan watched as they dragged and carried Oudekerk out of the house.

A few minutes later, the third man returned and pulled Ryan up.

"You walk." He said as he untied the ropes around the ankles.

Ryan took a step and lost his balance. He held on to the chair and steadied himself.

"Get going." The man nudged Ryan in the back with something blunt.

Ryan walked slowly with the man one step behind him. As he stepped outside, Ryan saw a Land Rover with Marco behind the wheel.

"Get in the back." The man pointed to the rear of the vehicle.

Ryan sat on the edge of the truck, jumped up and propelled himself to the back. Next to him was a tired looking Oudekerk, with blood caked on his right cheek.

The man tied Ryan's ankles again and closed the doors. As the truck swerved violently and made its way out, Ryan's shoulder jammed against the wheel well. He tried sitting up but the jostling and the pain in his side made it difficult. He pushed his feet against the door and pulled himself up slightly. His head was now high enough to see out the window. At first he recognized some areas but they became increasingly unfamiliar as the truck drove through towns which he did not recognize.

He looked over at Oudekerk wondering how much pain the old man was feeling. Oudekerk's eyes were open and he nodded weakly. Ryan felt slightly relieved, at least he was conscious. Being aware of the indignities he was suffering could not be easy.

Still, it allayed Ryan's fears of Oudekerk being in a worse condition; unconscious, seriously injured or dead.

The drive was long; Ryan guessed it was more than an hour since leaving de Avondster. The ropes digging into his wrists were cutting off circulation. He tried to move his fingers but they were numb. The confined position was unbearable. It was a relief when the truck finally came to a stop.

Ryan felt relieved for the moment but terrified of what might be in store.

He looked around. The area seemed industrial. The smell of sea air told him they were somewhere along the coast. But where?

A rumbling noise made him turn. He could not see but

guessed that a garage door had just opened. The truck drove in and the door rumbled closed.

The space was oversized, too large to be a garage. Where on Earth was this?

The noise of the car doors opening and closing echoed in the cavernous space. It was an airplane hangar; thought Ryan. But there were no airplanes in it.

The rear doors opened. The man jabbed Ryan in the shin and said "You, out."

Ryan pulled himself forward on his buttocks. The man grabbed his sleeve and pulled him off the truck.

The muscle man wheeled a flat-bed cart towards them. The man holding on to Ryan turned him around and flopped him into a sitting position on the cart. He then began wheeling the cart toward the building.

Where were they taking him? What about Oudekerk? Ryan looked back. The remaining two men were dragging Oudekerk out of the truck. Ryan caught a brief glimpse of the slumped body.

The cart jerked as it was wheeled through doors and hallways. It finally came to a stop in an area with desks, chairs and stacks of cardboard cartons.

Ryan was pulled off the cart and shoved onto a chair. He flinched as some ropes were pulled tight around his waist and tied at the back of the chair.

Ryan licked his dry lips, suddenly feeling very exhausted. *Oh please, let this end.* He felt an overwhelming need to break free.

He looked down at his bound wrists. There was no way he could break free. He had to cope somehow. He closed his eyes and took deep breaths. He pictured the gushing North Sea surf hoping the images would help calm him.

*I must have passed out.* Ryan awoke to noises in the room and winced at the pain. He shifted around in his seat but moving only exacerbated the discomfort of the ropes around him.

Where was he? He looked around trying to understand. The memories came flooding back. The windmill, Marco and his men, the beatings.

And now the imprisonment. He looked down at his bound wrists.

With difficulty, Ryan turned sideways. Next to him, in another chair, sat a very lifeless looking old man.

# CHAPTER 32

Sheri lay in bed staring at the shadows cast by the moonlight and the floating curtains. The stillness of the night was punctuated by the calling of the crickets.

She closed her eyes in the hopes of falling asleep; she had not slept a wink. The crickets' chirping grew louder and louder until she could not bear it. She threw off the covers, ran to the window and pulled the pane down with force.

The crickets were shut out but the deafening sounds in her head did not stop.

Slowly, Sheri made her way back and slid under the blanket. The other side of the bed was not slept in and had not been for days. How long was it since Lars spent the night in their bedroom? A fortnight? A month? She lost track.

"What is happening to my life?" Sheri said aloud. She had been asking herself the question more and more in recent months.

The twenty seven years with Lars had not been the happiest but had many rewarding moments. As Sheri van Reef, life had been good with two wonderful children and an enviable career in television. But fun filled society life and all the trips abroad could not bridge the chasm between Lars and her.

Everything was coming unravelled since their argument during the ski week. *Argument?* She sighed. That was not the word for it.

That was the moment of truth. It had finally dawned on her that there was nothing left in their marriage. The denial was over.

She shivered thinking of the disdain in Lars' eyes when he accused her of straying with Jose Santiago. That was so unfair. She had been nothing but faithful.

Was it that hateful look which turned her against her husband? Or was it the sense of abandonment she felt as she watched Lars walk out despite her fervent pleas. Did his accusations drive her to turn the painting over to Janet?

Since then, She had tried to come to terms with the situation; that her marriage was over; where to go from there.

Something had happened in the last few days. Something of a very serious nature. Lars had not come home, not even to check on his beloved collies.

She had not seen him for days. Nor was there a message about him. Where *was* he? Was he dead? No. If he met with an accident, she would have heard about it.

There was one person in the household who would know, Maurice Flanders.

How surprised Sheri had been in the first year of her married life when she discovered that the butler knew her husband's business affairs far better than herself.

*Butler, what a misnomer that is;* she smiled wryly. Flanders had access to Lars like no one else. Initially, she had brushed it aside as Maurice's long standing association with the family. But over the years, his privileged status had become anything but diminished.

*Maurice knows.* She sat up. *Maurice knows and I have to get it out of him.*

*Damn;* she swore looking at the clock; 3am, she would have

to wait a few hours yet.

"Madam!" Maurice exclaimed as he pulled his dressing gown tighter around his waist. "Good morning. I'm sorry I..." He seemed at a loss for words.

"Good morning Maurice." Sheri began walking toward the kitchen. "I hope I did not disturb you."

*Listen to what you're saying*; she chided herself. Flanders was her employee and if she wanted to talk to him at seven in the morning, that was all-right. *No, that isn't me. It's the anger talking*; she reminded herself of her rule to treat the staff with respect.

"Not at all Madam." Maurice had recovered from the shock.

He followed her into the kitchen. When she stopped at the work table, he spoke. "Is something the matter?"

*Is something the matter?* Sheri wanted to scream at him. *How can you say that? My husband hasn't been home for days.*

*No, shouting won't do.* The situation was delicate and a threatening tone might simply shut him up.

She leaned on the table and turned around to face him. "I want to know what's happened to Lars." It was embarrassing that she had to ask the butler about her own husband.

"He is not home?" Maurice pointed toward the bedroom upstairs.

*You know very well he isn't there;* the anger was mounting but Sheri said simply, "no, he hasn't been home."

"No?" Flanders' typically expressionless face showed surprise.

*He doesn't know either?* Sheri wondered if it was all an act.

233

"I think you know Maurice." Sheri kept her anger in check. "You're keeping it from me."

"Madam!" Maurice sounded genuinely alarmed.

Why was he so shocked? Was it because she had not heard from Lars? Or was it because she accused him of holding back information?

"Mr. Van Reef has not called?"

*He really doesn't know.*

Anyone in the household could not have missed the tension between Lars and her but it was a relief that Maurice did not know the extent of the discord. Could it mean Lars did not confide in him about personal matters?

Sheri searched the face of the man standing before her. Perhaps he *was* being truthful.

"Mrs. Van Reef." Maurice continued. "I would never hold back such news. You are my employer but more than that," his eyes were tender, "you remind me so much of my own Elisabeth."

Sheri had not forgotten. Flanders' oldest daughter and she were of the same age. When Thomas and Karina were young, Elisabeth's two boys often spent the day with them, paddling on the lake or cycling on the dyke behind the house.

Sheri tried to remain composed but emotion got the better of her. Tears rolled down her cheeks.

"Please Madam," Maurice fidgeted, "can I get you something? A glass of water?"

"Thank you but no." Sheri said awkwardly.

"Please, at least have a seat." Maurice walked to the kitchen table, pulled out a chair and waited.

"Thank you." She sat down.

Maurice continued to stand.

"I will find out whatever you need to know, Mrs. Van Reef."

"Thank you Maurice."

This was so bizarre. All these years, because of the close association between Maurice and her husband, Sheri had viewed Maurice as an adversary.

Now, strangely he felt like an ally.

# CHAPTER 33

*What was that?*

The noise of a vehicle brought Janet back to the present. She did not know how long she had been sitting on the sofa.

Someone was in the yard. Had Marco and his men had come back to look for her? Could this be the Land Rover? She jumped up and rushed to the front window from where she could see the yard.

Janet sighed with relief, the sign on the side of the truck said Huisman bakery. At this time? It was late in the day for the bread delivery man to be coming around. What if it was not someone from the bakery?

The front door! Had she left it open? Her head jerked to the left to check. *Good*; the door was latched. What about herself? Should she hide?

Peering through the frayed curtain, Janet decided to remain where she stood; wait and see what or who came her way. A short man wearing a white baker's coat stepped out. He went to the back of the truck and pulled out a white box. As he walked to the windmill, Janet saw with relief that the chubby face did not belong to either of the two men who had accompanied Marco.

The doorbell clanged. "Delivery from Huisman bakery."

Should she stay still and just let him go away?

*No wait!* A thought occurred to Janet. Maybe this was the

transport she needed to get out of there. She had considered walking but it was possible Van Reef's cars were trolling for her on the streets. Could she leave in the delivery truck to some point of safety?

Where would that be? *I'll have to cross that bridge when I get to it.*

Janet opened the door to see the man holding a cake box. She smiled; it had to be the Huisman apple cake. Oudekerk knew how much she liked it and must have called in an order while she slept that morning.

"Mr. Oudekerk is not home. Thank you on his behalf."

*Think fast*; she said to herself, *get the man to give you a ride.*

This was her chance. She had to leave in the bakery truck. And take the painting with her. She hoped the man knew Oudekerk well enough to oblige.

"Mr. Oudekerk was called away in a hurry. But he has asked me to take something to a friend." She pointed to Ryan's car. "You see, I have a small problem."

"You need a ride?" The round face smiled amiably.

"Yes."

"Okay, I can drop you somewhere on my route."

Things were looking up. But Janet needed some time to get the canvas from under the floorboards.

"I need get some things ready. And change my clothes." She pointed to the caked mud on her pants.

"How long?" He frowned and looked at his watch.

"Do you have fifteen minutes?" She pleaded. "I have to get Mr. Oudekerk's package ready. It is really important. I'm sure he will appreciate it very much."

"I have lots of deliveries." The frown turned into a scowl.

Janet was not about to give up this chance. "Is there any way you can come back in a short while?"

"I'll pick you up after I'm done in Oude Ade." He pointed in the direction of the village North-East of the de Avondster. "It will be about half hour, give or take."

"Thank you so much."

The man was already on his way back to the truck.

She had enough time to package the Mauve. Janet shut the door. Alone again, the panic resurfaced. Some part of her expected Marco's men to be hiding in the house waiting for her. Nervously, she scanned the space. Everything looked as it did before.

She hurried to the kitchen and placed the cake in the refrigerator. *Hope they will be back soon to enjoy it.*

The sight of coffee cups on the table stopped her. They were left there from the morning when Oudekerk, Ryan and she sat together.

What fate were her friends suffering?

In spite of the beatings, Oudekerk had not flinched. He had maintained that the painting was not in his possession. But now they had him and Ryan. Were those men trying to break them to find out where the painting was? And where *she* was?

Right now Janet had one task. She had to get the painting safely to Zalm.

She walked up to the second level, all the while listening for sudden noises. She tugged at the heavy carpet by the bed and pulled it away from the floorboards. Squatting down, she slid her fingers in the space between the planks and lifted. One by one, she picked up and moved the three planks.

It took her several minutes to get the painting out and put

239

everything back in its place. Before the half hour was up, the Mauve was back in the same cardboard tube Sheri had handed her.

Janet stepped into the bathtub and brushed the dirt and mud off her clothes. The clothes still looked dirty. She needed a change but could not muster the strength. Besides, she had to be ready in case the delivery man was finished a few minutes earlier. She was certain he would not wait.

Clutching the tube in one hand and holding on to the rope for balance, Janet made her way down the steps. The shopping bag with the supplies Ryan had brought for her was still leaning against the wall behind the sofa. Gathering her belongings, she thought it was safer to hide outside, in the garden. In case those men returned to the windmill.

Janet shuddered to think what might happen if Marco found her with the painting.

Outside the front door, she reached into one of the wooden shoes and pulled out a set of keys. She had seen Oudekerk use them. She found the key which fit and was about to lock the door but stopped. It was better that she left the door unlocked, just as she had found it. If Marco came back and saw the locked door, he might suspect she had returned and intensify his search for her. She placed the keys back in the shoe.

She stood behind a tall shrub where she could see approaching vehicles without being seen. Was the bakery truck really coming back for her? Several minutes elapsed before a vehicle rumbled over the gravel.

At the sight of the Huisman sign, Janet stepped from behind the shrub. She was not going to show herself until she could be certain the same delivery man had returned. As the chubby face came into view, Janet moved forward to meet him.

"Thanks for doing this." She smiled, trying to conceal the anxiety.

"No problem." He took her hand and helped her onto the high step, then walked around and sat down in the driver's seat. "Where do you want to be dropped off?"

"Some town centre on your route? Where I can catch a bus or a train?"

Riding silently in the truck, Janet was filled with doubts. What *was* her destination? She had to entrust the painting to Zalm. He was the one. He would have been the Mauve's custodian, had the scheduled meeting taken place that afternoon.

A frightening thought entered her mind. If Marco was a part of this affair, could Zalm also be connected? After all, they both were employed by the museum.

No, that could not be. Zalm was the curator and had been associated with the museum for decades. Oudekerk and he had been lifelong friends. Oudekerk trusted him enough to put the matter in his hands.

At this point, Janet felt she could not count on anyone. But she had to take a chance with Zalm. He was the sensible option, the only option.

She looked down at the package on her lap, it felt more and more like a ticking time bomb.

# CHAPTER 34

"Don't!" Ryan shouted but the jabbing did not stop.

He reached to push the hand away but the sharp pain in his side jolted him awake. He realized he was still bound as his wrists tugged to break free. The cold, damp air reminded Ryan where he was. Slowly opening his eyes, he looked around and began to remember.

The horror returned; the ambush, the beatings and now, being kept hostage in a hangar.

Something blue drifted in front of Ryan's eyes. He looked with fear at the apparition before him. It took him a few seconds to be able to see in the dim light. A small person stood inches from him.

Was more torture coming his way? Ryan closed his eyes and braced himself.

"You okay son?" A soft voice floated toward him.

He looked up to see a woman leaning, her face close to his. The sea of blue his eyes saw was the janitor's apron she wore.

The gentle voice was soothing, a change from the abusive barking he had heard until now. It must be a dream; Ryan drifted off.

"Jongen, wakker worden." The voice was telling him to wake up.

Ryan opened his eyes to see the woman holding a bottle to

his lips. He took several quick gulps. The water was heaven sent.

"Thanks." He said hoarsely.

She moved to Oudekerk and leaned close to his ears. "Hey Mister."

Oudekerk was still at first but seemed to respond to her persistent coaxing. Water dribbled down his chin.

"Mr. Oudekerk," Ryan tried engaging him but all he received was a nod. Then the body slumped. "Lady." He pleaded. "Can you cut these ropes?"

As if not hearing him, the janitor put the bottle away in one of her apron pockets and pulled out a paper bag from another. Ryan smelled food as she slid the contents on to her hand.

"Here, son." She supported his chin and shoved the sandwich into his mouth.

How long had it been since he last ate? Ryan took a large bite, chewed and swallowed it within seconds. He looked up and thought it was the kindest face he had ever seen.

Who was this angel of mercy?

"You want another one?" She asked when the sandwich was gone.

Ryan shook his head. "No, but thanks."

The blue apron moved back to Oudekerk. "Mister, wake up, eat this." She whispered and shook him gently. The old man took a bite and drank from the bottle.

The stillness was broken by the clanging of a heavy, metallic door closing. The noise reverberated through the building and echoed in the hangar.

The woman jumped. "I have to go." She whispered. "I'll

come back later, when they're gone."

"Lady, please untie me." Ryan urged but his plea was lost as she scurried away and disappeared into the darkness.

*Damn*; Ryan swore. The physical and emotional pain of being tied up had him aching to break free. The angel's presence had afforded him a brief ray of hope. With her gone, it was dashed.

It had to be far worse for a man twice his age. Ryan turned to Oudekerk, "How are you holding up?"

The old man nodded. He seemed slightly better; perhaps the food and water had helped.

What in hell was happening? Ryan's mind revisited the events of the past two days. It felt like some strange story which was happening to someone else, not to him.

The pain was unbearable. "What's going on Mr. Oudekerk?"

"Something very crooked Ryan." The elderly man mumbled.

"What happened to you after they brought us here?"

"Nothing good, I'm sorry to say." The old man began recounting. "Remember when the Land Rover drove into the hangar and parked?"

*How could I forget?* Ryan nodded.

"After they wheeled you away, Van Reef's lackeys started with me."

Oudekerk described what transpired during the three hours Ryan and he were separated.

»«

Oudekerk was helped off the truck, untied and marched into the building. Along the way, Marco continued his barrage and accused Oudekerk of being the culprit in what happened with the Mauve painting. At the door to an office, Marco

245

paused, nodded to someone inside and left.

"Please come in." A short, bald man received Oudekerk into a plush office. "Can we offer you a cup of coffee?"

*This isn't afternoon tea. What's going on?* Oudekerk wondered. *I am being treated more like a guest than a captive.*

He did not refuse the coffee.

"Would you like to use the wash room?" The only one to speak, the short man pointed to a door at the back of the room. The second man busied himself with the coffee maker.

Splashing cold water on the face and washing away caked blood felt refreshing. Coffee tasted good. Oudekerk felt his energy creeping slowly back.

He wondered what was in store next. He examined the faces of the two men waiting. He was sure he did not know them. And yet, they seemed to know much about him.

The small man perched on the edge of a desk, addressed him.

"Mr. Oudekerk, we apologize if those men have been rough with you."

The man's genteel demeanour was a surprise. Was he for real? Or was this a tactic? He found himself staring at the short, bald figure.

Oudekerk felt as though he should know the man but could not place him. He was polite and soft spoken, quite unlike the thugs who had abducted Ryan and him. Nonetheless, he seemed to be involved. He even had the appearance of authority.

"Mr. Oudekerk," The man clasped his hands. "I was asked to help by an associate. Unfortunately he cannot be here to speak to you personally."

*Or he wants to be conveniently anonymous.* Oudekerk wondered if the associate was in the next room listening.

"It seems his employees," The man pointed to the garage area as if to say, 'those men who brought you here', "are looking for a valuable painting." He cleared his throat. "They believe Sir, that you are in possession of it."

*Tell the bastard the painting is not his.* Oudekerk kept the comment to himself.

"They tell me the painting was taken and that you have it." The even tone continued. "At this point, the details are not clear to me."

*You bloody well know all the details.*

The exaggerated politeness was grating on Oudekerk's nerves. He was in no mood to gratify the man with a response. He glared at him without saying a word. The man shifted his position and waited a few seconds.

"Perhaps it is not clear to you Mr. Oudekerk. You see, this painting is very sentimental to its owner and he wants it back." He leaned forward and looked directly at his captive. "At whatever cost."

Oudekerk grunted his disapproval.

"My associate is indeed sorry for his employees' actions and wishes to compensate you for any pain they may have caused you."

At this point, Oudekerk had to say something. "I already explained to your thugs that they are talking to the wrong man. If you want to kill me for this painting, go ahead. All you will have is a dead man on your hands."

"Please sir, we have no such intentions. The owner of the painting only wishes to recover what belongs to him."

*You tell that son of a bitch the painting is not his to keep.*

Oudekerk watched the man before him. Despite not getting what he wanted, the man remained calm.

"I will inform my associate of our conversation."

"You do that."

"In the meantime, please think about our request."

Oudekerk scowled and made no effort to conceal his contempt. It was evident to him that the man was a part of the organization. He was much more than an 'acquaintance', as he claimed. Perhaps he was the boss's advocate. That would explain the smooth, controlled talking.

As the short man left the room, he jerked his head toward someone by the door. Oudekerk could only see the back of his head but was certain it was a signal to stay and keep watch. He heard low voices in the next room. He listened but heard nothing discernible.

The goons came back into the room. "Please come with us."

*What, no more barking 'get up' or 'move' orders?*

Oudekerk staggered as he stood up. The one with the shaved head grabbed his sleeve. "Here, hold on to me." He held out his elbow. They walked through three offices and a corridor but this time without prodding and pushing.

Why suddenly the respectful behaviour? Oudekerk looked around. Were they being watched? But there was no one else. He looked up at the offices on the second level.

Someone was behind those dark windows. Someone was watching.

Who *was* he?

Within minutes, they were back in the hangar. The men pushed him down on a chair.

*We are back where we started;* the controlled behaviour was gone. The men said nothing as they tied his arms to the armrests. His ankles were then bound and the rope was fastened to the chair's post.

Once tied down, Oudekerk was wheeled to a cubicle in the back of the hangar. There sat Ryan, also bound to the chair, seemingly asleep.

Since the beatings he received, Oudekerk had been in and out of consciousness. He was not aware of what happened with Ryan. Now they had been separated for some time. With sadness, he looked at the young man next to him.

What inhumanities had *he* endured?

# CHAPTER 35

The large, round clock hanging from the ceiling of the train station showed forty minutes past seven.

*Two long hours;* Janet shook her head in disbelief. Bus and train connections had been poor due to the remote location of the village where her journey began.

She remembered the Huisman deliveryman's annoyance at having to return to the windmill to pick her up. It meant deviating from his route and prolonging his day. *As if I don't have enough to do already*; his eyes seemed to say.

Still, he had complied with her request. As a special favour to Mr. Oudekerk; he had said.

It was a relief to be dropped off somewhere, anywhere. And to be out of de Avondster which was miles from public transportation.

Janet was swept along the stream of commuters leaving the train station. People exited the building in different directions and the crowd thinned out at the plaza outside. The air was thick with smells of street food and cigarette smoke. Janet weaved her way through the pedestrians, all the while clinging tightly to the precious cargo.

Her immediate task was to contact Zalm at the museum. As she walked, she scanned both sides of the street for a phone booth. The first one she came to, had a person inside and two more waiting in line. *This could take forever. The museum will be closing soon*; Janet quickened her pace to look for

251

another one. Four minutes of nearly running brought her to the second phone booth. Someone was on the phone but appeared to be waving goodbye to the voice at the other end.

As she waited, Janet's one hand was on the door handle and the other jingled the change. Her left foot was in the booth even before the man had stepped out. Ignoring the man's annoyed reaction, she dialled the number which she had memorized during the train ride to Amsterdam Centraal.

The recorded message at the other end announced that the museum was closed. *Dammit;* she slammed the phone down; *why didn't I make the call sooner?*

*Maybe he is at home.* The heavy phone book felt unwieldy as she balanced it on the small shelf. Leonard Zalm; she muttered, going to the Z's at end of the book. She gasped at the ten or so pages of listings of the name Zalm. Her index finger ran down the columns looking for a Leonard.

*One, two...seven, ten...seventeen;* the number of Leonard Zalms were down to seventeen. *This I can handle.* Janet dug out all the change from her purse and piled it on the stool. She then began working her way through the list.

"No, I don't work at the museum."

"There is no Leonard living here."

She had exhausted the seventeen entries without success. Why was he not listed? How was she to get in touch?

It would have to wait till the morning when Zalm would be at work. As badly as she wanted to unload the painting, she had to be patient.

Janet felt depleted. Pressed by the urgency of the situation, she had been scrambling on adrenalin to get the painting to safety. All that running was for naught.

Her thoughts turned to Ryan and Oudekerk. *Where were they*

*taken? How can I find out?* She picked up the phone. *Should I try Sheri?*

The thought of calling the mansion left her palms sweaty. What if someone other than Sheri answered the phone and recognized her voice? What if they were able to somehow figure out where she was?

*No that won't do.* Should she telephone Mrs. Steen? Yes, that was the answer. Mrs. Steen could in turn ask Sheri. If anyone could get through to Mrs. Van Reef, it would be her beloved housekeeper.

*Please be home.* The phone at the Steen house kept ringing. After a dozen rings, Janet gave up.

*I'm running out of options;* she sighed as she put the phone down. She picked up the bag and stepped out.

The noise of the crowds at Dam Square was deafening. *I have to get away from this.* She darted onto a narrow alleyway and headed in the direction of Rijksmuseum. With the city streets thronged with tourists and revellers, she knew Amsterdam was the best place to hide. She would need accommodation for the night. She walked from block to block looking for a hotel.

*De Gouden Eeuw;* wryly, Janet noted the irony. *The Golden Age*; the name of the hotel read. That was the period of the most acclaimed Dutch art.

There she stood, below the sign, clutching the original Dutch masterpiece by Anton Mauve.

*Clean rooms, reasonable prices;* the sign claimed. She followed the arrow down the path to the entrance.

"Welcome to The Golden Age."

The dingy lobby was far removed from the hotel's elegant name. The tattered rugs and stained walls were depressing.

253

But it was of little importance. Janet wanted to get off her feet. She wanted a place to crash.

Janet wanted the day to end.

"I'd like a room please."

"Single?"

"Yes." she nodded. "No. Make that a double room. I need some space to spread out."

*And have a little extra room for Ryan and Oudekerk.*

"One night? Sixty guilder."

"Sixty?" That was a lot for the dump. She hesitated. She knew she could not go on much longer. "Okay, I'll take it but for just one night."

"If you stay two nights, I'll give it to you for fifty." The grin revealed two rows of tobacco stained teeth.

Seeing Janet nod, he slid a pad of paper toward her. "Here, put your name down and sign at the bottom."

*Thank goodness he isn't asking for identification.* She registered as Carol Hayes and paid for the first night with cash.

The shower stall was small and dark but with endless hot water, the room felt worth the fifty guilders.

Janet felt relieved to have a bed for the night. Leaning on the wall, she stared at the neon sign on the building next door. The red and yellow flashing was mesmerizing. She drifted off within seconds.

》《

*What was that?* Janet bolted up in bed, awakened by a loud clanging noise. She ran to the window but it was too high. Looking around for something to step on, she saw a white plastic chair in the corner. Dragging it into the room and standing on it, she noticed that a garbage bin had been knocked over. But there was no sign of anyone. Whoever caused it to topple, had made a fast exit.

For a brief, panic stricken moment, Janet wondered if that someone was after her. *Van Reef's thugs might be out there looking for me. And they could come bursting in any moment.*

*No;* she shook her head; *How could they possibly know where I am?* Still, the anxiety was mounting. She looked at the door and decided to place something heavy against it. The television stand made loud scraping noises on the floor as she dragged it to the door.

*Is the Mauve still here?* She rushed to the shopping bag by the side of the bed. Picking it up and feeling around for the tube, she let out a sigh. The painting was where she had left it.

Was there another way out of the hotel if she needed one? The window perhaps. Janet climbed back on the chair and turned the latch but it did not budge. Rocking the handle back and forth a few times, she was able to slide the latch. Bracing for cold air, she pushed the window open and leaned out.

The fire escape was not far from her window. *About ten feet;* she guessed. It would mean taking a dozen steps along the ledge to the landing. At least, the ledge was wide and flat. Still, the room being on the third floor, the steps to the fire escape would be difficult. Janet hoped it would not come to that.

The air was frigid but she left the window open, wedging in a towel at the hinge to keep it from closing. Just in case she needed the emergency exit.

# CHAPTER 36

Linden held Van Reef's gaze. He could not let Lars know his true feelings. He was not going to show fear.

"We have not stopped searching. You know that Lars." The tone was restrained.

Linden watched the towering figure pace before his desk. Even with Van Reef's back to him, Linden could sense the cold eyes. He felt a shiver. Why did this man frighten him so?

Linden was after all Van Reef's counsel and had been for a decade. He knew things that could be seriously injurious to Van Reef and his empire. It was probably such an awareness that made him tread with caution.

Van Reef returned to face him, "Why then is it taking so long?" He spoke in an even tone as he always did, with little emotion or anger. But Linden knew the Simmons business was getting to him.

"Yes, I know Lars." He nodded sympathetically.

It was best to agree at this point. Anything else would only stoke the fire. He needed to calm Lars and get rid of him quickly. He had enough to worry about. The last thing he needed was Van Reef's wrath.

"We seem to get real close and she slips past us." Linden leaned back in the chair. "The men are out looking, day and night."

"We have the old man and her boyfriend."

"Yes, in the Big Tower." Linden pictured the corner in the grey building where the two men were held.

'The Big Tower' was his nickname for the first of four Van Reef shipping buildings. It was the place where Lars and his the top echelon had their offices. The Big Tower was where important planning took place. That was where the action was.

Only hours before, he had been there questioning Oudekerk on the whereabouts of the Mauve. What a waste of time that conversation had been.

Van Reef's voice snapped him back to the present. "They are out of sight there?"

Linden nodded. "Out of sight and out of reach."

*That's an understatement;* he said to himself; *It's fucking impossible to get near that fortress.*

Van Reef sat down and pulled the chair close. Linden recoiled at the smell of cigar smoke.

"Georg," Lars paused as if waiting for Linden's complete and undivided attention, "keep the two men there until I say otherwise."

"Yes, of course Lars."

*After that? What then?* Linden's pulse quickened.

"What other leads are you following?" Van Reef persisted.

For a man who did not typically bother with details, Lars was asking a lot of questions.

"We have made repeated visits to the neighbourhood and the newspaper. Someone is in her place at all times in case she comes back for something."

"The painting?"

"For example." Linden nodded. "She may have hidden it with another neighbour. We know it's not in the windmill, we've turned it upside down." Linden's eyes narrowed. "There has to be someone else shielding her."

Lars gazed off into the distance. He was quiet for a few seconds. The silence was excruciating.

"Has she gone to the police?" Van Reef's pacing resumed.

"Not since she filed the complaint in Amstelveen. If the police get another visit from her, we'll hear about it instantly." Linden smirked. "Our friends have their instructions."

"How many men do you have looking for her?"

Suddenly, Linden felt cornered. As Van Reef's lawyer, it was *he* who tried to get answers. Now, *he* was the one being grilled.

He said simply, "Two of my guys, Bakker and Neelen."

"Get some men from the warehouse."

Linden pursed his lips. This was risky business, even for Van Reef. "Not a good idea Lars. We need to keep this low key. There's been too much damage already."

"You mean that artist."

*That artist?* Linden stifled a grunt. *Why don't you just say, that guy we put out of commission, permanently.*

Aloud, he spoke in a voice trained to be soothing, "He was a dope smoking nobody. He won't be missed."

"How do you know these two men will keep their mouth shut?"

"They will. Because of what we have on them. Bakker's brother is in prison and we're trying to get him out with the assistance of our friends."

259

"And the other one?"

"He's dug himself a very deep hole and won't survive without us."

"Get the damned painting back Georg. This has gone on too long to be funny."

Linden needed more time. More resources. He thought of Maurice Flanders. If Van Reef wanted another man on the job, he could perhaps give up his trusted butler.

"How about Flanders?" He asked. "Is he busy at the mansion?"

"Busy?" Van Reef's lips curled. "The house has run itself for years."

If Flanders was so useless, why then was he still enjoying the cushy job, the easy living in the mansion? Linden wondered.

"Can we employ him in our search for the girl?"

"No, absolutely not." Van Reef shook his head. "The old man's losing it. I could trust him in the past but I don't think his memory is reliable anymore. He might let something slip."

So, that was it. Lars was better off keeping the butler employed at the mansion. If Flanders worked elsewhere, he might reveal something about the Van Reefs, past and present.

"We'll intensify our efforts. And I'll make some calls." Linden took a deep breath and locked eyes with Van Reef. "Is there anything else I should know?"

"Such as?"

"Is there more to the girl and the painting?"

Van Reef stood up. "Georg, if there's anything I think you

should know, you'll hear it from me."

"Yes, of course Lars."

The point came across loud and clear. It did not matter that Linden was counsel; he had to know his place.

Lars was the boss and had made certain it was not forgotten.

# CHAPTER 37

Janet stood at the doorway of the dining room and leaned in. Was every hotel guest looking directly at her? She was being paranoid; she dismissed it. Hungry as she was, it was a good idea to skip breakfast in the hotel. The less her face was seen, the better.

Dressed with woollen hats and scarves, people on the street were not easy to identify. She hoped her own winter clothing made her face unrecognizable.

She had to contact Zalm immediately. There was no time to waste. With the Mauve in her hands, neither she nor the painting was safe.

She stepped into the telephone booth and dialled the number and waited to be connected.

A female voice spewed out a mechanical greeting, "Good morning, welcome to Rijksmuseum."

"I would like to speak to director Zalm."

"He is not in yet. Can I be of help?"

Janet suppressed her irritation. "I must speak to him personally." Her voice was tinged with urgency.

"He should be in within the next hour. Perhaps you can call then?"

"It's a pressing matter. Could you give me his home phone number?" Janet knew the answer but it was worth a try.

"No Madam, that is not possible."

"Could you call him and tell him I need to speak to him?"

"I'm sorry Madam, please call back later."

Click; that was the end of the conversation. Frustrated to be still saddled with the Mauve, Janet began walking in the direction of the museum.

Perhaps this was the time to fuel herself with breakfast. Many cafés were open for business. Janet chose a quiet one, walked in and ordered coffee and a croissant. The seats along the window looked tempting but she chose a table past the bar, at the far end of the café. From there, she could watch people without being seen.

She ate the croissant and ordered another one. She realized she had not had a bite to eat since about 10 the previous morning. She bought a newspaper and sipped coffee while turning the pages and appearing to look for something in the paper.

A church clock bonged nine times. The chimes sounded out of place amidst the cacophony of city noises. Three quarters of an hour had passed; it was time to call the museum again. She paid for her breakfast and crossed the street to a phone booth at the end of the block.

"Zalm speaking." The voice at the other end sounded frail.

Janet felt relieved to finally speak with him but at the same time, nervousness set in.

"Mr. Zalm, I am a friend of Mr. Oudekerk." She had to come to the point quickly. "I have a painting he wanted me to give you."

"Who are you?" The frail voice turned hostile.

Janet recoiled at Zalm's harsh tone. She had not known what to expect but had hoped the news of the painting would be welcome.

"I'm a friend of Mr. Oudekerk."

"Why are *you* calling instead of him?"

Why did he sound so angry? Or was that fear she heard?

"Look Mr. Zalm, I will give you the painting and I'll explain about Mr. Oudekerk when we meet, it's too complicated."

She wondered how much she could tell him. Could she trust him? Would revealing too much further jeopardize her friends? The waters were just too muddied. Her head was spinning.

"You come here and give it as soon as possible. Don't mess with it, do you understand?"

She understood completely. "I will see you at the museum in fifteen minutes."

She began running. Suddenly, a thought occurred to her. What if Marco was in the museum? She would have to be careful; she decided. Even if he was there, with thousands of people milling around, she would hardly be noticed.

Ten minutes later, she stood on Stadhouderskade, across the street from the museum. The building's turrets towered over the neighbourhood and seemed very close.

She began to cross the street but stopped in the middle of the pedestrian crossing. The knot in the stomach was back. Something told her to turn around.

She changed direction and was back on the side walk. Leaning on the canal wall, she waited, trying to collect herself.

Perhaps she ought to look around first. She pulled her camera out of the bag and attached the zoom lens. Walking along the canal, she paused where the museum's entrance was in clear view.

Guarding the shopping bag between her feet, she scanned the area in front of the museum. The archway was teeming with people, even at the early hour. From the distance, the faces were not discernible.

Something black and shiny jumped into the view finder. It was a vehicle stopped on the street, perched partly on the side walk. She picked up the bag and moved along the canal for a better look. Concealing herself behind a vendor's cart, she re-focused the zoom.

She froze. The shiny object was the Land Rover which had been in de Avondster's yard. She could not make out the person behind the wheel but the vehicle's presence was enough to convince her that someone was on the lookout for her.

*I'm not waiting to find out.* Grabbing the shopping bag, camera still in hand, she turned away from the museum onto Spiegelgracht bridge. A large tour group was heading East and she fell in beside them. When the group paused, she bolted from them and ran, weaving her way through the alleys and one-way streets.

Zalm would be waiting. She had to let him know she had not disappeared with the painting.

"Mr. Zalm, this is..."

"Why aren't you here? It has been close to an hour since your call." Zalm voice shook.

"I cannot come to the museum. We have to meet somewhere else." Janet tried to sound calm and not upset him further.

"I'm calling the police."

What? Was he trying to intimidate her? If so, he was not succeeding. It was a thinly veiled threat to force her to go the museum immediately. Did he think she was about to disappear with it?

*I want nothing more than to get rid of it.*

"Don't do that Mr. Zalm. It will only worsen the situation. I cannot explain now but please, can we meet in another place?"

"I'm calling Oudekerk. I don't know who the hell I'm dealing with here."

She kicked the wall of the phone booth. Being treated like a small time criminal was wearing on her.

"Now listen Mr. Zalm," she kept her voice even. "I don't know what is going on either. But things have happened to me and Mr. Oudekerk. Bad things. I don't think he will be answering your calls any time soon."

She waited for a response but Zalm was quiet. "I am really afraid." She continued. "Somebody is after me and the painting and I'm running out of options. If you are not interested, I'll disappear. So will the Mauve."

"Wait just a moment."

Janet knew she had his attention.

There was a faint noise of footsteps and a door closing.

Zalm was back on the phone. "This is not good. Okay, you probably should not come here. Can you go to the police?"

"I've already done that." It was clear Zalm did not realize the gravity of the situation. "I have been to the police. I'm telling you, it didn't do any good. In fact, just the opposite."

The pause lasted a few seconds.

"I might have a solution. Do you know the Bijenkorf on the Dam?"

*You have to live in a cave not to know the department store.*
"Yes," she said, "I know it well."

"My daughter Annetta works there, same surname. Please hand over the package to her. I'll call her now and tell her she can expect you. How much time do you need?"

"Twenty to thirty minutes, less if I can catch a tram."

Another stranger, more explanations, more uncertainty. Janet was weary.

"Listen Miss Simmons,"

Janet stopped. Zalm addressed her by her surname. She had never told him her full name.

"I'm sorry for your troubles." The tone was gentle. "Call again later. Maybe I can help."

At that moment, Janet knew she could trust him. She had to. There was no choice. Zalm was a friend of Oudekerk and that meant something.

"Thank you." She hung up.

Thirty minutes would be enough time to walk to the Dam. But her legs felt weak. She would have to travel by tram. She crossed the street to the tram-stop and leaned on the shelter. She did not wait long. Within the next minute, the no. 4 tram rumbled down.

>«

The guard at Bijenkorf called for Zalm's daughter.

Annetta Zalm arrived carrying something in her hand.

She greeted Janet in a soft voice, "Thank you for delivering the package for my father."

Janet nodded but said nothing.

"Can I get you something? Coffee perhaps?"

"No." Janet managed a smile.

After the trauma of the past few days, it felt good to be

treated with kindness. In another place and at another time, she would have liked to get to know this woman. But now, the only thing she wanted was to be rid of the package.

The more distance she could put between her and the painting, the better.

"My father asked me to give you this."

The woman gave Janet a slip of paper and an envelope. Zalm's home address and phone number were written on the paper.

"What's this?" Janet looked inside the envelope.

She gasped at the thick wad.

"My father thought you might need it."

Zalm had believed her. He had grasped the gravity of her predicament. Janet squeezed the bundle in her hand. She would not need to visit the bank for many days, perhaps weeks. She folded the envelope and slid it into her coat pocket.

Janet left the Bijenkorf feeling relieved. A huge weight had been lifted off her shoulders.

Now she needed to disappear, be away from people, safely locked up in her hotel room.

She had to plan her next move.

She had to find out what happened to Ryan and Oudekerk, where they were taken.

*Should I go to the police?* She asked herself again and again. The answer was *no*.

There was one person who just might be of help. Janet would telephone soon. But now, she simply wanted a few minutes of peace.

# CHAPTER 38

11:00am, Sheri *had* to be at the television station by now.
That is what the assistant had said during the call fifteen
minutes earlier.

As she waited, Janet examined the passers-by. With the glass
wall of the phone booth nearly opaque with the salt of the
North Sea air, she did not think she could be seen. Still, one
could not be too careful. She bent her head and held the
large, black receiver across her face.

The brisk, business-like clacking of high heels sounded very
much like Sheri's.

"This is Sheri van Reef." The cool voice carried with it the
image of a woman perfectly put together. Janet could almost
smell Sheri's favourite perfume.

"Mrs. Van Reef, this is Janet. I need to speak with you."

Getting out the words required effort. The trauma of the past
two days had left her depleted. The sleepless night had not
helped.

"Hello there Janet." The tone was gentle. "How can I help?"

"This is something we need to discuss in person. It's
complicated. Besides, I don't think it's safe to talk about this
over the phone."

"I see." Janet pictured Sheri flipping the pages of her desk
diary. "Why don't you come to the station? We can talk
without being interrupted. In fact, I'll clear out the next

couple of hours. When do you think you can get here?"

Sheri's eagerness to meet was a surprise. She was an extremely busy person but was anxious to talk. And immediately.

Did she know something?

Janet estimated the travel time to Hilversum. "I will need close to an hour I think."

"I'll be waiting. Come up to my office. I'll leave instructions with the receptionist."

Janet arrived earlier than planned but Sheri's assistant had expected her. She walked Janet to a meeting room. "Mrs. Van Reef will be with you right away."

Within minutes, Sheri arrived, waved to Janet and spoke to the secretary. "Some coffee please Sonja and no phone calls."

Sheri walked to the table but did not sit down. "Something is wrong." She stared.

Janet too had been shocked by the dishevelled appearance and the dark pools around the eyes, when she caught a glimpse in the mirror in the lobby.

She did not get up to shake hands. "It's a mess Mrs. Van Reef." Janet began, but paused as Sonja came in with the coffee.

Sonja filled the two cups and left the room, shutting the door behind her.

"The last two days have been hell."

Janet's words came pouring out, sometimes confused, sometimes with clarity. She could see Sheri trying to digest the information as she narrated the painful events.

Her eyes welled up when she spoke of William. "My,

neighbour Wil," she spoke haltingly.

Sheri got up, walked over and put her arm around Janet's shoulder.

"He was severely beaten." Janet continued after a few seconds. "He died from blows to the head. He was only trying to help me. He had nothing to do with any of this."

Sheri's face was ashen.

*I have never seen her like this.*

Janet watched Sheri walk back to her chair and sit down. The seldom ruffled Mrs. Van Reef simply sat, staring into space.

She seemed lost.

Now more than ever, Janet believed that Sheri had no part in the events which had rocked her life so violently. Despite her own pain and anger, she felt sorry for Sheri.

It was a minute before Sheri spoke, her voice barely above a whisper. "What about you? Where are you staying?"

"At a hotel."

Sheri nodded. She seemed to understand Janet's reluctance to divulge anymore.

"The painting is now with a friend's friend, someone who knows what happened."

Unloading the painting had been a huge relief. But the feeling was short lived when Janet thought of her friends languishing somewhere.

"I am here now to find Ryan and Mr. Oudekerk."

"The Oudekerk who lives in the windmill?"

Janet nodded. "They were taken from there. I escaped because I happened to be outside."

"Who took them?"

Your..." Janet paused, searching for a way to describe the men other than *your guards*, "two guys who work at the mansion."

"Who?"

"I only know one first name, Peter. The other one I don't know. They work as guards."

"I see."

"There was a third person, someone I met recently, a man called Marco."

"Marco Haarlemmer?"

*How did she guess the Haarlemmer name?* That meant Sheri knew Marco. What was the connection between them? Did Sheri know how or why he was involved?

Janet was suddenly afraid. "You know Marco?"

"Not really. I met him just once."

So, it was not as though they were close associates.

"How did you know him?" Sheri had her own questions.

"I went to the museum and talked to him. Shortly after noticing the Mauve painting in your..."

"Yes, yes." Sheri cut her short as though she did not want to be reminded that her husband had been in possession of the painting, the property of the Rijksmuseum.

"I could not believe it was the same Marco who showed up at the windmill." Janet shook her head. "He had me fooled. He came across as someone utterly dedicated to the museum."

His righteous rhetoric still echoed in her mind. And now, she felt embarrassed by her attraction for him during those few weeks. And deeply ashamed for thinking of Ryan as a less than exciting companion.

"We've all made mistakes Janet." The sadness in Sheri's eyes seemed to speak of her own regrets. "Okay." She sat up straight and her tone turned business-like. "Have you gone to the police?"

Janet realized that Sheri was in the dark about many facts. This was another indication that Sheri did not have a hand in the actions which had caused Janet such anguish.

"Yes, I have been to the police. I'm sorry to say it has only made matters worse."

"How do you mean?"

"Everything unravelled after that. The mansion guards seemed to know every move I made." Janet paused. "There is a definite connection Mrs. Van Reef."

The vacuous look returned to Sheri's eyes. *She is beginning to put the pieces together, just as I have.* A minute passed, two. What was she thinking? What did she know?

"Mrs. Van Reef," Janet wondered if she should to continue.

Sheri seemed out of sorts, disconnected. But this was probably Janet's last chance to get it all out in the open. And to ask Sheri for help.

"I've been running ever since." She continued. "At this point I can't trust anyone. Certainly not the police. If I file another complaint, I'm sure they won't let me leave. I might find myself locked up or dead."

Sheri sat, still staring at the wall.

Once again, Janet interrupted the silence. "Mrs. Van Reef, I don't know where they've taken Ryan and Oudekerk. I don't know what to do. So I came to you."

Finally Sheri looked up. "I am so sorry Janet. For everything that has happened to you and your friends. I don't know what's going on. But I feel responsible. I will see what I can find out." She picked up the pen. "How can I contact you?"

"I'd rather not say where I'm staying." Janet could not afford to divulge her hideout to anyone, not even Sheri who was offering to help.

"After everything you've been through, I don't blame you." She paused for a moment. "You could call me here but I'm not always at the station. How about I contact you via Mrs. Steen? I know you trust her."

Janet nodded. Mrs. Steen ought not to be dragged into this but there was little choice.

Janet departed feeling as hopeless as when she had arrived. Perhaps her expectations had been unrealistic but the meeting with Sheri had not solved anything.

There had been no magic pill, no silver bullet.

# CHAPTER 39

An eerie darkness enveloped the house. Driving into the compound, Sheri wondered why no lights were left on. She parked the car under the portico and walked to the front door. The collies could be heard all the way from the back corner of the house. No one stirred despite the dogs' noisy greeting.

*Shh*; she whispered but Rocky and Coco paid no attention. *Glad you two are happy to see me.* Ten minutes went by before the dogs calmed down and returned to their corner.

Sliding off her high heels, Sheri walked upstairs barefoot. Pausing outside the bedroom door, she listened. But for the noise of a ticking clock, the house was still. Gently, she turned the door handle. *I needn't have bothered;* she sighed. The bed was not slept in. Spending nights next to Lars had become a distant memory.

*Why do I torment myself?* She questioned. It was no secret he no longer loved her, if he ever did.

She changed out of her business suit and splashed her face at the bathroom sink. The ice cold water was invigorating. She felt a second wind coming on and decided sleep could wait.

Buttoning up the blue flannel night gown, she walked to her office at the end of the corridor, all the while trying to unravel the tangled web closing around her life and that of Janet.

Events triggered by the painting had led to deadly

consequences. William's life weighed heavily on her conscience. And now, the lives of two more men hung in the balance.

Perched on the windowsill seat, Sheri watched the shimmering water. It calmed her, as it had, during many a crisis in the past. *I wish I knew where to begin with this one;* she leaned her head on the window frame. Time was of the essence and she had to begin somewhere.

Once again, she knew Maurice was the man.

Could he really help her? she wondered. The last time she appealed to him, his concern seemed genuine. As well his promise of help. However, the information with which he returned was superfluous and of little use.

He had to do better this time. Even if that meant approaching Lars and putting the question directly to him. Maurice had nothing to lose. He was safe in the Van Reef empire.

*That's more than I can say for most;* Sheri stared into the darkness.

>«

The hour was early and the house still, as Sheri walked downstairs looking for Maurice.

"Good morning Madam." Maurice appeared from the corridor at the sound of footsteps.

"Could I have a word with you Maurice?"

"Of course Madam." He pulled out a chair but Sheri continued to stand.

"Maurice, a few days ago, I asked you to find out what was going on with my husband."

Despite the awkwardness she felt, Sheri was composed. *I wear that mask well.* Her career in television had helped master the art.

"I'm about to ask you for more."

Maurice stiffened. "I am at your service, Madam."

"Something happened when we were in Switzerland."

The ordeal began when they were away at Davos. Sheri remembered the confrontation with Lars and the abrupt end to the ski vacation. The painful memories were vivid as if the day was yesterday. The turning point had cruelly put an end to her denials. She was unsure if she would ever recover from it.

*I do have to get back to the present;* she reminded herself of the problem at hand.

"You know we rushed home from Davos." The anger was still raw but she kept it from surfacing. "I did not know why we cut short our vacation. I still don't. I also do not know why Janet was sent packing."

How strange it was that she, the owner of this house, was talking to an employee and alluding to her own diminished role in the household. "What's going on?"

Maurice looked down at his feet. It was an uncomfortable situation. Sheri also knew he was torn between his loyalty to Lars and consideration for her, a woman 'much like his own daughter' as he had sometimes said.

"I know this is delicate Maurice. I have no quarrel with your wanting to maintain Lars' confidence."

*How pathetic that sounds.*

Sheri knew she had touched a nerve.

"Mrs. Van Reef," Maurice appeared to arrive to a decision. "I will tell you what I know."

"I think it was late summer or early autumn." Maurice began

with Janet Simmons. "Mr. Van Reef found her snooping in his office."

"She had asked my permission."

"But Mr. Van Reef did not like it."

Lars had declared it unacceptable and Janet had been asked to leave. "Not too long ago, a painting in his office went missing. Mr. Van Reef is sure Miss Simmons stole it."

Sheri's heart dropped. Janet may have been looking around in the office upstairs but it was Sheri who caused the painting to disappear.

In a moment of blind rage, she had made the decision to take the painting out of the house and pass it on to Janet. Lars had wounded her deeply and this was her retaliation.

She had her revenge but at great detriment to Janet.

"Did you report it?"

She needed to find out if there was collusion with the police.

"You know Mr. Van Reef does not like publicity. He wanted to find the painting quietly."

By quietly, did he mean harass, intimidate and brutalize? Sheri's jaws clenched. Was keeping it quiet really to avoid publicity? Or was there more?

"So, what's the latest?" She pressed even though she was certain she knew more at the moment than Maurice.

"The painting has not been recovered. At least as far as I know. They have been unable to speak to Miss Simmons."

*They may not have spoken to her be she got the message.*

It was time to let Maurice know how dangerous the situation had become.

"Janet came to see me recently."

*Should I fill in the when and where?* No, she could not ignore the probability that some of the conversation might make its way to Lars.

When she next spoke, Sheri did not take her eyes off Maurice, "Someone has died because of all this."

He gasped and steadied himself on the table. *He looks like a ghost.*

"Why don't you sit down?" She held out her hand for support.

Maurice sat on the chair and cradled his head in his palms.

"A glass of water?"

*This can't possibly be an act.* Sheri knew then Maurice had been in the dark about William's death.

"No, thank you." Maurice said hoarsely as he stood up. "It is horrible. A life was lost." He shook his head.

"I beg you to tell me everything you know about this situation. What you don't know, I want you to track down." Sheri thought of the ragged looking Janet. "First and foremost, find out about Janet's friends. Where they have been taken."

She stepped closer and looked into his eyes. "Ryan Parks and Meneer Oudekerk are in grave danger."

"Madam." Maurice had recovered from the shock. "Please give me an hour or two. I will make some calls. I might have to leave the house for a bit."

"And Maurice, please don't bother Lars about this."

The thought that her husband might learn of her enquiries was terrifying.

"I shall not speak about it Madam. You have my word."

»«

281

Time seemed to be at a standstill. *What else can I do?* Sheri ran her finger down the list. The top four items were checked off. Perhaps she could busy herself whittling down the mounting pile of fan letters.

*I wish Maurice would return with some news.* Finger nails rapped on the mahogany desk.

The flash of sunshine reflected by a passing car made her look up. *It must be Maurice.* As she ran to the front window, she heard a car door slam.

*Please no bad news;* she leaned on the wall and took deep breaths. A minute later, she was at the end of the corridor but Maurice was already halfway up the staircase.

"Good afternoon Madam."

"Good afternoon Maurice." The frown on his face sent her pulse racing.

"I have some information." He stopped to catch his breath.

"Let's go sit down." Sheri walked back to her office.

Maurice spoke as he followed her. "They have been trying to contact Miss. Simmons but there is no trace of her."

"I told you I saw her." She pointed to a chair. "But you did not know when." She hesitated but added, "Janet came to see me yesterday."

"That means she is still around." He scowled. "Yes, you did tell me. I kept that bit of information to myself."

*Good man*; Sheri's shoulders relaxed. With each of the recent conversations, the feeling that she could trust him had strengthened.

She asked, "What are these men's names?"

"Bakker and Neelen."

"The guards?" Her eyes narrowed.

282

Maurice nodded. "We have hired them as guards but they work for Mr. Linden."

Sheri clenched her teeth. With his silver tongue and long list of titles, Linden had carved himself a powerful position in the Van Reef operation. The first time they met, Sheri had seen through the suave demeanour.

*Be careful*; she had warned herself through the smiles; *be very careful of this snake.*

Maurice continued. "They suspect Miss Simmons is out to make money by selling the painting. They think she may even have gone to a neighbouring European country."

This account of Janet was not a surprise. By painting her as a thief, the chances of catching her were better.

"Something else." Maurice checked his notes.

Sheri felt a shiver. What *else* could Lars have found out? Did he know of her own meetings with Janet?

"They feel that in addition to the painting, she might have taken other things. Some papers from the office. Information sensitive to the business, material she could sell to newspapers and such. This could be damaging to the family."

Sheri breathed a sigh. Her meetings with Janet had gone unnoticed.

The idea that Janet might have stolen personal information was a stretch. But Janet did work for a newspaper and the picture they painted was believable.

She felt that Maurice was relaying the story he had been fed. Whether or not he knew any of it to be true, he was simply repeating it.

"What else?" She pressed.

It was a balancing act. She had to get him to tell her everything he heard. On the other hand, if she pushed too hard, Maurice might become nervous and withdraw his cooperation. Sheri sensed continuing conflict. His loyalty was to Lars and to the late Mr. Van Reef. That was just how things were in the family.

"You know, lives are at stake." She hoped he believed her side of the story.

Maurice cleared his throat. "There is something going on down at the Big Tower."

"What do you mean?" She glared. "What's supposed to happen at the Big Tower?"

"I'm not entirely sure." Maurice shook his head. "But here is why I think something is about to happen. You know I pitch in every now and then with clerical chores. Last week I helped with coordinating the schedule. Today I was told some of the planned work had been postponed. Friday is not a holiday but the workers have been given the day off. No one would tell me why."

This was abnormal. Not even Maurice, one of Lars's most trusted men, was given an explanation.

"I don't know if it has any connection with Janet Simmons's disappearance. But something unusual is taking place. They were evasive. The best I could do was to read between the lines." Maurice's shoulders sagged.

*He looks like he was ejected from the game and told to sit on the side-lines.* The picture was becoming clear to Sheri. He no longer belonged in Lars van Reef's inner sanctum.

Maurice appeared to have come to the hard realization.

"Thank you. I have to see what I can do."

*But what?* She felt bewildered.

"I will keep looking Madam. If there is something I can do in the meantime, please let me know." He waited to be dismissed.

"I will need your help. And Maurice, don't worry, this conversation will remain between us."

She wanted to allay any fears of repercussions from Lars. She dismissed the idea immediately, Maurice had no such worries.

*She* should be the one concerned.

As the last of Maurice disappeared around the doorway, she tallied up the situation. A valuable original masterpiece thought to be stolen from the house. No police report. A fired employee. An interrupted vacation. A trail of brutalization. The horrific death of Janet's neighbour William.

Sheri's image of her husband was crumbling.

# CHAPTER 40

Sheri was out of breath from running as she slid into the driver's seat. There was no time to rest. She let up on the clutch and eased the Mercedes out of the mansion.

The diamond studded wristwatch glinted in the sun. *Thirteen minutes, not bad*; she had driven to Mrs. Steen's house in record time.

The front door opened before she had a chance to knock.

"Good evening Mrs. Steen. I'm sorry to disturb you at dinnertime."

"Don't you worry schatje. Come in." Only 4'11", the host reached up to help the much taller Sheri with her coat.

Sheri hesitated, "I'll keep it on, this shouldn't take too long."

"Nonsense. You'll stay and have coffee." Mrs. Steen did not wait for an answer and proceeded to the kitchen.

Sheri did not argue. No visitor to the house was leaving without a cup of coffee. No matter what time of day. She slipped off her coat and hung it on an already used hook.

"Thank you." She bent down and hugged the diminutive figure. It was comforting to be in the housekeeper's company. "Thank you." she repeated, grateful to be welcomed.

Grateful to be sheltered from the cold world outside.

"Talk to me love." Mrs. Steen handed her a cup.

"It's about Janet." Sheri began.

The housekeeper stopped stirring and looked up. "Where is that child?" She frowned. "I haven't seen her in ages."

"She came to see me yesterday. She is having serious problems and I need to help her."

"Is she all right? She's not hurt, is she?"

Sheri reached across the table and patted the old lady's hand. "She's not hurt. But things have happened to her."

"What things?"

It was clear to Sheri that Mrs. Steen had no idea of the painting or the disastrous events in its trail.

"Her friends have been hurt. She's worried for them. She is frightened that something might happen to her also."

"Sheri my love, you are talking in riddles." Mrs. Steen crossed her arms.

"I'll come to the point then." Mrs. Steen sounded testy. Sheri thought it best to be direct. "You see, she is in trouble with Lars. You know what happened, with her being dismissed and all that."

"Janet was very upset about that." The elderly lady shook her head. "I don't understand what happened."

"Lars thought she took a painting from the house."

"I heard that but didn't believe it for a second."

Sheri leaned closer, "I can tell you she did *not* take the painting."

"I knew it." The elderly lady thumped the table with her fist.

*She deserves to know everything that happened and someday I'll tell her. But not now.*

Sheri continued. "Mrs. Steen, I'm asking for your help. I

didn't think it was a good idea to discuss this on the phone."

"You are always welcome here. And you can talk to me about anything."

*She understands more than she is leading on.* Sheri felt saddened that Mrs. Steen was left in the dark. Sheri resolved to tell her the whole truth. But now was not the right time.

"I've asked Janet to be in touch with you."

Sheri did not have to explain further. Her housekeeper knew what that meant. Janet was to call here. She was in no way to contact Sheri at the mansion.

"Here's what needs to happen." Sheri picked up her purse off the floor.

Mrs. Steen was quiet but the scowl had not left her face.

"I promise I'll tell you everything someday. But for now, you must trust me." She dug in her purse and pulled out a leather pouch. "These are keys to the Big Tower."

Mrs. Steen stared back. She said nothing.

"Please Mrs. Steen." Sheri took the old lady's hands in hers. "This is serious. Janet is in trouble and it might get a lot worse. If you insist I can tell you everything. But for your own sake, the less you know the better."

*Knowing more puts her in an awkward if not a dangerous situation.* Sheri needed her help but was not going to put her at risk. *In case Lars gets to her*; she shivered.

"All right. I won't ask questions." The frown eased slightly. "My concern is for that child. She has no family here, none."

"When Janet comes here, give her this." Sheri unzipped the pouch and pulled out two keys. "This one is to the gate and the other to the door on the North side. Her friends are in there."

"Is Ryan one of these friends?"

"I really should not say anymore." The look in Sheri's eyes confirmed Mrs. Steen's suspicion. "Would you give her the pouch and explain the Big Tower?"

"Yes, yes." She sighed, resigned to being in the dark. "I'll tell her where the buildings are."

"I have drawn a rough sketch of the docks and some directions."

Sheri unfolded a sheet and smoothed it out on the table. Mrs. Steen peered at it.

"Janet's friends are in there? I don't like this one bit." She shook her head. "How did they..." she began but checked herself, "all right. When she calls, I'll tell her to come get the keys."

"And please tell her I am working on it." Sheri stood up and planted a kiss on Mrs. Steen's cheeks. "I'm sorry to put you in the middle of this."

The housekeeper's face softened. "I'm sorry for being impatient schatje, there are too many things I don't understand. But you can call me, no matter what time of day."

Sheri sighed. She did not like disappointing her housekeeper. She loved the dear woman and knew her to be a true ally.

The pendulum clock bonged six. It was late. She would be missed at the mansion.

*Well, not missed exactly, just noticed as being absent;* she thought ruefully.

Noticed but not missed; that had become the recent tag line in her life.

On her way home, Sheri pondered her own actions.

Why had she given the painting to Janet? Why had she not confronted Lars with everything she knew? Was it because she knew deep down that she would not be satisfied with the answer?

Assuming Lars would even bother to give her an answer.

The feeling that she should have come clean had long been gnawing at her. She should have faced her husband and had it out in the open. She shivered remembering his chilling expression during their last exchange.

It was a look that haunted her for days.

Now was not the time for regrets. It was too late. Sheri's actions had resulted in a chain of tragic events. Now, she had to undo that damage.

»«

"I've been worried about you. How are you Janet?" Mrs. Steen's concern came through the phone lines.

It warmed Janet's heart but she did not lie. "I've been better."

*My Ryan isn't well and neither is Mr. Oudekerk.*

Now she had to find them and get them to safety. "Do you have any news?"

"Yes. Mrs. Van Reef paid me a visit. You have to come here and pick up a few things."

The instructions sounded cryptic.

"Anything else?"

*Please tell me Sheri knows about Ryan and Oudekerk.*

"It's better you come to my house Janet. You'll understand better and you'll need what Sheri left for you."

*More riddles*; Janet pursed her lips. "I'll be there soon, less than two hours."

Sheri had indeed told Mrs. Steen something important. It *had* to be information on Ryan's whereabouts. That meant they were alive. They had to be. Otherwise, Mrs. Steen would not hold back the news.

Janet felt her spirits lift.

»«

The schedule board in Centraal Station announced the train to Hoofddorp leaving in twenty minutes. Could she get something done in that time? She wondered.

Perhaps there was some news about the painting. She could call the museum and ask director Zalm about any development.

She walked back to the phone booth on Spuistraat and dialled the direct number Zalm had given her. The director announced himself. She felt relieved she did not have go through explanations with the assistant.

"Meneer Zalm, this is Jan..." The voice at the other end cut her sentence short.

"I don't know who you are. Stop calling here." Zalm's voice was low and the sentence was choppy.

"It's about..."

Click; the line went dead.

Zalm hung up on her with no explanation. What was that all about? Janet stared at the receiver. Her hand suddenly felt clammy. The phone fell with a thud as she let go of it.

The men had caught up with Zalm. They had got to him.

She grabbed her bag and stepped onto the side walk. The blur of pedestrians streamed past her as she ran into the train station and up the steps to the platform without stopping.

They got to him; they got to Zalm; the record in her head

kept playing.

The net was being cast far and wide.

Yet another man had become a casualty.

»«

The boots felt like lead as Janet trudged the last few yards from the bus stop to the Steen house.

The gloom did not abate despite Mrs. Steen's warm smile.

"You look terrible. Come in and rest for a while."

"I can't really stay. What did Sheri have for me?"

"Let's get to it."

Janet followed the housekeeper into the kitchen.

"Here are some keys and a sheet of paper with instructions." Mrs. Steen handed Janet a leather pouch and an envelope.

Keys? Keys to what? To the place Ryan and Oudekerk were taken?

Sheri got her these keys? She had come through. Even though she seemed detached at first, she *had* been working to help Janet.

"What are these keys?" Janet unzipped the pouch and counted six.

"These two," Mrs. Steen separated the keys marked with nail polish, "are to the Big Tower, the clunky one to the gate and the other to the office door."

"Where is this tower?" Janet pictured a lighthouse.

"It isn't an actual tower." Mrs. Steen shook her head, "It's the nickname for a building in the Schiedam docks. It will become clear in a minute." She pointed to the envelope.

The last time Janet was handed an envelope, there was a wad of bills in it. This time it was a neatly folded sheet of paper.

Her hands shook as she slid it out.

"Here." Mrs. Steen took the paper, unfolded it and smoothed it out on the table.

The two women sat next to each other and examined sketch. It was a hand drawn map with wavy lines and branches snaking in and around it.

"This water," Mrs. Steen pointed to the lines. "it's the Nieuwe Waterweg. You know what it is?"

"Yes." Janet nodded, remembering her trip to the area. How impressed she had been when she first stood on its North bank and watched the intense level of activity.

Her finger moved to the small branches snaking in and out of the waterway.

"And these things marked 4000, 5000, 6000 and so on?"

"Those are docks." The housekeeper explained. "This is where the Big Tower is, at the dockyards." She poked the red dot with a toothpick.

Janet studied the map. "It seems to be somewhere between docks 6000 and 6500. Very close to 6000, possibly dock 6100 or thereabouts." She turned to Mrs. Steen. "What exactly is this Big Tower?"

"These buildings belong to Mr. Van Reef's shipping business. The dot is where his and other offices are." Mrs. Steen took Janet's hand. "Your friends are in there."

Janet's heart dropped. "They are in this building?"

"Sheri says they are kept here."

Ryan and Oudekerk were alive. Locked up but alive.

Janet fell silent.

"Now, now, we have work to do." Mrs. Steen tapped the table.

*Yes, I have to find them and quickly.*

How on Earth was she to do that? They were in a fortress somewhere. These docks, there were thousands of them. Could she navigate her way through them? Was it safe for her to be walking there?

"How am I going to find them Mrs. Steen?" Janet rubbed her forehead.

"Not easily. Can you get someone to help you?"

"No." Janet's voice trembled.

The last time she sought someone's help, he was murdered. Two others who were involved had been badly beaten and locked up somewhere.

"You've been to the police already."

*Yes. And everything came crashing after that;* Janet began to speak but hesitated. She had to be cautious about throwing accusations of collusion. Perhaps it was paranoia that made her suspect it. No, she decided, it could not be. How else did they know her every step?

She said. "I did go to the police but it was no use."

"What about your newspaper people?"

Janet shook her head. She had thought of her editor Boris when she first realized she could not handle the problems on her own. He had been her closest thing to a friend at the newspaper. Someone with authority and influence. When she approached him, he had not minced words and told her to go to the police.

Janet shivered, recalling a subsequent phone call to the office, once again to appeal to Boris. The secretary's mention of Janet's brother's visit had sent the alarm bells ringing.

*What brother?* She wanted to scream.

She knew then Van Reef's men were lying in wait for her at the Daily's offices. Just as they were at her apartment building.

"Now listen to me Janet. The map looks complicated but the building is easy to find. During the day, the gates are open and you can sneak in." She tapped the map. "Vehicles are driving in and out constantly."

Janet did have options. She could scope out the building and the surroundings during daylight hours. Once certain the premises were accessible, she could wander in. Of course, she would have to blend in. That meant tucking the long, auburn hair under a cap and dispensing with the high heeled boots.

The paralyzing feeling began to ease.

"How do I get to these docks?"

*6100, 6100;* she kept repeating. It had to be the one.

"I can get Jacob to help you."

"No." Janet spoke sharply.

Her eyes were wide with fear. Too many people had paid dearly already. She was not about to jeopardize another life.

This gentle woman had no idea what they were up against. "No Mrs. Steen," Janet reiterated, "we can't do that."

"All right." Mrs. Steen scowled but relented. "You can do this Janet. I know you." She looked up to see Janet's reaction.

Encouraged by the nod, she continued. "The docks are marked along the main road in Schiedam. The access roads have signs that say *Havens* 5000 to 5500 and so on. Once you get close, you'll see the orange and yellow Van Reef logo."

"I must get going." Janet folded the sheet delicately as if it might shatter if she shook it.

"Janet, I know you have questions but I don't know much more. Mrs. Van Reef will be able to answer them. But don't call her at home, yeah?"

It was clear. Sheri was not to be reached at the mansion. Janet looked at the clock. Home is where Sheri would be at this time of the night.

*I have so many questions.* The answers would have to wait till Sheri was at work. That meant mid-morning the next day. That could be too late.

"Is there anything else you can tell me?" she made one last effort. "Something about the Tower?"

"It's a storage building. I got a tour when they opened. I remember huge rooms, like airplane hangars. There are smaller rooms too, used as offices. The buildings sit right on the channel. Trucks drive in and deliver the containers and cranes load them on to barges."

Ryan and Oudekerk could be anywhere in the tens of thousands of square feet. Finding them in that large area felt impossible. But she had to do it. She had to start somewhere in that building.

She stood up. "I have to get down to Schiedam."

"Be careful Janet. It's isolated down there."

*And a miserable place for Ryan and Oudekerk.* Janet put the keys in the backpack and slid the map in the flat, outer pocket.

Mrs. Steen walked to the key rack and lifted off a ring. She took Janet's hand and put the key ring in it. "Take Jacob's car."

She was lending Janet her son's vehicle? "What about

Jacob?"

"He won't need it for a few days. He and his father are at the cottage, fishing."

Janet stared at her, not knowing what to say.

"Take it Janet. You will need it to drive around the havens. You won't find too many buses that go there. Or from here at this hour." She paused. "Of course you could stay here tonight."

Janet stifled a gasp. *It won't be long before they come looking for me here.*

Aloud, she said, "Thank you but I'm safe where I am."

Janet left feeling strangely charged. Hopeful of seeing her friends. Afraid but encouraged. She wanted to drive down and find Ryan and Oudekerk immediately.

*No*; she thought. That was beyond foolish. She was unfamiliar with the area and did not have a clear idea where the Big Tower was. A lone car exploring in the middle of the night might be noticed. A lone woman walking around the docks was asking for trouble.

She also knew she could not go on much longer. In her exhausted state, she could get careless and be discovered.

Sleep was elusive but Janet stayed in bed. Perhaps the situation would seem less grim in the morning.

# CHAPTER 41

With the map in one hand and a coffee cup in the other, Janet sat in the café next to the hotel. The toast and eggs she ordered were going to waste. She had little appetite.

Schiedam looked to be 50 miles away, she would need at least an hour. From there she would have to find her way through the docks and locate the storage facility.

*Should I update Sheri on what I'm about to do?* No, she decided. She was on her own. That is why she had been given the map and the keys.

*The keys!* Janet reached in her backpack to make certain they were still there. She breathed a sigh as she felt the jagged edges.

Sheri had done her part. She had taken pains to find out Ryan and Oudekerk's whereabouts. It could not have been easy. Surely, it was a risk even to ask questions. Even though Sheri's promise had sounded feeble, she had come through.

And now Janet was in possession of the location as well as the keys. She gathered her things and got up from her seat. At the cashier's counter, she stopped and paid for the breakfast.

Next to the till was a plate piled with sandwiches, covered by a glass dome.

"They're fresh miss. Just delivered." The man smiled.

"I'll take three ham and cheese sandwiches." She pulled out

more money.

One for herself in case the day turned into a long one. The others for Ryan and Oudekerk. Hopefully, they were well enough to want food.

*Let them be well.* She pleaded. *Let them at least be alive.*

Three quarters of an hour had elapsed before she began seeing signs for the *Havens;* the docks. At the first turn off for Schiedam, she exited the highway. It was time to get closer and narrow down the location of pier 6000.

She reached over and touched the handmade map, it was still there. She had memorized the names and numbers. Still, the map was crucial.

The piece of paper was the key to unlocking the cruel mystery.

Rush hour was not yet past and traffic moved steadily but at a slow pace. As the road took her through a densely built up area, she committed the landmarks to memory. The frequent stops afforded her the time to look around. Two miles down the road, she saw signs for the centre of Schiedam.

That was it. Schiedam was the town on the edge the dockyards. The pounding in her temples intensified.

Soon she would have to leave the busy road and find Van Reef shipping. Turning left and heading South, she drove past an odd combination of run down businesses and well maintained homes and apartment buildings.

The residences were out of place in such close proximity to the grey industrial area. She made a note of the signs in front of the apartments; Oceanus, Proteus, Nereus; Gods of the seas.

At another time, the mythological touch would have been an amusing diversion. Right now, it was a reminder that her destination was nearing. And the impossible task she was up against.

Her eyes scanned every signboard indicating access to the docks. *Ship building repair, dock maintenance*; she read the descriptions aloud. *An orange juice company?* That seemed out of place but it was simply another business. The *Nieuwe Waterweg* was after all a shipping channel.

The roads branching off in the Southerly direction were signposted with dock numbers. As she drove, she noticed the numbers increasing.

Soon the numbers were in the 6000s. She was getting closer. She licked her dry lips. Dock 6500 flashed by but Janet kept driving.

After a mile, she reversed the car and began driving back toward Schiedam for another look at the 6000s. She had expected the docks to be dark and seedy. The yards looked grey and industrial but not dangerous. Perhaps it was the residential area not far away which made it seem less grim. Or was it seeing cyclists on the road? Or was it simply wishful thinking?

As the church steeple came into sight, she reversed direction again. After going back and forth three times, the layout of the docks became familiar.

Many businesses had fences and gates. Some in addition had sentries. Why were some properties wide open? She wondered, looking at several unguarded premises. Perhaps some businesses were in no great need of security.

Janet had expected to find a series of fortresses. Seeing open businesses eased the anxiety. There was a good chance she could get close.

It was time to get close to dock 6100.

She had been told the Van Reef property was secured but hoped the gates were open. The car slowed and stopped close to dock 6000 but Janet did not see the green and orange Van Reef sign. Mrs. Steen had specifically mentioned the colours. It would perhaps become visible closer to 6100.

The knot in her stomach tightened as the car moved closer. The number 6100 was carved on a small wooden signpost, four feet off the ground. In contrast, the Van Reef logo towered above the property. The red dot on the map was on the mark.

The gates were open. A car drove out without stopping. She turned to get a better look at the sentry post. It was unmanned. *Should I drive in? No*; she clenched the steering wheel. It was premature. What if the guard was on break? He could be on his way back any minute.

She kept driving. Just past 6200, the road widened with pull-outs on either side. Janet stopped the car in the space and forced herself to take deep breaths. She needed to calm down to make the right decisions.

She then turned the car around and drove past the Van Reef property, thinking of a way to get closer and explore on foot.

Parked trucks occupied the area between the length of the buildings and the fence.

There it was, the first building, the Big Tower. The adjacent parking area was nearly full, with thirty or forty passenger vehicles.

Janet drove on. She sighed. 6100 was behind her, out of sight.

A half mile further, a parking lot on the right had several empty spaces. It was a good place to leave the car. The Volkswagen rocked over ruts and small boulders on the unpaved surface of the parking lot. She felt relieved it was a small car as she squeezed into a space on the end, half on the grass and half on the muddy ground.

Janet stepped out and looked around. There were no signs saying 'private', 'keep out' or 'no parking'. Some cars appeared as though they had been there for months.

She grabbed the dog leash and began walking to dock 6100. No dog was attached to the leash but it gave her an alibi for being in places where she did not belong.

Walking briskly, she took ten minutes to get to the Van Reef property. The buildings sat directly on the North side of the waterway.

A narrow canal separated the adjacent property from Van Reef's. Janet walked past the Van Reef gate to the far side of the separating canal. She stood before a jetty which was wide open. If possible, it was a good place from which to scope out the Big Tower.

Would she be conspicuous? *No;* she decided. Not far from where she stood, she had seen a dog and its owner. A few minutes earlier, two cyclists. She clenched the leash, it was a good disguise.

A sudden smell of dead fish hit her as she wandered onto the jetty. Hurriedly, she pulled the scarf up around her nose.

One, two, three; she counted the businesses along the jetty. A few of the people milling about did not seem like workers. Perhaps they were residents of the apartments out for a walk. There weren't any parks near those buildings; she surmised; this was the nearest open space to which they had access.

Janet's shoulders relaxed. She could stroll along the canal for a better look at the buildings next door. The leash was unnecessary; no one took notice of her.

The wide shipping channel came into clear view as she took

a few steps onto the jetty. As she walked further and stood on the edge of it, she wanted immediately to examine the buildings to her right.

Lars van Reef's property was clearly visible as she turned to face it. Only a narrow canal separated her from it.

Janet shuddered; the Big Tower loomed a little too close.

She stood next to a wide, decorative lamp post. Certain she was obscured by it, Janet drew out her camera. The viewfinder showed the skyline dotted with cranes of different sizes. As she swept the zoom across the waterfront, she counted thirteen cranes. The variety of shapes was surprising. Some looked threatening, like fire breathing creatures from science fiction films.

The loading areas along the channel were packed with containers. One neatly piled stack with containers of many colours looked from the distance like a giant puzzle cube.

Gradually, Janet panned the camera to her right, onto the Van Reef property. The zoom made the building suddenly jump closer, sending a shiver down her back. Pausing the lens on different areas, she looked for signs. What she was looking for, she did not know. But there had to be something, perhaps a Land Rover or a black Mercedes which might be parked close to a door. That door would have to lead to the offices.

Four grey and red cranes were perched as if ready for action. Mrs. Steen had described the business as a shipping and storage facility. That is how it appeared. Just as Mrs. Steen said, the main building had a series of garage doors but bigger, much like airplane hangar doors.

*Where's the main entrance?* Looking back and forth, she counted four heavy, metallic grey doors. If there was a primary access to the building, it was not in plain view.

*This is the Big Tower;* she whispered to herself. She hoped Ryan and Oudekerk were in there. She hoped they were alive.

The parking lot did not reveal any people or vehicles she recognized. Nothing remarkable or unusual stood out. Many people were going in and out of the hangar doors.

*Too many people;* she cursed. Even dressed almost like a man, she could not go in there now. Her only chance was when the workers had gone home.

*In the dark?* She felt the hair on her neck stand up. But what choice did she have? Walk in there now and be confronted by someone or return in the dark and get into the building?

The gates would certainly be locked. She sized up the cold, grey metal. She did not have a clue how to climb over it.

Disappointed that she did not get much closer, Janet headed back to Amsterdam. She would rest for a few hours in her hotel room. She had to be patient and wait out the hours till dusk.

# CHAPTER 42

"We really should not been seen talking to each other." The tall, stocky man set his drink on the mantel. He lit the cigarette dangling between his fingers and threw the match into the fireplace.

"We are two guests at a private party." Van Reef smiled and glanced around the room.

"Just the same Meneer." With his back to the room, the man appeared to be staring at the flames. "If you and I were connected, it would not be good." The tip of the cigarette glowed as he inhaled deeply. "It would be, be," he spoke haltingly, "the end. For both of us."

"You are overreacting Dijkstra." Van Reef jabbed at the ice cubes repeatedly with the stirrer. "In the three years, we have been seen in the same room only a handful of times."

Van Reef looked around and returned the wave from the host at the far end of the lounge.

"I feel we are losing our grip on the situation." He continued, still smiling at the host. "There are too many unexplained things."

"We are watching their every move."

"Not well enough Dijkstra."

"Meneer Van Reef." The man breathed heavily. "We have to be extremely cautious." He held the gaze steady. "I have already risked a lot."

"Yes, yes." Van Reef's tone eased. "Damn." He muttered as he caught sight of Mrs. Martin walking toward them.

She would want to go on talking about something or the other. But he needed the time with Dijkstra. He would chat with Mrs. Martin for a few minutes and then get rid of her somehow.

Van Reef turned to the man next to him and added quickly, "I'm convinced there's a leak Dijkstra. I urge you to..." he cut the sentence short as the lady moved within earshot.

"Darling Lars." The host held up her bejewelled hand.

"Mrs. Martin." Van Reef took her fingers, bent down and kissed both her cheeks. "You look radiant."

"You are always a charmer darling." She smiled at Dijkstra. "Lars, have you met Mr. Dijkstra? The Superintendent of police?"

"We just introduced ourselves." Lars's smile was disarming. "We were wondering if we've met before."

"I am certain you have." Mrs. Martin's face turned serious. "Lars, why is Sheri not here this evening?"

"She has been a little under the weather. She sends you her regrets Mrs. Martin."

"But she has missed many parties. What is the matter?" The host persisted.

"We think it's a case of the empty nest." Van Reef's brow wrinkled. "It hasn't been easy on her."

"Oh, the poor dear." Mrs. Martin nodded. "Well, I want to see her as soon as she feels well enough." She patted his arm. "She is lucky to have you Lars." Her eyes turned wistful. "Sheri and you, so devoted to each other."

"She misses you." The disarming smile returned.

As Mrs. Martin glided away, Van Reef turned to face Dijkstra. But the superintendent had picked up his drink and was headed for another guest.

"It was nice to meet you Meneer Dijkstra." Van Reef made certain he was heard by guests nearby.

The superintendent stopped, turned around and shook hands. "My pleasure Meneer Van Reef." He smiled. Leaning closer, he spoke softly. "That leak you mentioned," he paused, "you should perhaps examine your own organization."

Dijkstra walked past other guests and out of sight. Van Reef stood watching, his jaws clenched.

Janet Simmons was a thorn in his side.

A leak in his camp spelled disaster.

# CHAPTER 43

The twinkling airport lights visible from a mile away now seemed dulled by the descending fog as the car went around Schiphol and headed South. It would be fully dark by the time Janet reached Schiedam. The fog would be a curtain behind which to hide.

Exiting the highway near Schiedam, she checked the street signs. Everything looked different. Had some of the landmarks changed?

*Yes, things always look different at night;* she reminded herself. Houses which looked unique earlier were indiscernible with shades pulled down. The darkness had changed the landscape almost beyond recognition.

*At least the silhouette looks the same.* The docks had a familiar feel from the morning's exploration. It was quieter but Janet was surprised at the level of activity.

Her heart began to race at the thought of getting close to the Big Tower.

For the second time in a day, the car pulled into the same run down parking lot. It was half full with many of the vehicles familiar from the morning. A car with a missing wheel looked as though it had been left there permanently. Janet eased the Volkswagen into the wide spot between the third and the fourth cars.

"Ouch!" She let out a cry but caught herself and ducked low.

She had almost fallen as she stepped out and her left foot

went deep into a rut. She lifted the foot gingerly, fearing a twisted ankle. It seemed unharmed. Staying low, she closed the door softly and waited.

Hearing no sounds, she moved to the back of the car. *Should I take the leash?* She wondered. *No*; she decided. At the late hour, it was a flimsy alibi.

She stopped at the edge of the parking lot, looking for signs of people or cars. Besides the noises from the docks in the distance, she heard nothing. Keeping a lookout for approaching headlights, she shone the light on the ditch along the road. Good, it was dry. She could walk in it and duck down at the first sign of a vehicle.

The hum of working machinery in the shipyard became louder as she walked the half mile in ten minutes. As the road curved, the high gates of the Van Reef property came into view.

The anxiety mounted as her eyes wandered up the imposing entrance. The cold, grey metal was meant to keep people out. It was working on her.

Janet wanted to turn and get as far from there as possible but she knew she could not.

Checking for cars in either direction, she ran across the street and dropped down in front of the gates. In the crouching position, the latch was too high to reach. She stood up, still on the lookout for headlight beams.

The latch slid with little resistance. The clanging sound seemed to travel quickly in the stillness. Janet hurriedly put both hands on the metal to dampen the sound.

She pushed on the gate. It was locked. *Please let it be one of the keys;* her hand shook as she fished out the key bunch from her coat pocket. *The clunky one*; Mrs. Steen had said. Janet pushed in the key and gave it a quarter turn.

Click. She stood still. The key worked. It had unlocked the seemingly impassable entry.

She nudged the gate open and listened. Stepping quickly inside, she turned to close the latch. *No*; she stopped. That was not a good idea. Not for a quick exit. She hoped the gates stayed closed even without the latch holding them in place.

A rectangular cement block stood just past the edge of the driveway. She scurried to the structure and dropped down behind it. Looking at the plates bolted on to the cement, she knew it was a power distribution housing.

Janet was now officially on Van Reef property. The thought was frightening. If she were caught here, she was certain to end up in the canal behind her. Never to be found.

Peering from behind the cement block, she looked for a way into the facility. The driveway was the length of one or two city blocks. Vehicles were parked at the end of it, adjacent to the first building.

She examined the driveway. It was a long way to walk without being seen. With the moonless sky, darkness was on Janet's side. Still, it would be better to make a dash for it.

She ran quickly and squatted down by the first car in the parking lot. As she waited to catch her breath, her eyes became accustomed to the darkness and she was able to see more details.

Should she walk in between rows of cars? No, she decided. It might conceal her but she could accidentally bump into something and make a noise. Not fully standing up, she walked and crawled slowly behind the last row of cars. As she approached the first building, she looked for a spot from which to scope out the entrances.

The drainage pipe on the side of the building provided slight cover. She stood behind it and leaned for a better look. Light streamed out of two open hangars.

The hangar was the way into the building. Lights were on which meant people were still in there. Or were they?

She waited and listened. It seemed quiet at first but she heard a faint jumble of voices. The sound seemed to come from the second hangar. Looking around and seeing no one, she began inching toward the first hangar. Her ears amplified every noise. Once inside the hangar, she stepped behind a crate and stood still.

The voices could no longer be heard. They had either stopped or the sound did not carry into the hangar where she stood. Janet came out from behind the crate and looked around.

Nothing seemed out of the ordinary; a jeep, a forklift, carts and crates of different sizes. All seemingly typical in such a place. On the wall where the building met the hangar was a door.

What was behind that door?

If anyone lurked in the hangar, he hid himself well. Janet stepped further in and tiptoed behind the row of crates. Still, no sign of anyone. Why was the door open and lights left on? Where were the workers? Were they in the other open hangar? Or were they behind that door?

Soon Janet stood at the edge of the row of crates, a short distance from the wall. She crawled on all fours toward the door. Leaning closer with her ear against the cold metal, she listened for activity inside. She heard nothing. She guessed that the muffled sounds came from outside and not from behind the door.

She stood up and turned the handle gently. The door was not locked. She opened it an inch and waited. No sound came from behind the door. She pushed hard on the heavy metal and opened the door fully.

Could this be the office? The space was narrow and plain, like a passageway. She stepped in, shut the door softly and took a few steps. The lighting was dim but sufficient for a good look.

Was this the Big Tower?

It had to be, from Mrs. Steen's description and the red dot on the diagram. The words 'Big Tower' had led her to imagine a fortress. An impenetrable one.

But she was inside. And her entry seemed to have gone completely unnoticed. It had been so easy.

Too easy.

Was a welcoming committee waiting in the wings?

Janet did not move a muscle. After a minute of no dramatic sounds, she took a few more steps.

Across from the door she had just walked through, was a stairwell. To her right, past the stairwell, was a corridor with doors on both sides. She walked down the passage and counted five doors, three on one side and two on the other. None of the offices had any lights on.

Janet had not known what to expect in The Big Tower. She had no real plan. Suddenly she felt very overwhelmed.

*I have to start somewhere.* She stopped at the first door. It was quite possible Ryan and Oudekerk were in one of these office rooms. Where else could they be? In a container? She shuddered at the thought.

The first office was locked. Was this the one? She looked through the window and saw only darkness. The keys Sheri had given her were in the right coat pocket. She cupped her hand around them to dampen any jingling noise. One by one she tried all the keys but none unlocked the door. The next office was the same. The third and last office appeared L shaped with the door on her left.

Click. The third key unlocked the door. She waited to see if anyone heard the click. Stepping in, she lowered herself to the floor. She waited, looked around and listened. No lights were on.

What was that intermittent clicking? It seemed to come from a piece of office equipment. What was the hum? Was something just turned on? *No.* she guessed it to be from a refrigerator.

She stood up and scanned the room. It was lavishly furnished, quite unlike a typical office. No family photos were on display. Who were the faces behind these desks? It was a relief in a way that she did not know.

She walked through the length of the office and came to the second part of the L shape. It was long and narrow, a corridor. Bits and pieces of office equipment were on tables lining the wall.

At the far end of the corridor was a door, much like the connecting door she had come through minutes before. She walked to it, constantly looking through the glass windows for signs of employees. She tried the door, it was locked.

The same third key unlocked it. A blast of cold air came in as she inched the door open. The door lead to the second hangar. Janet hesitated, wondering if this was where the voice was coming from. What if someone was working in that hangar? What if they heard the door open?

She held her breath. But there was no sound. No movement. She counted to ten and stepped out of the corridor.

The hangar was at least three times the size of the first one. Unlike the first hangar, the doors of this one were closed.

She detected no sign of recent activity. Where did the voices come from?

The wide space was lined with several industrial sized shelves along the walls. Different types of crates and pallets occupied the room. The majority of the crates looked tidy, buttoned down and ready for shipping. Others appeared to be in various stages of being packed or unpacked.

Something glinted on the far side to the left. It took her eyes a few seconds but Janet was able to make out the shape. It was a vehicle. *Wait*; she thought; *it's the Land Rover*.

It was the same Land Rover which was at de Avondster. The same one waiting for her outside the Rijksmuseum. This was a confirmation that Ryan and Oudekerk were brought here.

She gasped. Did it also mean that Van Reef's men were still around? But she smelled no fumes and felt no heat radiating from the vehicle. It had been left there for some time.

Her eyes moved to the right. The empty space next to the Land Rover meant another vehicle was usually parked there. Lars Van Reef's?

Further to the right were two rows of crates. She turned to look at the Land Rover again. Could Ryan and Oudekerk still be in it? She wanted to run to it but held back. Someone streaking across the space might be noticed. By whom? She looked up and around. The offices she had just left had an upper level. The upstairs rooms might have windows with a view of the garage.

By taking the long way along the wall to the right, she would be less conspicuous. Janet took slow, deliberate steps, looking out for obstacles. The crates did a good job of hiding her from plain sight. As she passed the first open crate, she looked in. She shone her pocket flashlight which showed the crate half filled with smaller wooden boxes.

Janet kept walking and reached the hangar door. A cold draft seeped through the crack between the door and the ground. She tightened the scarf around her neck. She now had to get through the exposed width of the hangar. She got down and started on all fours. When she reached the Land Rover, she stood up slowly. The rear window revealed an empty cab. She moved forward for a glimpse through the side windows. The vehicle was empty.

She looked past the Land Rover. The offices ended several feet to the right of the door, exposing a recessed space. Chest-high cubicle walls bordered the space. What was in those cubicles?

She went to the back of the vehicle and walked all around the edge of the hangar. The path was narrow but unobstructed. The wall was lined with shelves and tool boxes. As she moved, she kept her hands and elbows close to her body to avoid knocking anything off the shelves.

Finally arriving at the cubicle wall, she paused and listened. Besides the hum of equipment, she heard no sounds. She stepped into the first office. It was 6'x6' and contained storage cabinets. A few coats and sweaters hung on the coat stand. That was a sign that people could still be around. She strained to see the rest of the office. Plain desks filled much of the room and were topped with ledgers and papers. Convinced no employees were around, Janet walked past the desks to the cubicle furthest away.

Then she saw them.

# CHAPTER 44

The men were seated in chairs on either side of a table, their wrists strapped to the armrests and feet tied together. Ryan's head was tilted to his left. Oudekerk was slumped forward.

Janet approached Ryan, he was the one closer to her. She knelt down for a look at his face. His eyes were shut but he was breathing. Ryan was alive.

He seemed to sense something and his eyes flickered open. He looked at Janet but appeared dazed and confused.

"Mevrouw?"

*He doesn't know who I am.* Alarmed, Janet spoke his name, "Ryan, it's me, Janet."

He stared at her face. After a few seconds, he seemed to recognize the person before him. "Janet." He tried to sit up but could not move. He winced in pain.

"I'll cut the ropes." Janet unzipped the backpack's side pocket, dug her hand in and felt for the knife.

Ryan spoke, his voice a hoarse whisper. "Janet, what are you doing here?" He looked around slowly. "How did you find us?"

"Long story Ryan." Janet began slicing through the ropes. They were already worn and gave in easily.

She examined Ryan's swollen face. "Are you hurt?"

Ryan licked his lips caked with blood. "I'm all right but the old man, he..." He tried to turn to his left but clutched his side in pain.

Janet walked to Oudekerk and touched him on his shoulder. She heard slow breathing. She spoke as she positioned the blade under the ropes. "Mr. Oudekerk, it's me, Janet. Can you hear me?" There was no response. "We'll get you out of here very soon."

"I'll give you a hand." Ryan stood up, wavered and dropped back on to the chair.

"Here, drink some water." Janet stopped cutting and walked over to give him the water bottle.

He gulped several times before pausing for a breath. She slid her hand under his arm and pushed up. She waited until he was steady and let go of his arm.

The two walked over to Oudekerk. "He looks so weak."

From the corner of her eyes, she saw Ryan nod. The elderly man slumped in the chair bore little resemblance to the strong, burly miller Janet had come to admire.

As she cut the ropes, Ryan held Oudekerk's shoulders to keep him from sliding off the chair.

"Mr. Oudekerk?" There was a slight movement of the head but he said nothing. Janet looked at Ryan. Both wanted to know how badly he was hurt.

Ryan held the bottle to Oudekerk's mouth, some water made its way in but most of it dribbled down his chin.

"So glad you're okay." Janet leaned close to his ear and whispered. "We'll get you out of here. Do you think you can walk?"

He appeared to nod but made no effort to stand.

"Don't think he needs to walk Janet." Ryan pushed Oudekerk's shoulder gently back on to the chair.

"You're right. We'll wheel him out of here." She looked for a way out. "The shortest way is through the hangar door. Then it's some distance to the gate through the parking lot and driveway."

"The doors will make a lot of noise." Ryan grimaced. "We came in through there. It was pretty loud during the day."

"You're right." She agreed. "Besides, the doors might be alarmed."

"How did you manage get in here?" He shot her a puzzled look.

"From back there." She pointed to the door of the L-shaped office. "Let's go back the way I came. That other hangar was open."

*And I hope it still is*; she thought nervously. But it had to be. She had not heard it close. In fact, she had not heard any noise since being in the building. Perhaps no one else was around. But what if there was? And she simply did not hear them?

Janet shivered at the thought that Van Reef's men might be lurking.

"Let get the hell out Ryan."

She pulled Oudekerk's jacket tighter around him and fastened two buttons she could get her fingers around.

"We'll follow you." Ryan's left arm held Oudekerk's shoulder from falling forward as his right guided the chair.

"Let me make sure the coast is clear." Janet ran across the hangar to the connecting door. She put her ear to the keyhole but heard no voices. She motioned to Ryan to come.

Ryan moved the chair slowly. The waiting felt excruciating. Knowing it was not easy for Ryan to manoeuvre the large man in the office chair around the obstacles, Janet walked back to them. With one person on either side of the chair, they were at the door within seconds.

Janet turned the handle and held the door open with her left elbow. The two lifted the heavy chair on to the small step. Janet ran ahead to the end of the corridor. She heaved a sigh of relief. The coast was clear. She moved briskly as Ryan wheeled the chair a short distance behind her.

»«

"I don't believe it." Janet's voice shook as she slid the latch. "We're out of there."

"I can't believe it was that easy."

Janet nodded. "Too easy." She shivered. "Can't help thinking it's a trap."

"Me too. Let's get the hell away from here."

Janet pointed up the street, in the direction of the parking lot. "We have that far to go before the car."

"Yes. My car." Ryan automatically patted his pockets for the keys.

"Not yours Ryan." She began pushing the chair.

"Your van?" His voice tinged with disbelief. They had agreed not to use her vehicle as it was too recognizable.

"Not that either but that's another long story."

The uneven road combined with Oudekerk's bulk in the chair kept them from running. Fearing that some vehicle would come screaming after them, Janet strained to listen.

Every screech made by the chair sounded like thunder in the quiet of the night. Janet kept looking around for signs of headlights.

"Thank God we're off the road." She exclaimed as they steadied the wheelchair on the pot hole ridden ground of the parking lot.

"Stay here." With Ryan holding the chair, Janet reversed the car out of its space.

She stepped out and opened the back door for Oudekerk. The two struggled to get the large man into the back seat. Janet took off her coat, folded it and placed it under Oudekerk's head.

Janet wanted to drive away from the docks as fast as the car would allow. But that was not sensible. If Van Reef's people missed their captives and were on the lookout, a speedy, errant car would most definitely draw their attention.

Neither said a word as Janet drove slowly and they were a few miles from port 6100.

"Mr. Oudekerk needs medical attention Ryan. I think we should take him to a hospital now."

"Hmm." Ryan mumbled.

Janet looked sideways and saw him fast asleep. She had yet to find out everything that had happened. But first, she needed to get Oudekerk to a hospital. The old man's condition weighed heavily on her mind.

She stopped on the side of the road and unfolded the South Holland map. A big, red H indicated a hospital. How far was it, five or ten miles away? They could be there in fifteen minutes.

As she put the car in gear and pulled out, it occurred to her that the hospital staff would ask questions. How did Oudekerk suffer the injuries? When, what and where. She was certain police would be called in.

Contact with police was extremely risky. Fear began to creep in. Van Reef's reach was long. She knew the net was being tightened.

No, she could not risk being discovered.

What should she do? Oudekerk needed help. So did she. Driving slowly, Janet began to look for a phone booth.

She had to contact Rosie. Her friend was her only hope. But what if Rosie was somehow a part of this? What if she too had turned bad?

What if *she* was Van Reef's connection inside the police department?

*No, absolutely not;* Janet screamed silently. Rosie had been nothing but a good friend.

»«

"Hello." Rosie picked up on the third ring.

Janet hesitated. Doubts about Rosie crept back in.

"Who's there?" The voice was stern.

Janet had no choice. She whispered, "Rosie, I need your help. It's urgent."

"Where are you Janet? What's going on?"

"A friend, an elderly man is hurt and needs to be in the hospital."

"Who is this man? Where have you been? I haven't heard from you since Amstelveen. I've called Ryan's number a dozen times."

The barrage of questions was terrifying. At the same time, Janet realized that Rosie mentioned Amstelveen as Janet's last location, not de Avondster. The windmill is where Janet stayed after the police interview. That was the place to which Van Reef's men came looking for her. That meant Rosie was not aware Janet's whereabouts after she left the police station.

*So, she isn't the one telling them where I am.*

324

The realization was a relief.

"This man, he knew what was going on with me and the painting."

"What happened to him?"

"He was beaten by the same men. He needs to go to a hospital."

"It might be fastest if you call emergency."

"But I'm terrified of doing that. It means the police come next. They haven't exactly helped me Rose. I can't explain now. Please, I need your help. I need you to take care of this."

"I'll do my best."

"We are in Rotterdam."

"Rotterdam. Okay, can you get to Erasmus?"

"Yes."

"Go to the emergency parking lot, the main one will be closed this time of night. I'll meet you there."

"Rosie, can this be an anonymous call?"

"Don't worry Janet. Everything will be all right."

Janet hung up, still filled with scepticism.

»«

Pulling into the hospital at Erasmus, Janet looked for a police car. Rosie had not arrived.

"Ryan." Janet prodded Ryan awake. "Can you stay here while I get help?"

Ryan nodded. His eyes were wide from being awakened from his slumber.

Janet left the two men in the parked car and walked through

the entrance.

"There's a man outside." She pointed. "He's badly hurt."

"Lead the way Miss."

Two attendants followed her to the car. One wheeled a stretcher while the other peppered her with questions; *'what happened?' 'Is he breathing?'*

Ryan and Janet watched from a distance as one of the medics spoke to Oudekerk.

"Meneer, can you hear me?"

They continued their exchange. Oudekerk was lifted on to the stretcher.

"We would like you to come in Miss." The older of the two addressed Janet as they began wheeling Oudekerk away.

"A family friend is on her way to take care of things." Janet walked behind.

"We need your information for the paperwork."

"We will meet her here and come in."

"Okay." One turned his head and shouted.

Within seconds, Oudekerk was inside the building and out of sight. Her friend was now in safe hands.

"Let's get out of here." Janet wanted to disappear.

Even as she uttered the words, Janet knew she could not leave until Rosie arrived. They moved away from the glaring lights of the hospital entrance.

The long wait came to an end with flashing lights. Janet and Ryan stayed in the shadows until they could be certain that the person stepping out was Rosie. Janet called out softly.

Despite lingering doubts, she felt relieved to see Rosie walking toward her.

Janet dropped down on the lumpy hotel bed and pulled the covers over her face. The peace was not to last.

"You must be very tired Janet."

Ryan's voice sounded in her ear like a buzzing mosquito. Her body ached for sleep but she could not ignore him.

"There is a hell of a lot going on in that building and we ought to go back there."

She remained still, not knowing what to say.

Ryan paused for a response, then continued. "We should go to the Big Tower now, before the night is out."

Janet turned her head to look at him. With difficulty she opened her eyes.

Did he really suggest going back to that hellish place, where he was held captive? Why would he want to do that after suffering such trauma in there?

It was as though Ryan heard her silent questions.

"I'm going tell you what happened to us and you'll know what I mean."

Janet no longer felt sleepy as Ryan began narrating the events of his past forty-eight hours.

# Chapter 45

"That's unbelievable."

Yet, Janet believed it. Everything she had experienced thus far had reinforced her opinion of Van Reef. His powers were mighty, his reach far and wide.

"So you see Janet, there are very strange things going on in there. And we'll never get as close as we are now to finding out."

"Yes, I don't think we'll get another chance." Janet agreed reluctantly. "I guess we should do it now. But aren't you tired?"

She felt weary. The day had been tension filled and physically exhausting. It had to have been far worse for Ryan. But she knew he was right. Once the escape of Oudekerk and Ryan was discovered, the building would be bolted down and security increased many fold.

"I'm okay." He stood up. "This is our only window. I don't think they'll miss us till the morning. They certainly haven't cared if we lived or died." Ryan recalled with feeling the cleaning lady. "Except that angel of mercy."

"You've convinced me. I'm worried about you, that's all."

"I'm all right except for some aches and pains. I'll swallow down some aspirins." He looked at his watch. "We have another four to five hours of darkness."

"For a change, I'm glad for these short winter days."

Janet checked her backpack once again. She had all the things she might need; camera, flashlight, snacks and water.

They set off for The Big Tower. Forty five minutes later, Janet pulled into the same deserted parking lot where she had left the car earlier. With the two trips behind her, she was becoming familiar with the area. She felt she could find her way out quickly if they had to depart in a hurry.

Ducking down and walking low behind cars in the parking lot now felt routine. On the long stretch of the road, there was no sign of traffic. They began running but dropped down into the ditch at the flash of headlights in the distance. A large black sedan whizzed by. Not too far from them, it came to a sudden stop.

Janet looked at Ryan and saw in his eyes the fear she felt. He grabbed her arm and pulled her lower into the ditch.

There were no car sounds. What was happening? Janet could not breathe. They stayed low and remained still.

Soon, the car revved its engine and drove away.

"Let's wait a few minutes. Let's be sure they aren't coming back." Ryan did not let go of Janet's arm.

Finally, they were at the entrance to Van Reef shipping. The key worked but the gate did not budge.

Janet pointed to the padlock on the latch. "This wasn't here earlier."

"Maybe the night watchman locks it up?"

"Or..." Janet had a sudden, sickening feeling. "Do you think they've discovered you're gone?"

"Maybe." Ryan pursed his lips. "That would be closing the barn door after the horse?"

"You're right." Janet agreed. "Besides, if someone escaped,

why would they come back?"

The logic was reassuring. Padlock or not, they had no choice. Janet walked to the edge of the gate and looked through the slits by the hinge.

"I don't see anyone patrolling."

"We go over the top." Ryan stood next to the concrete stoop and leaned his body against the gate. "Use me as a ladder."

Janet stepped onto the stoop and balanced as she grabbed the top of the gate.

"Come on, put your feet on my shoulders."

Having Ryan as support was comforting. Being with Ryan felt right, natural. Despite the missteps, bad decisions and everything that went wrong, Ryan had been nothing but supportive.

"Glad you're with me."

Climbing on his shoulders, Janet propelled her upper body over the top of the gate. On the other side, she was staring at a long drop.

*The sooner the better;* she muttered to herself as she went over the gate and dropped down onto Van Reef property.

Her backpack hit the ground and something in it clanged against the asphalt. She froze. Even the slight sound seemed to reverberate in the quiet night. She lay still and waited to see if the noise was heard.

Certain it was not, she stood up. The winter clothing had provided sufficient padding, she felt no bruises.

"I'm okay." She whispered.

Ryan was already dropping himself on to the pavement next to her. She grabbed his hand and pulled him toward the power distribution housing.

Was the coast clear? She scanned the property. The red and grey cranes which were conspicuous during the day were mere silhouettes in the dark.

"Let's go."

They sprinted the distance and were on the parking lot within minutes. In contrast to earlier in the day, only half a dozen cars were parked.

They moved toward the hangar and stopped behind the parked half of a tractor trailer. Janet leaned to get a look at the hangar doors.

"Not a single hangar door up." She had expected that to be the case but still felt disappointed. They would have to find another way in.

They walked past four hangar doors. Janet remembered the first three.

"This is the one where I found you guys." She pointed to the second one.

"It looks like there are two sets of hangars."

"What's this narrow part between them?"

Sandwiched between the set of hangars was a narrow block, not wide enough for a hangar but too wide to be a passageway.

A fence enclosed the width of the solid block. A sturdy chain locked the gate. Ryan jumped up on the fence and dropped to the other side.

"Come on Janet, it's quite easy. You've had practice already"

Janet threw her backpack over the fence to Ryan. The panels in the fence provided convenient footholds. As she jumped down to the concrete, she caught sight of an entry into the building.

"A door." They said simultaneously.

"I think this is connected to the offices."

She spread out the keys in the palm of her gloved hand.

Ryan examined them. "This one might work."

He turned the key in the door. It made a clicking sound. They looked at each other.

Janet watched Ryan turn the knob as she returned the keys to the backpack. He inched the door open, they waited and listened. Janet heard the same eerie hum of engines and machinery running at some distance.

They stepped into a dusty room with shelves and cleaning equipment. The shelves were laden with tins of paint, brushes and rollers. Janet and Ryan crossed the cleaning pantry to another door.

"I'll bet this opens to the office." The door was unlocked. Janet pushed it open and saw an office similar to the one she had seen earlier.

"The office I was in was just like this. Only more posh."

They walked through the room and stepped into the corridor.

"It was just as quiet then." The silence was unnerving.

"My absence hasn't been discovered." Ryan whispered.

"Otherwise there would be people here turning the building upside down looking for you." Janet added. "We wouldn't have made it this far."

Now they were back and had work to do. But what? What were they looking for? Where were they to begin?

Ryan followed her into the L-shaped room. "You're right. It looks like a nice office. A plush one a CEO might have."

"You see that door at the end of the corridor?" She

whispered. "That is the hangar where I found you."

"I guess that's a starting point." Ryan's voice shook.

The two walked single file through the narrow corridor to the connecting door. At the door, Janet stopped and listened. She frowned; this was becoming a habit.

Tiptoeing, whispering and listening at doors was happening all too frequently.

They heard no discernible sounds, only the hum of machinery. Janet opened the door to a dark hangar. They waited to let the eyes adjust to the dimness.

"That is where you and Mr. Oudekerk were." She pointed to the furthest corner of the hangar.

"We were brought here from the windmill." Ryan's expression changed. "Oudekerk could have died here."

"They must think you're still here."

"If not, they're out there looking for us."

"And not here. This is the last place they'd look."

Suddenly Janet felt better. They were safe at the Big Tower, at least for a short while. A very short while. In a few hours the workers would be trickling in.

"What shall we look for?"

"Whatever it is, if there is any place they'd keep it, I think this would be it."

Ryan pointed to the first open crate in the first row. Janet switched on the flashlight and pointed it to the floor. The path was free of obstacles.

She shone the light into the crate. The back of it was packed tightly with smaller wooden boxes. The crate was half full.

*Look*; Ryan pointed to a label inside a plastic sleeve. Janet moved closer and peered at the text, it read, 'Tools'.

Ryan tugged at the wooden box closest to him. *Heavy*; he mouthed the words and stepped inside the crate. With both hands, he lifted the box and placed it on the floor. He looked around for something with which to pry open the box.

Janet leaned close to his ear. "There are shelves stacked with tools along the other wall."

Ryan nodded and walked softly, feeling for obstacles along the way. After a few steps, he pointed to something. Janet saw him bend down and pick up a long, black item. He turned around and walked back with a crowbar in his hands.

As he pried open the small wooden box, the cracking noise echoed through the hangar. He paused for the noise to die down. Janet listened for footsteps or any noise of someone approaching. Feeling it was safe to continue, she nodded. After four more attempts, the box was open.

Ryan reached and grabbed Janet's torch. Clenching it between his teeth, he peeled off the straw-like packaging and began examining the contents of each package inside. Tools were piled on top of more tools. Janet stood watch, her eyes and ears keen for signs of someone else in the hangar.

Not taking his eyes off the contents, Ryan waved for Janet to come closer. She wedged herself in the narrow space. Her eyes followed the light.

She stifled a gasp. "These are not tools."

"You're right, they aren't tools." Ryan whispered. "Well, not conventional ones anyway." He picked up a heavy plastic box and shook it. "I bet I know what this is." He flipped open the latch and held it in front of Janet. "Rifle ammo."

Rifle ammunition? What did that mean? Did the crate contain firearms? But the contents were labelled *tools*. The box however, was packed with weapons.

The crate was in a Van Reef shipping building.

Lars Van Reef was shipping illegal firearms.

Janet stared wide-eyed. She had not expected to make such a horrific discovery. It was beyond belief.

She had to document this cargo. She pulled out the camera and focused the lens. *Wait*; Ryan motioned, removed his sweater and held it above the camera to keep the flash from lighting up the room.

He then pointed to longer and wider oblong boxes at the bottom. Janet knew what the contents were; *rifles*.

"We have to open one." Ryan wiped his brow.

Janet looked at her watch. "It's not safe for us to be here too much longer."

"Listen." Ryan moved the boxes as he talked. "I'm getting the hang of opening and closing these. It won't take long. I really think we should look at it."

Even though she was nervous, Janet knew he was right. She too wanted to find out. "What can I do?"

"Just stay out of the way." Ryan reached for the row of oblong boxes.

Janet kept a lookout for signs of activity. The night would soon turn into day. They should be out of here before daybreak. Well before daybreak. Before the morning shift began.

If they were to be discovered, it would be the end.

Janet was recovering from the shock. Van Reef shipping was much more than what it seemed. Was Sheri aware of what went on?

Janet's mind drifted to Sheri's strange behaviour. Mrs. Van

Reef's actions were against the well-being of her own husband. What was her motivation?

"Look at this."

Ryan's voice snapped her back.

"More rifles." They looked deadlier than the first batch.

"These are automatic rifles." Ryan dug his hand into the side of the box. "I'm sure one of these boxes also has the magazines."

Rifles and ammunition in a garage in Holland; it was such a contradiction. Janet snapped more photos.

"We could dig further and find more and more."

"I think we've seen enough weapons."

Ryan nodded. "Let's hurry and put the boxes back in the crate." Janet followed Ryan's lead, putting the lids back on and tapping them closed.

As they had walked along the crates, Janet noticed that everything looked the same as during her visit earlier. Mrs. Steen had hinted that something big was going to happen. Janet had dreaded the idea of the place swarming with people. But it was not.

Perhaps the distraction of kidnapping Oudekerk and Ryan had slowed down the operation.

One question kept coming up.

What was the Van Reef organization really all about?

The next open crate they walked by contained large wooden boxes with a narrow profile.

They checked their watches at the same time and looked at each other.

"Very quickly."

Ryan was already leaning into the crate toward one wooden box which did not seem completely sealed. Together they eased it forward.

Janet recognized the packaging instantly. "I know what this is."

It was the kind in which paintings were wrapped for shipping. Ryan was ready with the open blade of Janet's Swiss knife.

"Careful." Janet worried about being hasty and causing damage to the painting.

Ryan worked the knife with slow deliberation. One by one, he peeled off the layers of packaging and slid the painting out of the housing.

"Can you see through the plastic?"

Janet shone the light up and down. The painting looked dark and heavy. She squatted down to look for the signature. Shivers ran down as she read tidy scrawl beginning with a full R.

"The scribble says it's a Rembrandt."

They exchanged looks. Was this painting another original? First the Mauve, then the Chagall. And now, a Rembrandt?

"I can't believe it." Janet could not take her eyes off the signature.

She did not know how long she had been staring at the painting when she felt Ryan's tap. He held out his hand and pulled her up.

"First guns and now this." It was mind boggling. What else could there be in the other crates?

While she snapped photos, Ryan walked around examining the outside of others crates. He returned with something in his hand.

"This appears to be paperwork for the cargo."

The two peered at the text.

"Spanish?"

Ryan nodded. "Names. They could be people or places. We should make a copy."

"No time." Janet said looking at the brightening skies.

They both knew it was time to leave. Quickly but quietly, they put the painting back in the crate. At least on the outside, the crate looked undisturbed.

Ryan slid the paper in his pocket. They made their way back to the door on the side of the building through which they had come in.

The area outside the building was quiet. The only loud noise was from the waking sea gulls. Even though dawn was about to break, the parking lot was still cloaked in darkness.

"If we can't see anyone that means we can't be seen." Janet felt reassured.

Still, they walked softly, stayed low and close to parked vehicles.

So much needed to be said but both remained quiet during the ride back to Amsterdam. It had been a long and exhausting night.

# Chapter 46

"They should be here any minute now Sir." Maurice Flanders addressed his boss from the doorway.

Lars Van Reef looked up from his desk but said nothing. His face was rigid. The eyes were devoid of expression.

Maurice had seen Lars this way before. That incident too had been very unpleasant.

Maurice's eyes darted from his boss to the window at the end of the corridor, looking for signs of a car pulling in.

Bakker and Neelen had been near Leiden when they called. They should have been here already. If they were delayed much longer, Van Reef's simmering anger was likely to bubble over.

Maurice had rarely seen his boss express anger outwardly. However, over the years he had learned to read Van Reef's mood. Lars' voice remained calm but the face told another story.

*I'm getting too old for this.*

Maurice fidgeted. Living in the same house and being in Lars' confidence, he was regularly asked to convey news; sometimes good news, many times the opposite.

Lars' voice caused him to look away from the window.

"Sir?" He was not sure if a question was asked.

"This has already gone too far Maurice. We should have ended the situation before it got to this point."

Maurice stood wringing his hands, not knowing what to do. With Van Reef's present mood, the less said the better; he decided.

"I am baffled. Tell me, how did they get out?"

The question was not unexpected. Maurice looked at Lars but turned away quickly. Facing those eyes was uncomfortable.

*I hope he doesn't know about my conversations with Madam.*

Beads of perspiration trickled down Maurice's back. He felt he had better say something to deflect the focus.

"I hope Bakker can give us a detailed account Sir." He could think of nothing else to say.

*God, why don't they hurry up?* He leaned into the corridor and looked down the hall at the window.

"First of all, we can't seem to get our hands on one person." Van Reef continued. "It is not as if the Simmons girl knows many people. We have men looking for her full time and we cannot locate her."

Lars tapped the table with the ball point pen. It went on for what seemed like minutes. Every click was excruciating.

Maurice stood still. It was pointless to say anything. Why stoke the fire?

"Now we find out the two men are not in the Big Tower. Even though they were tied up. Even though the property is secured. What are the odds of that?"

Maurice swallowed. He suspected Janet Simmons had been given the keys.

*By Madam.*

After he had divulged to Mrs. Van Reef where the two men were being held, she must have given someone the keys.

That someone was most likely Janet Simmons.

"And the girl is still missing." Van Reef slammed his fist on the table.

Headlights flashed in front of the house. It was not a moment too soon. Maurice hurried down the steps to the front door.

"What took you so long?" His sharp voice reprimanded the two men. "Mr. Van Reef is waiting."

"Sorry boss, bit of a mess on the highway." Bakker looked down as he wiped his feet on the mat.

"He's waiting in the office." Maurice pointed upstairs.

The two men stiffened, the real boss would be demanding explanations. They paused, as if to hold off the encounter.

"What are you waiting for?" Maurice demanded. "Go on upstairs, first door on the left."

He walked behind them up the steps and to the office. He stood far away from Van Reef but close enough to hear and watch Bakker and Neelen.

Van Reef glared at the two men.

"Meneer." Bakker's voice was barely audible.

Maurice took a step closer.

"What did you find out?" Van Reef shot the question.

"I went to check on them as soon as I got in this morning. It was early, seven o'clock."

Van Reef did not move a muscle. Bakker's eyes darted to avoid the chilling stare.

"They were gone. The guard and I walked around to see if they had been moved to another room. But we couldn't find them anywhere. We looked in all the offices and in hangars 13, 14 and 15. We talked to the foreman when he came in at

8. He didn't know anything. Then we made calls." Bakker began listing the people he called.

"What did you find out?" He was cut short.

"We called the police station but the agent on duty wasn't the one Mr. Linden said we should talk to. We then decided to call the hospitals. So we asked if an old man and a young guy had been brought in. Erasmus Hospital had admitted someone fitting Oudekerk's description. But they would not give details."

Neelen pointed to Bakker. "He called me at home and I went immediately to Erasmus. I said I heard my great uncle had been missing." He beamed as if pleased at his quick thinking. "Yeah, he was in the hospital all right, but no visitors, they said. Only his immediate family members could see him."

"What about Parks?"

"No sign of Simmons or the boyfriend." Bakker continued. "We are still checking, near her place and his." Bakker answered the next question he thought the boss might ask.

"Did the hospital say anything about who brought him in?"

"No boss. I tried but the staff is tight lipped."

"Police records?"

"They are not saying. We are waiting till later when the officer, our friend, reports to work."

"Check the hotels in the cities." Van Reef spoke with no change in his voice. "Where else could she be so well hidden?" He turned to look at Maurice. "Mrs. Van Reef must have the girl's photos in her files."

"I will go and check right away." Maurice left, relieved someone else now faced the fury.

He rambled down the steps to the kitchen. As soon as he felt he was out of Van Reef's reach, he leaned on the wall and paused to calm his breathing.

Madam would not be home for a bit but he could busy himself in the kitchen pretending to look for a photo of Janet.

Maurice Flanders was out of the line of fire. At least for now.

# CHAPTER 47

Janet wanted the agonizing day to end. Once safely back behind hotel doors, she simply wanted to lay down on the bed and close her eyes.

Ryan and she were weak and in need of food. Reluctantly, she left the security of the hotel room to find breakfast as Ryan went to shower.

The world seemed to have woken up; the street was bustling with people. Where were they all going? What lay ahead for them?

What her own day was to bring, Janet did not know. The night had revealed much but she still did not get it. What was it? She asked herself; what was *it* she was trying to get?

Janet had seen a lot in the past few hours but the picture was fuzzy. Some things were apparent; Van Reef shipping was transporting firearms. Illegally? That was not obvious. The label said *tools* but did that prove anything? Why did she jump to the conclusion that the firearms were illicit? Perhaps they weren't actually being shipped but were simply stored in that crate.

What about the Rembrandt? She had automatically assumed that it too was an original. Nothing she saw confirmed the painting's ownership one way or another. She actually knew nothing of the Rembrandt's status. The photo she snapped was not exactly evidence.

Evidence of what?

Slowly, the answer became clear as she pieced together the fragmented thoughts.

Janet needed clear evidence of Van Reef's wrongdoings. She had suffered because of her discovery of the Mauve. The painting had been in Lars' possession but he was by no means the rightful owner.

Lars van Reef had to be exposed.

It was self preservation.

»«

Janet returned to the hotel to find Ryan fast asleep. She looked at him with sadness, regretting having involved him in the mess.

Three people close to her had become accidental pawns in the cruel game playing out around her.

If only for a brief time, the hot shower melted away the pains, physical as well as mental. Janet sat on the bed. It was time to study the cargo declaration.

She leaned back on the wall, resolved to study the Spanish text on the piece of paper. Only seconds later, her eyes closed and her head slid slowly onto the pillow.

A rumbling sound awoke Janet. What was it? She bolted into a sitting position. It was the noise of doors opening. Someone was coming into the hangar. She would be discovered. She had to run. Or at least hide from whoever was approaching.

Janet rubbed her eyes and looked toward the source of the noise. No, it was not the rumbling of a hangar door but a rapping sound just outside the hotel room. Someone was knocking at the door.

They had come for her.

348

Janet froze. What was she to do? Where was she to run? She looked at the high window.

"Housekeeping." A female voice declared.

Was it really housekeeping? Janet walked to the door and peered through the peephole. A cart and a maid stood in front of the door. The knocks became louder.

"Can you come back later?" Janet responded in a low, disguised voice.

"Yes, Ma'am." The figure moved away from the door, pushing the cart down the hall.

If rooms were being cleaned, the hour was late. Janet looked around for a clock. The red digits on the bedside clock told her it was half past one.

She took a few short steps into the room. It was very late. She had overslept. A frantic feeling began to set in. She stopped. What was the hurry? Where did she have to go?

She had to pull herself together. Janet sat down on the bed. Slowly, the events of the night replayed in her mind. The rifles, the Rembrandt; she remembered the shocking discoveries.

She felt Ryan stir and turned to see him checking his wristwatch. He then sat up with the same look of alarm she had felt. He looked around the room bewildered.

The night had been a strange one for both of them. "It's all right Ryan." She leaned over and touched him. The unfamiliar surroundings seemed to add to his confusion. "We are in a hotel. Remember?"

Ryan nodded but still looked perplexed.

"Come on. Let's have some breakfast." Janet pointed to the food on the table.

Slowly, Ryan stood up and walked over to the table. Janet followed him. They sat in silence as they ate stale croissants and drank cold coffee.

"Want to talk?" Janet asked, anticipating Ryan's need to make sense of recent events. Just as she needed to understand them.

Still reticent, he stood up and opened the window. Along with the cool air came the clatter of city streets.

"So what do we think is happening down there?" Ryan began abruptly.

"Whatever it is, it doesn't seem legal." She pictured the automatic weapons.

Ryan nodded. "Those were some serious firearms."

"I've been thinking about this." Janet said. "We don't know for certain they're illicit."

"Because the label said tools, my guess is the weapons are not declared." He now seemed wide awake. "They are changing hands with the help of Mr. Van Reef."

"Firearms trafficking?" The mere words were disturbing.

"That's what I'm saying."

"You may be right." She nodded. "With his connections, he's probably able to do it with ease."

"I remember you mentioning famous guests who attended the Van Reef parties."

"Yes, many people in high places." She recalled the famous faces.

"Getting back to the hangar," Ryan gulped down the last of the coffee, "the painting, what if it's an original Rembrandt?"

"Let's assume for the moment that it *is* an original and Van Reef is not its owner," Janet analysed, "that means somewhere else, a fake is taking its place."

"Just like your Mauve." Ryan nodded. "It's all making sense now."

At least a part of the puzzle was taking shape.

"If the transport of the paintings *is* an authorized one." Ryan paced in the small space. "Don't you think there would be more paperwork?"

"You mean official documents from the museum?"

"Place of origin for example. It's hard to imagine any museum had any part in this shipment."

"I also think a masterpiece would be secured better and on the shortest route with armoured escort."

Ryan nodded in agreement. "It wouldn't be left lying about in that hangar."

Janet suddenly remembered the camera. "Ryan, I took photos."

"We need to get the pictures developed or put the film in a safe place."

"Yes. Let's go." She picked up her bag. "Now."

In less than five minutes, they were dressed and walking on Spuistraat in search of a post office.

»«

Janet slid the roll of film into a padded envelope. On a piece of paper she scribbled;

*Photos at Van Reef shipping and storage facility:*

*-'Tools' as marked on crates, actual contents: firearms*

*- Rembrandt – also packed for transport.*

*Both found in crates at wharf 6100, Schiedam/Rotterdam.*

She addressed the envelope to herself at the Daily office. Next to her name she wrote, C/O Boris van den Bergen.

"This way it won't fall through the cracks if something happens to me." She let out a nervous laugh.

Ryan's unsmiling eyes expressed his disapproval. The pain of William's violent death was too raw.

"You're right." She guessed his thoughts. "I shouldn't be flippant."

"Let's head back to the room and talk." Ryan took her hand and the two walked back to the hotel.

"That's a relief." Janet kicked off her shoes and leaned back on the dingy wall where the headboard once had been. "At least the photos will be safe."

"I feel we don't have the big picture." Ryan sat at the table.

"That's exactly what I've been thinking." Janet shared her confusing thoughts. "We don't really know what's legal and what's not."

"It's apparent that some or all of that cargo is headed to a foreign country."

"A Spanish speaking country." Janet added. "That could mean Spain or any number of countries in Latin America."

"Okay, let's start at the beginning and string together what we know so far." Ryan picked up the pen.

*I've gone through this scenario a thousand times.* Even her dreams about paintings and museums were becoming too frequent.

Sorting out the confusing thoughts with Ryan was a relief. "We can start with my trip to the Rijksmuseum."

Janet began listing significant events; Mauve sighting at the museum – stumbling upon an identical one in the Van Reef household – museum's confirmed as a counterfeit – harassment and intimidation by Van Reef's goons.

"We know they want you off the trail."

"At this point they want me off the face of the Earth. But before that, they want to get the one thing that could hurt them."

"Yes. *The morning ride on the beach.*"

"I wonder how much Sheri knows. She's the one who gave me the painting. That's a strange thing for her to do."

Giving away such a prized possession was a peculiar thing for anyone to do. It was an act that could be detrimental to her husband. Why would Sheri do such a thing? What was her motivation?

*What does it mean for me?* Janet asked herself. She could never go back to the obscure life of a small time reporter. The Van Reef men had already come dangerously close to her. The next encounter could mean certain elimination.

The thought of a brush with Lars Van Reef struck terror.

What about the new evidence Ryan and she had unearthed? Was it enough? No, something was missing. She needed to find out more. She needed something else, one crucial piece to complete the picture.

She had to find that key.

"You know, I just don't think we understand the whole story." Ryan's voice snapped her back to the room.

"That's exactly what I was thinking." Janet echoed. "Based on everything that's happened till now, we can guess that original paintings are being switched for fakes. If the likes of Marco are involved, it could very well go unnoticed for a long time."

"Or forever, never to be discovered. It was mere coincidence that got you thinking."

"I'm sure only a few people knew what happened with the Mauve."

Among those, Oudekerk was incapacitated; Ryan and she were on the run. What about Zalm? Was he all right? If something happened to him, the switch may never be brought to light. It was a depressing thought.

Janet sat up. "We have to get to Zalm."

"I agree. That Mauve was one painting. He needs to be warned that there might be dozens more."

Janet nodded. "I've felt all along that the Mauve was the tip of the iceberg."

"What we saw in those crates confirms it."

"We can follow up on the Rembrandt. We have photos."

They sat across the table, both digesting everything that had happened and what needed to be done.

"That other cargo," Ryan spoke after being quiet for a few seconds, "crates full of rifles. That's deadly serious."

"It has to be illegal. This whole thing reeks."

Janet drew sketches on the paper, as though trying to connect the dots. Minutes ticked by. A church bell rang somewhere.

"Janet," Ryan leaned close. "What do you think about going back there tonight?"

She stared at him. She knew it had to be done was too terrified to propose a return visit to the Big Tower.

"Yes, I know. If we're caught, that'll be it for us." He paused. "But Janet, you *were* there."

*That's right. I did go back to the Big House. I made it out of there.*

Did that logic make the Big Tower any less dangerous? What if during the day, the captives were discovered missing? If that were the case, dock 6100 was the last place they would look for them. The terrifying feeling eased slightly.

"Yes," she said slowly, "I think we need to go back. To get concrete proof."

Despite the danger, they *had* to return. It was the only way.

It was survival.

»«

Dusk was falling, Janet checked the time; 3:45pm.

"It should be quite dark around five." That would leave them enough time to drive to the docks.

She stepped in to the revolving hotel door. Ryan grabbed her arm and pulled her back.

"Let's go the other way, through the laundry room and out the service entrance."

"Did you see something?" Her heart began to race.

"Just a precaution." He turned around.

They walked through the service entrance to a small back courtyard. A garden gate led them to a narrow passageway between the hotel and the building next to it. Three minutes later, they were on the side walk behind the block on which the hotel was situated.

As they walked the long way around the buildings to the car, Janet went into a corner store and bought two sandwiches and a bottle of water.

"Preparing for a long night Janet?"

She smiled but with great effort, "I hope we won't need

355

them."

Twilight had all but faded as the car pulled into the same parking lot an hour later.

"It's even darker and quieter than when I parked here last."

Was it darker or just more eerie? Janet's nerves were more frayed with each visit.

"Here we are once again." Ryan whispered as they dropped into the ditch outside the Van Reef gate.

The premises were even more still than the night before.

"It's much too quiet Ryan." Janet had felt aware of every sound and every flash of light.

"It's not unusual for Sunday night."

Was it the Sunday calm or was Van Reef lulling them into a sense of security?

"It could be a trap." She clenched her teeth.

"Surely they don't think we're coming back?" Ryan spoke softly, in a calm tone. "Janet, you have the keys to the building but they have no way of knowing that."

Ryan's statement was reassuring. He was right. Van Reef had no idea she could gain entry into the building. Besides, no escaped captive in his right mind would think of returning. Van Reef would not be expecting them. Janet was counting on it.

"So, as today is a day off, it's possible they haven't discovered our rummaging early this morning." The idea was comforting.

They followed the same path as the night before. Even fewer vehicles were parked on the premises.

Janet unlocked the door and pointed to the room which she had thought might be the boss's.

"Let's start with the posh office."

They stood at the doorway and looked around. The large, mahogany desk and the leather covered chair were clearly the room's centrepiece. The top of the desk was clean but for a small stack of papers. Janet walked to it, picked up the sheaf and began scanning the text.

Ryan walked past her to the wall. "I'll look at the file cabinets."

Janet heard him tugging on the handles of the drawers.

She heard a low, soft whistle. "This one isn't locked." Ryan whispered as he slid out the first drawer. "Only stationary supplies." The drawer was shut and another opened. "More stationary."

*What am I searching for?* Janet looked for a  hint, a clue, something. Nothing she read on the pages in her hand seemed extraordinary. She placed the sheaf back on the desk, just as she had found it.

Janet moved around the desk to the drawers. She pulled on the first handle. The contents were unexciting, pens and small notepads. She picked up a pad and read the small print on the bottom, *VR and Sons*.

From the other side of the room she heard a sigh and turned toward Ryan. He was looking in her direction and appeared downcast. She too felt discouragement setting in.

An hour passed by. Nothing jumped out. Janet read and re-read every piece of paper she found. Some were correspondences more than ten years old. Some were receipts for various items; stationary, paint, invoices for cleaning and repair.

"I have nothing so far." She said with disappointment. Ryan did not seem to hear her. "Ryan?" She called louder.

He was deeply engrossed in something. What was it? Janet walked over to him.

"Take a look." His eyes sparkled.

Ryan showed her a sheaf of stapled papers in his hand.

"It's some kind of a shipping document. A cargo document, what do they call it?"

"A manifest?"

Yes, it was a cargo manifest. They walked to the mahogany table. Ryan flattened out the paper.

Janet pointed the flashlight. "Judging from the ink, it's quite recent."

She touched the paper; it felt crisp. She was sure it was printed within the past two or three months.

Ryan placed his index finger on the text in a box on the left. "Shipping date?"

"Huh." Janet mumbled in agreement. "It's only a couple of weeks away. This is a list of items being shipped in the very near future."

"This cargo manifest was buried with all kinds of out-dated documents." Ryan had not taken his eyes off the paper. "Somewhat disorganized?"

"Or it was placed there by design. You know, camouflaged." Janet slid off her backpack and placed it on the table. She reached in and felt around for the small ring notebook.

"Look." She stopped on one page. "These are numbers I wrote off of the crates. Does the manifest have this one? G8211-455."

"No." Ryan's finger moved down the cargo list. "How about G6233-683?"

Janet tried not to shout. "I have that one."

She placed the notebook next to the manifest. Ryan held down the paper flat while she ran her index finger down the numbers. They searched for matching items. There were two.

The rectangle on the top of the paper appeared to show shipping details.

"Look." Janet pointed to an address. "Registration?"

"Shipping company: VR and Sons, Rotterdam." They looked at each other. "VR for Van Reef?" Ryan asked.

Janet nodded. "It was also on a notepad."

Ryan read the next line aloud, "Consignee: Guillermo Paulo in Santos, Brazil. Port of discharge; Paranagua."

"So the cargo in that crate," Janet pointed in the direction of the hangar. "is being shipped to Brazil."

"Look at the description of goods next to G6233-683, *tools*."

They both knew what that meant; firearms.

"The next item G6233-684 is described as planks; hardwood."

"Isn't that taking coals to Newcastle?"

*Tools* was a disguise for firearms; *wooden planks* translated to paintings.

"We both know what's actually packaged." Ryan echoed her thoughts.

The picture was becoming clear. "If the authorities are told to look the other way, it doesn't really matter what they write on it." Janet picked up the papers carefully. "Let me make a copy."

Ryan nodded. "I'll look through the rest of this file cabinet."

The drawer screeched loudly as he pulled it all the way out. Both Janet and Ryan stopped to see if the noise had attracted attention. She nodded, convinced no one had heard it. Ryan continued searching.

As Janet returned with the photocopy, she saw Ryan lift the last folder from the back of the drawer. She handed him the original cargo manifest and slid the freshly made copy into her backpack.

Ryan placed the crucial piece of paper in the folder lying on the floor. He then closed the bottom drawer, opened the one above it and slid the folder in the middle. "This is where I took it from, I think."

He reopened the bottom drawer and pulled out a large envelope from the back. It was stuffed with articles cut out of newspapers and magazines.

"Scrapbook?" Ryan removed a handful and spread it on the floor.

Together, they scanned the articles. They comprised of headline news, some recent, some ancient. A few articles appeared to be from a shipping newsletter.

"Election news Janet." Ryan whispered.

She leaned closer and read the headline. "I've seen a million of these."

The article contained no news. Why would they save an ordinary story? Her eyes moved quickly to scribbles on the margin to the right of the article.

"Someone's making editorial comments on an article?" Ryan shot her a look. "That seems odd."

Janet tried to discern the handwritten scrawl. She stopped at a set of underlined letters, *J.M.E.S.*

Janet felt herself go numb.

"What's that?" Ryan asked.

She did not answer.

"What is it Janet?" Ryan nudged her.

"Not *what* but *who*." She looked up at him. "Jose Miguel Eduardo Santiago."

"Jose Santiago." Ryan's eyes were wide.

Neither said anything.

The silence was deafening.

"Do you think he was an associate of Van Reef?" Ryan asked. "A friend?"

Janet looked at the paper as though it was made of poison.

"What is it?" Ryan turned her shoulder so she faced him.

The murder scene was vivid in Janet's mind, as if it happened the day before. She remembered the lights flashing, sirens screaming. She pictured Santiago lying in a pool of blood.

Ryan tugged on Janet's sleeve as if to shake her out of the trance.

"Van Reef was no friend of Santiago." She finally spoke. "But there is a connection. All of this is connected."

Jose Santiago was a rising star, one expected to win the biggest political prize in the land. He was the most outspoken crime fighter. He was gunned down in a parking lot in Amsterdam.

What was the link? There was a connection; that was beyond doubt. But what was it?

She sat down on the floor. "You remember his death?"

Ryan nodded.

"Santiago swore he would clean up the country, from crime filled streets to corruption at high levels. That was his election promise."

"There was talk of a contract killing." Ryan added. "For weeks, the media was going on about conspiracies."

"The murder was never solved." Janet's eyes were dull.

Santiago never received the justice he deserved.

*In what way was he involved?*

She turned the page. "A hand written note." She peered at the words. "JS, reception on waterfront." She translated aloud the Dutch text as she read. "6 April – Wednesday."

"What happened on that day?"

*The date will be imprinted on my brain forever.*

"It was the evening Santiago was gunned down." She tried to suppress the gasps as she spoke. "It was a Wednesday."

"This note." Ryan pointed to the handwritten date.

"Someone was informing Van Reef of Santiago's whereabouts on that day."

"Or Van Reef was letting someone know."

"Santiago had gotten close." Janet nodded mechanically. "Too close."

She recalled the Spanish text they had read. The names would have been that of ports and addresses, possibly in Brazil, Venezuela or Argentina.

"Whether or not Santiago knew of what was going on, he was clearly in the way."

Jose Santiago was an obstacle.

"And had to be eliminated." Ryan added to Janet's train of thought.

She stared into space as though the picture was finally taking shape before her. It was clear as day. All the dots were now connected.

A chill ran down her back.

"Let's get out of here Ryan." All of a sudden, she wanted to leave.

*Get out while you still can;* her mind screamed.

Janet was lost in thought as they drove back to Amsterdam. They now had evidence of illicit transport of state property and of illegal firearms trafficking.

They had evidence linking Van Reef to Santiago; possibly to his murder.

*Why would Van Reef keep the incriminating information?*

The piece of paper contained the article on Jose Santiago. Next to it, the orders to eliminate him.

The parchment was a memento.

Van Reef's decree drawn in ink was a trophy.

# CHAPTER 48

A loaded gun.

That is how the papers felt in Janet's hand. She looked down at photocopies of the cargo manifest and the original newspaper article. In the article's margin were scribbles in someone's handwriting, possibly Van Reef's, detailing Santiago's whereabouts on that fatal evening in April.

The two pieces of paper might prove to be the link between Van Reef and Santiago's assassination in Amsterdam.

Janet turned to Ryan, "We must find a place for this."

"Yes." He agreed, "as soon as possible."

Janet leaned back in the seat and closed her eyes but the buzz of thoughts denied her the respite. The bombardment of images of the Mauve, Santiago, the mansion and the man with the shaved head would not stop.

She opened her eyes. "I finally have it Ryan. The questions which plagued me for months, the apparent coincidences – it all fits now."

The past day had filled in many blanks. Slowly but surely, the picture was taking shape. Most of the pieces of the puzzle had fallen into place.

"I too am understanding it." Ryan turned sideways and looked at her. "I'm sorry if that hasn't always been the case."

"See, I wasn't crazy after all." It was a relief to have Ryan completely on her side.

He had shown only polite interest in Janet's theories. At first impatient and dismissive, his attitude had changed when the stalking began. Then came the threats. Now he had endured beatings and kidnapping. Worst of all, they had lost a dear friend.

"It's falling into place." He shook his head in disbelief. "Who would have thought this of the famous Mr. Van Reef?"

How ironic that the Van Reef name was much revered in Dutch society. If the world only knew of the shocking goings on behind the cloak of that surname.

How much had Santiago discovered? Evidently enough to deeply wound Lars van Reef.

"Then came Jose Santiago." Ryan echoed her thoughts.

"Yes." She recalled with sadness the blood soaked torso.

"It's mind boggling Janet."

"Yes, it is."

Mr. Van Reef, the eminent businessman, respected member of the community, involved in such illicit activities? A criminal and a murderer, he had Santiago killed.

Was Van Reef the crime boss to whom Santiago had alluded?

"All the prominent citizens who had rubbed elbows with Van Reef," Ryan continued, "how would they feel if they knew?"

There were many, the stars, the mayors and most of all, the Royals. Being close to important people must have opened many doors and afforded Van Reef special privileges. Sheri's celebrity had also given him access to people well connected.

*Sheri.* Janet's heart just sank. Did she know? Janet remembered the sadness in the large blue eyes. *How could a woman who had everything be sad?* She had wondered then but quickly dismissed it as fatigue and stress. Now, Janet understood. Sheri must have been aware of at least some of her husband's questionable dealings.

"I was thinking about Sheri." She shared her thoughts.

"She must have known Janet. You can't live with someone for twenty odd years and not know."

Still, Sheri could not have been a willing participant. Her actions were evidence to that. She had produced the original masterpiece. By giving Janet the keys to Lars' fortress, she had enabled Ryan and Oudekerk to be free.

"Without her help, I would not be here talking to you Ryan."

"You're right. If she hadn't given you the keys and shown you how to find us, Oudekerk and I would still be back there, tied up and miserable. Maybe dead."

"I can't wait this to be over." Janet clutched the papers.

In her hands was evidence, the crucial information which could put an end to this.

"Okay, here we are." Ryan slowed to look for a vacant parking space.

The car had entered Amsterdam city centre. They were within a few blocks of the hotel.

"There's one." Janet pointed but Ryan did not stop. "Why didn't you take that spot?"

Instead of slowing down to park, Ryan accelerated the car.

"Head down Janet." He said sharply.

Immediately Janet bent her head down to her knees. What was happening? Her heart pounded. What was it that rattled Ryan?

Minutes went by before he spoke. "We are not going back to that hotel."

The sinking feeling returned. "What did you see?"

"Two men, standing near the hotel entrance."

"Could they have been tourists?"

"No." The tone was unbending. "I recognize that look. Standing at attention, looking left and right, waiting."

*Waiting to pounce.* They were expecting her. Janet felt hopeless. They had traced her to the most obscure hideout imaginable.

"I can't be sure but I think I've seen them before." Ryan's voice shook. "At the Big Tower when we were tied up."

"So they know I'm staying at the hotel."

"Correction, you *were* staying there." He emphasized. "It's time to get the hell away from that hotel."

Janet held on to the door handle as the car swung left and right on the narrow Amsterdam streets. Ryan checked the rear view mirror frequently. His rigid face was unnerving. She had never seen him so afraid.

The frenzied driving continued. Fifteen minutes went by before the car exited the outer city ring.

"Okay, I'll calm down." Ryan's face relaxed. "It's not likely they can be following us now."

He approached an empty space on the side of the road and pulled in the car. Turning to her, his face still tense, he asked, "What now?"

"I have been thinking that myself."

*If you can't hide in Amsterdam, where else can you hide?*

"How about we get on the highway and head South for the airport?" She paused, expecting an argument.

"Suits me." Ryan put the car in gear. "But my passport?"

"Both are with me." Janet was glad for the habit of carrying important documents with her at all times. "I have yours since that trip to Rome."

"I have no money."

She patted the backpack. "I have a wad of bills given to me by Zalm."

"The museum director?" Ryan sounded incredulous.

"Yes. There's more I have to tell you." So much had happened. She had to bring him up to date.

"What if the airline people think it's a bit fishy?" Ryan's logical mind worked through the logistics. "How do we explain the sudden departure?"

He was right. Dishevelled and wanting to depart immediately would raise eyebrows. "I can make up some story about my mother taken ill suddenly."

"Let's see how it goes." Ryan comforted her. "We'll approach the airlines. If we get cold feet, we can leave and look for a train leaving for Rome or Paris."

"That's good." They had options.

"Where do you want to go?" The tension in Ryan's face had eased.

"As far from this place as possible. The first train out of here to any city. Maybe a flight to Heathrow." In London, she could seek refuge with friends.

"Yes, anywhere." Ryan agreed.

Janet looked down at the sheaf of papers still on her lap. "What about this?"

"They must have a post office at Schiphol. At least a post box. We'll buy stamps from the dispenser."

"Yes, let's go to the airport, Rome or anywhere else."

Janet dreamed of being free of Lars Van Reef but the suddenness of the departure was unsettling.

The thought of staying behind however, was chilling.

»«

"Flight to London in a few hours." Ryan waved the tickets.

With the majority of airline desks open even at the midnight hour, several flights to London were available. Janet's act about the family emergency had elicited sympathetic nods.

"It can't happen quickly enough."

Janet looked at the clock. It had only been ten minutes since the last time she checked the time. The wait for the flight seemed unending. She tried to rest but sleep was elusive.

She could not escape the images of a man with a shaved head and tattooed arms coming after her.

# CHAPTER 49

"How is everything Boris?" Janet was glad to finally speak with her editor.

"Janet, this is dynamite." Boris was almost shouting. "Just unbelievable."

"And the photos, did they come out well?"

"It's everything we need. I put together a composition and just came out of a meeting with the Director."

This was good news. The higher ups at the European Daily were in the loop. There was no holding back. The story would soon be public.

"It is going to print ASAP. Janet, you'll never guess." Boris continued excitedly. Janet was accustomed to his grunts and half sentences. The talkative side of him was a surprise. "The big D has an emergency audience with the Prime Minister himself. Even as the story goes to print."

"Thanks for telling me that Boris. All the pain and suffering was not for nothing."

"I will also be visiting your friend Oudekerk. He is out of the hospital you know."

Janet fought back the tears. "Give him my love, I'll visit as soon as I can."

"One last thing Janet." The exuberance abated. "I'm sorry I didn't do more back then."

"I'm not sure you could have Boris. How were you to know?

They were everywhere."

Van Reef's men were everywhere, including within the police department.

»«

The morning coffee tasted extra special. "I know we've been running around but it feels like a holiday Ryan."

"I guess it's all relative. We're no longer running for our lives." He refilled their cups.

The quiet was interrupted by the telephone. "Who could it be at this hour?" Janet carried the telephone to the balcony.

"It's Boris." She whispered.

"I didn't think you wanted to wait for the mail for this." What news did he have? "Your dear employer, Mrs. Van Reef has been hailed as a heroine. Only after you of course." His laugh was hearty.

"And Lars Van Reef?"

"He is going down Janet. Along with a lot of other people. We're still awaiting judgement on Marco Haarlemmer."

Janet looked up to see a smiling Ryan.

"You two can relax completely. With the boss convicted and the organization falling apart, I doubt anyone will want to chase you now."

"Good news I take it." Ryan asked as the telephone conversation ended.

Janet's smiling face was an open book.

Special thanks to my friends at
The Gulf Beaches Writers' Group